24 Hour Telephone Renewals 0845 071 4343

HARINGEY LIBRARIES

THIS BOOK MUST BE RETURNED ON OR BEFORE
THE LAST DATE MARKED BELOW

Online renewals – visit libraries.haringey.gov.uk

published by Haringey Council's Communications Unit 973.16 • 08/12

D1341846

70001651610 2

THE DISAPPEARING CHILDREN

The Disappearing Children (Prime Minister Father & Son book 1)

ISBN: 978-1-907912-38-2

Originally published in Norwegian in 2012 under the title *Barna Som Forsvant*

First published in English by Phoenix Yard Books Ltd, 2015

Phoenix Yard Books
Phoenix Yard
65 King's Cross Road
London
WC1X 9LW

1 3 5 7 9 10 8 6 4 2

A CIP catalogue record for this book is available from the British Library
Printed in Great Britain.

www.phoenixyardbooks.com

PRIME MINISTER FATHER & SON
THE DISAPPEARING CHILDREN

Lars Joachim Grimstad

Translated by
Don Bartlett and Siân Mackie

THE VERY FIRST CHAPTER

EVERYONE'S GOOD AT SOMETHING. Finn Popps was good at remembering things. However, he wasn't particularly good at keepie-uppies, dancing, singing, skating, juggling or turning his eyelids inside out. Not that turning your eyelids inside out is something you have to do all that often, but you never know. You might find yourself in a life or death situation where being able to turn your eyelids inside out is what saves you.

But Finn Popps could remember things. It was like everything he had ever read or seen on TV had been written down on little Post-it notes and stuck to a giant memory wall inside his head – a wall he could examine whenever he needed to.

That was why he was so irritated with himself. Who was the big, old man sitting on his right? He knew his face. He had seen him on the news and in the newspapers several times. What worried Finn was that the images in his head were of stabbings, murder, assault and other crimes. Surely they didn't let murderers into the palace? He shifted a tiny bit to the left.

Finn looked around. There were a lot of other familiar faces as well. Not just his big brother, father and grandmother. The Crown Princess sat across the table from him, unaware of the

1

big white blob on her nose – a souvenir of the dessert she had wolfed down.

Finn had never been to the palace before. But, my goodness, that's where he was now – in the big, yellow banqueting hall sitting beneath some huge chandeliers with at least a hundred other stiffly dressed dinner guests. He had been given a new suit for the occasion even though there were still two weeks until Christmas, and he had stood for a long time in front of the mirror trying to coax his hair into submission.

'Oh, look, Finn-icky's finally done,' his big brother had said, noticing that Finn had given up trying to tame his wild curls. Finn was certain Bendik wouldn't have had any trouble getting into *Guinness World Records* as the World's Lamest Big Brother, if there was such a thing as world records for big brothering.

But even though Bendik was just as irritating as before, a lot of other things had changed, Finn thought. They had just moved into a new house, he was starting a new school on Monday and tonight he was having dinner with the King. And the big, scary man sitting on his right. Oh, and the Great Leader of North Boresia.

That's why they were really here. The mysterious little dictator from North Boresia was visiting Norway, and according to the menu this evening was the *Banquet in Honour of the Great Leader Kim Il-Ding*. His visit had been splashed all over the newspapers. The dictator rarely travelled, and then usually only to visit a dictator friend in another dictatorship to discuss dictatoring.

But after he had personally called them up and invited himself, the brand-new Norwegian prime minister didn't dare say anything other than: 'Yes, yes, my goodness, Mr Kim, of course you can come, we'd be happy to have you.'

The very same brand-new Norwegian prime minister was currently sitting four chairs away from Finn and trying to maintain a conversation with Mr Kim. Finn glanced in his direction. The brand-new Norwegian prime minister was called Teddy Popps and he was Finn's father.

Teddy was actually called Theodor Bjørnstjerne, but almost no one knew that. However, everyone knew that Teddy was actually a taxi driver. This had all started in his taxi. Every single day for years and years he had listened to Norwegians grumbling in the back seat about the price of electricity, bumpy roads, cold winters, short summers, narrow aeroplane seats and the fact that there wasn't anything interesting on the telly, especially on Mondays.

Teddy Popps knew how people felt. He felt the same himself. Especially after his wife had died – Finn's mother, that is – he had been angry and peeved and put out by this, then that and then the other.

That was why he had started the More Party.

Their manifesto was simple. The More Party would give people more of what they wanted and less of what they didn't want.

'Folks, we're talking fewer bills through your letterbox, warmer water in swimming pools, colder soft drinks in the supermarkets and more chocolate at the bottom of your ice cream cones! And I promise you thermal underwear that doesn't itch! There's nothing worse than itchy thermals!' Teddy had shouted at the television camera when being interviewed.

And it worked. When the general election came round in the autumn, the More Party surprised everyone by coming out on top. It was sensational. News of the taxi driver who had become prime minister travelled around the world and back. Other national leaders called to congratulate him, and both well-known and obscure TV channels from well-known and obscure countries came to interview the fat little man trying to hide his baldness beneath three long, straggly strands of hair.

Teddy Popps was a changed man. None of the grumpy, angry taxi driver remained, he had become a happy, beaming prime minister who smiled for photographers while checking that his three strands of hair were still where he had placed them.

However, Teddy's good mood wasn't doing much for him at the moment. Watching him converse with Kim Il-Ding was like watching someone trying to walk through treacle.

'Your ladies are very beautiful,' said Teddy in his best English.

The dictator had two women with him, one on either side. Kim Il-Ding squinted at him, and then he started to laugh.

'Hahaha, you tinking my head is very beautiful? You has also beautiful head, but not hair on it, heeheeheehee! You bald, but you try hide it, heeheeheehee!'

Kim Il-Ding shook with loud, hysterical laughter while glancing right and left to show everyone how funny he thought it was. He had a lot of hair, which stood on end and made him seem a bit taller than he really was. Well, so long as it didn't rain, thought Finn.

Teddy didn't seem to find this very funny. The whole point of his comb-over was to hide the fact that he was going bald. However, Teddy's mother, Baba Popps, was grinning from one pink earring to the other. She wasn't smiling because Kim Il-Ding was laughing at her son's hair, but because she was inside the Royal Palace. Finn's tiny grandmother sat next to her son beaming with pride among all the people she had only read about in her gossip magazines: the royal, the rich and the famous.

'Another iceberg, sir?'

A waiter in a white shirt appeared at Finn's right elbow. He held out a tray of desserts – vanilla ice cream shaped like mountain tops with little white chocolate polar bears clinging to the peaks. Finn stared at the dishes as if hypnotised, but he knew he couldn't manage another one. The chef had clearly got the message about the theme being 'Norway'. Finn had already eaten 'Elk with blackberry sauce', 'Deep-fried North Sea cod in oil' and three bowls of 'Queen Sonja's iceberg'.

Finn had just opened his mouth to say 'no thank you' when the man next to him took two dishes from the tray. The same fat, old man whose name Finn couldn't remember.

'One for him and one for me,' he growled.

However, after the waiter had gone, he kept both desserts for himself.

'You're only little, you don't need any more. I, on the other hand, have this to fill,' he laughed, patting his expansive stomach before attacking his icebergs with a spoon.

Then Finn remembered who he was. The voice brought it all back, and at last Finn put a name to the face as he located the Post-it note on his memory wall. He had to resist the urge to heave a sigh of relief. No wonder he had connected him with all kinds of terrible crimes. The old growler sitting next to him was called Malthe and he was Oslo's Chief Constable.

'Chief Constable' sounded a bit Toyland, Finn thought, but he was well aware that Malthe had a lot more on his plate than petty crime. There was now a greater chance of being robbed in Oslo than in New York, Finn had read, and it was usually gangs of young hooligans that were to blame. He could understand why the Chief Constable needed all the dessert he could get to console himself.

'You just eat, I'm full,' said Finn, not that it made much difference. The Chief Constable was already powering his way through iceberg number two.

Kim Il-Ding's laughter was getting louder and louder. He sounded like a cat with its tail caught as he shrieked with laughter at his own jokes about the prime minister's lack of hair.

Then he stopped laughing and starting frantically clapping his hands instead. As the entire banqueting hall turned to look at him he stopped that too, leapt out of his chair – and clambered up onto it. Then the Great Leader – who was actually rather small – cleared his throat. Prime Minister Teddy Popps' face lit up.

Finn knew that his father had been looking forward to this. Kim Il-Ding was renowned for giving wonderful presents on his rare international visits.

'Hello you everybody!' shouted Kim Il-Ding in not quite impeccable English. 'I want thank you for all food, it very good – but not elk, which taste toilet, heeheehee,' said Kim Il-Ding as he shrieked with laughter again, jumping up and down on his chair.

For a moment, Finn was afraid the dictator would fall and hurt himself. But Kim continued.

'You build beautiful country, and the Great Leader want thank you for fantastic visit and give two gifts. One gift for old king and old queen, and one gift for baldy prime minister, heeheehee!'

Finn could see his father was starting to get seriously annoyed, but he kept his mouth shut.

'For king and queen I has . . .'

He clapped three times and a door opened. Two North Boresians came in wearing military uniforms and carrying an enormous flat-screen television . . . made of gold.

Finn heard a gasp run the length of the hall. It was the biggest, thinnest TV set Finn had ever seen. As big as a ping-pong table, as thin as a comic, and encased in the purest, shiniest gold. Someone started clapping, and pretty soon everyone had joined in. It really was a magnificent gift.

Kim Il-Ding waved something that looked like an old DVD. On one side, there was a picture of him with his head on top of another man's ridiculously muscular body.

'For your Highnesses, my popular fitness DVD, *The Great Leader Gets Hunky* where I lifting the cars and throwing the big rocks that smash helicopters in air, heeheehee!'

He's mad, thought Finn.

'And now, my small bald friend.'

Kim Il-Ding pointed at Teddy, who flushed scarlet.

'I want be kindest person in world for you and give you fantastic present . . .'

He clapped his hands three times. The same door opened, and both Teddy and Baba turned round in eager anticipation. The two North Boresian soldiers came in again, but this time they were carrying an enormous package between them. The package was topped with a massive bow and looked like the world's biggest Christmas present. Baba started fanning herself with her hands in excitement.

Kim Il-Ding clapped his hands again and the package started to move. Teddy jumped. Baba gasped. Then the contents burst through the paper and rolled onto the floor.

The present was a small North Boresian boy.

'Kind me want give you . . . one of my son! Heeheehee! Take, take, I got lots and you only got two. And this one, he called Kim Il-Im, he love already Norway and he want live in this cold country, heeheehee!'

Teddy Popps was on the verge of tears. He shot a look of pure longing at the giant television next to the wall behind the king and queen. Then his gaze came back round to rest on the small boy walking towards him. Little Kim Il-Im walked straight over to Teddy Popps, grabbed his face, pulled it down towards him and kissed him on both cheeks.

'Hi, new popth. Ith it all right if I call you popth?'

Kim Il-Ding started laughing hysterically again.

'He learn Norwegian too, heeheehee!'

Except for the 's' sound, thought Finn.

Teddy Popps gathered his wits and flashed something that was probably meant to be a smile at his new son.

'Of course you can. Of course you can call me pops.'

Baba thpluttered.

CHAPTER 2

MEANWHILE, IN A DARKER, COMPLETELY CHANDELIER-LESS PLACE . . .

The two men leaned over the railing of the landing they were standing on and looked out across the enormous room.

'A beautiful sight. Right, Red-Cap?' said one.

'Nah, I've never been able to stomach them,' said the one called Red-Cap.

'Pfft, pull yourself together. These are different. These are . . . the future,' said the first. He had a big, curved beak of a nose and a stooped back.

The man with the red cap didn't say anything. Maybe he was doing what the other had suggested and was pulling himself together.

'Yes, Vulture, I hear what you're saying. But I won't believe it until I see it,' he said at length.

The one that looked like a vulture turned to Red-Cap, irritated.

'You'd better watch your tone. Especially if the Colonel's around,' he said.

They stood in silence for a few seconds.

'He said it all starts this week. First phase,' he added.

'Yep, this week. This is quite something, isn't it?' said Red-Cap.

'Yes, it really is,' Vulture said slowly.

There was nothing more to say. Luckily, there was quite a lot to see.

Below them, thousands of children stood lined up in rows. Occasionally they would hear a little cough or someone clearing their throat, but otherwise it was totally quiet.

'Oh well. Better be moving on up,' Vulture said after a while.

'Yeah, probably.'

For a moment it felt as if the floor was swaying under their feet. They shared a hurried glance before letting go of the railing and walking towards the heavy metal door, which stood ajar. After they came out, they closed the door carefully behind them and turned the big, metal wheel so that the room was locked and no one could escape.

CHAPTER 3

THE POPPS FAMILY, NOW including new member Kim Il-Im (or Camomile, as Finn's father persisted in calling him, and it had kind of stuck), sat eating breakfast around the big, round table at 18 Inkognitogate. Even though the prime minister's residence had been perfectly habitable, Baba had insisted on having the whole house redecorated before they moved in. The inspiration was Gran Canaria, which in Baba's opinion was the most beautiful place on earth.

The kitchen walls had been painted turquoise. Baba was thrilled.

'Just like the sea around Gran Canaria,' she said contentedly. It reminded Finn more of the last time he had thrown up. The world outside the window was as unlike the Canary Islands as it was possible to be. It had been snowing for weeks and heavy flakes were still drifting down from the dense, heavy clouds.

The yolk of Finn's fried egg broke, sending yellow goop running everywhere. It looked like a little sun had exploded. Right now it wouldn't really have mattered if the sun had actually exploded. Finn's father had decided that Finn, Camomile and Bendik were going to their new school in the extra long, extra shiny prime minister's limousine. Even though it would only have taken five minutes to walk.

'Times change, Finn, my lad. You're the prime minister's son now. If we were all the same, perhaps everyone would think they could be prime minister.'

'Yeah, and we couldn't have that, could we?' said Finn bitterly as his sun collided with the crispy bacon.

Arriving at a new school in an extra long, extra shiny prime minister's limousine was like turning up with a huge sign saying I AM DIFFERENT. Finn didn't particularly want to be different on his first day at school.

Unlike his big brother.

'I like how you think, Dad. I just hope some of the girls see. I hear there are a lot of great girls at Urra.'

Urra was Uranienborg School for students from the first to tenth class. Camomile sent Bendik an inquiring look.

'Great girlth? Great for what?'

Bendik responded with a withering glare and muttered 'numpty' under his breath.

Finn knew that of all the things in the world his dad wanted, a brand-new North Boresian son was pretty low on the list.

'Who on earth would pack a little boy into a box and give him away?' Baba had asked, miffed, when they were on their way home from the palace. She had probably been hoping for a bathtub or a huge, sand-coloured leather corner sofa.

'Someone completely stark raving cuckoo,' Prime Minister Popps had mumbled back.

In any case, everything had gone surprisingly well so far. Camomile didn't have any airs or graces, he just wandered around the house like a huge smile on legs. He would always suddenly ask the strangest things, but Finn was the only one who ever bothered to answer.

Finn also tried to teach him how to say 's'. It didn't go well.

'I can thay eth!' said Camomile.

'No, you can't. It sounds like eth,' Finn said.

'Lithen. Ethhhhhh!' cried Camomile, jumping up and down in a perfect imitation of his first father.

'We can practise some more another time,' Finn said calmly.

Even though it was a bit odd to be presented with a brother the same age as you on a Saturday evening visit to the palace, Finn was nevertheless grateful for Camomile's arrival. Both because he seemed a much better brother than the one he already had, and because he would no longer be the only new kid in class.

But even that wasn't a comforting thought at that precise moment. Finn sighed and tried once more.

'Do we have to drive, Dad? Pleeease?'

Finn's father put his cutlery down and looked at Finn in despair. Just as he was about to answer, a long shadow fell across the kitchen floor and everyone turned towards the door. A moment later a tall, thin, elderly woman stepped into the room. Or to be a bit more precise, a moment later a tall, thin, *ancient* woman stepped into the room.

She was wearing a dark coat, some sort of peaked cap and brown leather gloves. She was old, a lot older than Baba. Her face was full of deep wrinkles, many of them so deep that it was difficult to tell where her mouth was.

14

For a moment, Finn wondered whether her wrinkles were like the rings on a tree. If I count them all, I might find out how old she is, he thought.

Finn's father dropped his cutlery onto his plate with a clatter and quickly got up from the table. The woman was still quite a bit taller than him, not that she was ridiculously tall, but Teddy Popps was rather short.

'Err, everyone, this is Miss Syversen,' he stammered.

'Good morning,' she replied from a wrinkle Finn guessed had to be her mouth.

Miss Syversen nodded briefly and seriously in their direction, and they didn't know what to do except nod back in just as serious a manner. Finn remembered his father telling him about Laila Syversen, the Norwegian prime minister's chauffeur.

'She's driven all the Norwegian prime ministers all over the place in all kinds of weather at all speeds,' he had said, before lowering his voice as if to emphasise something: 'I know a little about driving myself. And I can tell you, Finn, my lad, I was sceptical about such an old lady driving someone as important as the prime minister, but that woman is the best damn chauffeur in this country. Maybe even the world. So there,' he added, nodding at Finn.

But this was the first time Finn had seen her with his own eyes. And even though his father had told him she was tall and old, he hadn't realised quite how tall and old she really was. Not that it mattered. Miss Syversen's seriousness seemed to make Prime Minister Popps nervous. He stood looking at her, waiting for her to say something. But Miss Syversen just observed them for a few seconds, then swivelled and calmly walked out again.

Teddy Popps regained his composure, smoothed down his comb-over and turned to look at his three sons.

'Okey dokey, boys. Time to go!'

Finn stayed where he was. First day in a new class, at a new school, in a new town. He looked at his plate. The yellow sun was everywhere.

CHAPTER 4

Bendik started to play the drums on his thigh as Miss Syversen did as she was asked. The car had a sound system worthy of a prime minister – there were loudspeakers everywhere. The music provided Finn with a welcome distraction, and he soon noticed that he was also tapping along. He glanced over at Camomile, but his new brother sat stock-still. He gazed straight ahead, still half asleep, in a world of his own.

'Here we are then,' said Miss Syversen as the prime minister's car came to a halt in front of the huge school building.

Finn peered out of the window. To his great relief, and Bendik's even greater disappointment, there wasn't a child in sight.

They understood why when they reached the playground.

'Go on, Viktor, whack 'im!'

'Don't let 'im win, Big Jimmy! Clobber that slimy git!'

Children of all ages crowded round like ants around honey, and even though Finn couldn't see, he knew what was going on. A fight. Some people cheered, but most people just stood and watched. Before Finn, Bendik and Camomile got close enough to see for themselves, the bigger of the two boys had managed

17

to sit on the chest of the other and pin his arms down with his knees. The boy underneath tried to struggle free, but he was stuck.

Finn quickly realised who it was. Even though he had never seen the boy before, he felt like he had seen his face countless times over the last year. The boy pinned to the ground had to be Viktor Krantz, and he was his father's son. Most boys are their fathers' sons of course, but Viktor was the spitting image of the arrogant Ernst Krantz, the deputy leader of the More Party. He had the same eyes, the same protruding top lip and the same smarmy hairstyle, which was still impeccable despite all the wrestling and rolling around.

A few weeks after Teddy Popps had decided to try and become prime minister, completely by chance, Ernst Krantz had clambered onto the back seat of the taxi Teddy was still driving. On the surface they were very different: Ernst was tall with dark, thick hair and wore fashionable Italian suits for his job as a lawyer. But it only took driving over a speed bump for them to discover that they agreed about most things, from the holes in the roads to the price of Coke.

Teddy needed a man like Ernst in the More Party. He could hardly be expected to fill in all the holes in the roads himself. No, he needed someone smart who knew a lot of people it was smart to know.

That was why Ernst Krantz had been at their house so much over the last year. And most of the time he talked about himself or his son Viktor – and how amazing he was.

However, Viktor Krantz didn't look that amazing lying with his face in the snow and an enormous, angry boy sitting on top of him.

'You've always been a bigmouth, you have, Viktor. Not so tough now though, are you, eh?'

Big Jimmy's voice was controlled, but Finn could hear the fury in every word. Viktor flailed like a flounder being pressed into the seabed – he tried to wind a leg around Big Jimmy's torso, but it was no use.

'You're gonna regret this, Jimmy!' Viktor shouted. 'And I'll have the last laugh, because you are and will always be a . . .'

He stopped writhing. Instead, he used the last weapon at his disposal. He spat. The gobbet hit Big Jimmy right in the face, followed by two words which hit even harder:

'. . . fat loser.'

The spit ran down Big Jimmy's face and his eyes smouldered. Slowly he lifted his right hand. Some of the girls turned away. Viktor looked scared and tried to avert his face to avoid the blow.

But it never came.

Big Jimmy's face betrayed his utter disbelief. His right hand had stayed where it was. He turned to see why it wasn't doing what he wanted and found himself eye to eye with Camomile.

'Didn't anyone ever tell you it ithn't nithe to hit people?'

Finn couldn't believe his eyes. Tiny Camomile had Big Jimmy's hand in a lock, and he made it look easy. Big Jimmy tried to pull his hand back, but he couldn't.

Then they heard a loud, shrill sound. It seemed to pierce the layers of Finn's clothes and his skin, not stopping until his very bones vibrated. The sound made everyone turn, half of them with their hands over their ears. Camomile let go of Big Jimmy.

A broad-shouldered man in his sixties was walking briskly towards him across the playground. He was wearing a shaggy fur coat and in his mouth he had a huge, metal whistle, almost as big as a tennis ball, attached to some sort of metal chain around his neck.

'Who's that?' Finn whispered to a boy next to him, who looked like a first-year.

'That,' said the boy, 'is Bojan, the gym teacher.'

The big man made his way through the crowd towards the two brawlers. Bojan looked from Big Jimmy to Viktor and back again without saying a word.

'Thank God you're here,' Viktor gasped innocently from where he lay. 'He attacked me for no reason,' he continued, getting up and brushing snow from his clothes. 'He's completely insane.'

'That's not true!' protested Big Jimmy. 'He called me a . . .'

Bojan shook his head in resignation. But still he didn't say anything; he just grabbed the boys by their jackets and dragged them towards the school building. A little girl ran after Big Jimmy with a red boot he had lost during the fight and gave it to him. Then the bell rang.

'What now? Will they get told off?' Finn asked the first-year as they walked towards the school building.

'Not by Bojan. He'll take them to the head teacher's office,' said the boy, turning to Finn. 'Bojan doesn't speak.'

CHAPTER 5

WHILE ALL THE OTHER pupils headed straight for their classrooms, Finn and Camomile had to look for theirs.

'How on earth did you do that?' Finn asked as they climbed the stairs.

'What?'

'What you did to Big Jimmy's arm in the playground.'

Camomile smiled slyly.

'Little frogth croak louder than big toadth, you know.'

'What?'

'Old North Borethian thaying.'

Finn paused and looked at Camomile for a few seconds before smiling and shaking his head.

'I'm going to have to teach you to say *s*.'

Finn and Camomile were the last two into the classroom, where they quickly found empty seats. A man in his late forties stood next to the teacher's desk taking books and sheets of paper out of a leather folder. Finn knew that this was their teacher; he had seen a picture of Amund Gulliksen on the school website. Gulliksen was wearing a woolly jumper with a picture of four reindeer flying through the air followed by a sleigh and Father Christmas. Nice jumper, thought Finn, trying to see if any of the reindeer had a red nose.

Then Gulliksen scanned the classroom, partly through and partly over the top of a pair of thick glasses, which were sliding down his nose. He managed to shove them back into place by wrinkling his nose, which Finn thought made him look like a mouse sniffing the air.

'Albert!' Gulliksen said, poised to put a cross by Albert on the register.

'Here,' answered a tall boy next to the window.

'Cato!'

'Yessir', said a boy with a long fringe.

'Einar!'

Except for Viktor and Big Jimmy, and Finn knew where they were, everyone was present. Gulliksen looked up from the list, his glasses so far down his nose that he had to wrinkle it *and* lean back a bit to see through them.

'OK, everyone, today there are two new faces in our class. This is Finn Popps and Kim . . . erm, let me see . . .'

Gulliksen glanced down at the updated register so quickly that his glasses fell off his nose.

'. . . Kim Il-Im Popps.'

Camomile jumped up from his chair.

'But you can jutht call me Camomile! That'th what the prime minister callth me.'

Some children laughed. Finn hoped it was because they

22

thought Camomile was funny and not because he lisped.

Gulliksen peered across the room at Camomile.

'OK, great. Camomile Popps it is then.'

Gulliksen cleared his throat as if to make a speech.

'As you all know, Finn and, erm . . . Camomile's dad is the Norwegian prime minister.'

Finn studied his desk.

'But it's not fair that we know all about your dad, but nothing about what everyone else's dads do. So I thought we could start by talking about that! Who wants to start?'

Thank goodness, thought Finn, who had expected to have to talk about himself first. He decided he liked all of Gulliksen and not just his jumper.

A hand shot into the air a couple of desks to Finn's right. It was Sunniva, a girl with dark hair who looked a lot like Pocahontas in a book Finn had read when he was little. She was so eager to say something it looked like she was about to take off from her chair. Gulliksen didn't even get a chance to utter her name before she had launched into a tirade. But she didn't talk about her dad.

'Come on, Gulliksen! Why only dads and not mums? Huh? Are dads more important than mums now?! You may not have realised, but there aren't only men working in this country. There are women, too. We're not living in the Dark Ages. And what about people like me who don't even *have* a dad?! What I do have is a mum who's a nurse and she often has to work nights to make hens meet.'

'Er, I expect you mean to make ends meet, Sunniva,' Gulliksen said gently.

He looked a bit nervous behind his glasses.

'What I mean,' said Sunniva, even more irritated after being corrected, 'is that not everyone in this country has loads of money to spend even though some idiot has gone around promising them the sun and the stars!'

Sunniva turned to Finn and pinned him with her dark Pocahontas gaze. He knew that what she really meant was the *moon and the stars*, and that she was referring to the promises his dad had made while on the campaign trail before the election. But even though he was the first to admit his dad said and did a lot of strange things, he didn't like anyone calling him an idiot.

Gulliksen held up his hands as if he was trying to calm a fire-breathing dragon.

'Now, now, Sunniva . . . I didn't mean it like that. Of course what mums do is just as important as what dads do.'

He smiled and pushed his glasses a bit further up his nose making his eyes look even bigger.

'But to keep this brief, I suggest everyone chooses one parent to talk about. Sunniva's given us a start, so we can continue with . . .'

He got no further because the door opened and Viktor and Big Jimmy walked in. They didn't even dignify Gulliksen with a glance; they just went to their seats.

'Ah, maybe you can begin then, Viktor? Everyone has to say what one of their parents does, and you can choose whichever one you want to talk about.'

As Big Jimmy sat down in one of the empty seats at the back, Viktor walked straight towards where Finn was sitting.

'I'm saying nothing,' said Viktor, not taking his eyes off Finn.

Finn felt himself go hot and cold. Viktor came closer, not stopping until he stood right next to Finn's desk.

'Shift,' said Viktor. 'This is my seat. Don't you go thinking you can do what you want just because your dad's the prime minister.'

Finn noticed the whole class looking at him.

'Sorry, I didn't know . . .' Finn started, but then gave up trying to explain and gathered his things.

He carried everything to the only empty seat, which was next to Sunniva. She narrowed her eyes as he came closer.

Finn slumped down onto his chair. All of a sudden he felt so tired. He just wanted to lie down and sleep. And wake up somewhere else.

CHAPTER 6

FINN GLANCED AT THE gunge-green clock on the wall for what felt like the hundredth time. It wasn't just the hour and minute hands crawling round – the second hand seemed to be taking its time as well. He had always enjoyed going to school, but now he couldn't wait to get away. Away from Uranienborg School, away from his new class, away from Viktor Krantz and angry Pocahontas girls, and away from flying reindeer, 18 Inkognitogate and every aspect of his new life. Finn wanted to go back to the life he'd had before, when they had lived in a crooked little house in a little village outside the city, when he had still had a mum.

It was a noisy class. Einar threw rubbers at girls' heads, and if that wasn't bad enough, Hedda talked them half to death afterwards. Cato with the fringe just did what he wanted, disappearing halfway through lunch and not coming back until they had Norwegian, a bar of chocolate in his hand. The twins, Morten and Magnus, slept through large parts of the afternoon. Ivan with the red hair rocked to and fro on his chair, crashing to the floor twice before the end of the day. Gulliksen wrinkled his nose and did his best, but Junita, a girl with long, blonde L'Oréal hair, was almost the only person who ever put her hand up when he asked a question.

'Times were hard in Norway after the war. People didn't know where to turn and the country had to rebuild,' started Gulliksen, opening a new box of chalk. 'N-o-r-w-a-y i-n t-h-e 5-0-s,' he said slowly as he wrote, pressing so hard the chalk screeched against the board.

Then the classroom door opened and everyone turned to see a small, well-dressed, elderly man standing on the threshold. His bushy eyebrows hung like two heavy balconies over his eyes, prohibiting any upward vision. The din in the classroom immediately subsided as the man walked towards Gulliksen, supported on a stick that hit the ground at the same time as his right leg.

Finn didn't have to wait long before Gulliksen told him who the man was.

'Headmaster Bentson, how . . . how nice! What can we do for you?'

The head teacher nodded to Gulliksen, surveying the knitted jumper with a look of deep scepticism. He was wearing a grey suit, the trousers neatly pressed, with a shirt and tie. Then he noticed the heading on the board.

'Ah, the fifties. Those were the days,' he said, smiling and shaking his head fondly in the direction of Gulliksen, who didn't know whether to nod or shake his head in response. In the end he just twitched awkwardly.

'Well, I have a message for your class that I wanted to deliver in person.'

Gulliksen's twitches became more animated, he was clearly

nervous about what the message could be. Bentson, however, turned to face the class and raised his voice.

'My dear pupils. We are going to hold a national general knowledge competition for six to sixteen-year-olds. Or, to use the word I gather you prefer, a . . . quiz.'

Finn lit up. A quiz! He loved quizzes! Capital cities, highest mountains, longest rivers. Historical battles, American presidents, Swedish pop bands – bring it on!

There were clearly others who felt the same way, if the sudden cheering and applause was anything to go by. The head teacher had to bang his stick on the floor and clear his throat before he continued.

'This is an old tradition which is making a comeback. National general knowledge competitions like this were normal in the fifties and sixties . . .'

Bentson nodded at the board.

'. . . and were designed to establish which school and which class had the most knowledgeable pupils in the country.'

The head teacher paused, pursed his lips and raised his voice another couple of notches.

'Uranienborg school is an old and venerable school. As the principal, I expect you to represent us in a manner that both you and I can be proud of.'

He extended a finger and held it in the air. The classroom was completely silent.

'That is why there will be a qualification round in the big gymnasium the day after tomorrow, where we will choose the best . . . quiz team from this school. Each team will comprise three people, and both genders must be represented.'

Finn swallowed. They would be in *teams. And there had to be at least one girl in each.* Of course he and Camomile would pair up, but asking a girl to be on a team with them? On their first day of school? He looked around. Many of the other kids were already forming teams.

'The winners will go on to the national final, which is to be held at Oslo Spektrum next week.'

The pupils looked at one another, and Bentson pursed his lips again. A hand shot into the air. It was Viktor's.

'Yes, young man?'

Viktor smiled his most charming smile.

'Umm . . . Headmaster, sir, will there be any sort of, well . . . prize?'

Bentson sent Viktor a sharp glare for a moment, and Finn thought he was going to get into trouble, but then the head teacher clapped his hands and smiled.

'But of course . . . the prize! How could I have forgotten?'

He paused for dramatic effect.

'The team that wins the national final . . . will win a trip to the South Pacific island of Bora Bora!'

The class cheered again, this time with even less restraint. Everyone liked the idea of holidaying on an island so beautiful they had named it twice.

Bentson sent Gulliksen a long stare, and Gulliksen tried desperately to get the pupils to settle down. It took a while.

'I recommend that you practise – this will not be . . . erm . . . child's play.'

He nodded at Gulliksen and the board.

'That is all for now. Your lesson may continue.'

But instead of leaving, Bentson stood for a few seconds studying the reindeer on Gulliksen's stomach. Finally, Gulliksen felt he had to say something.

'My, eh . . . my mum knits them. I have one for every day in December,' he said.

Bentson shook his head, then limped out, his stick thunking against the floor with every second step. Gulliksen watched him go, still staring after him even when the thunks sounded very far away.

The rest of the day passed with Finn unable to pluck up the courage to ask one of the girls to be on their team. When the bell rang for the end of the school day, Finn was the first out of the classroom. He waited for Camomile in the playground.

'Goth, Finn, I've got to thay, thith plathe ith amathing!'

Curious, Finn gazed at him as he explained:

'Lotth of new friendth. Lotth to learn. Lotth of clever girlth. What more could you want?'

Finn sighed.

'I've gotta hand it to you, Camomile, you're a positive person.'

Camomile's smile wrapped almost the entire way around his head.

'You think tho? Great, I juth read that pothitive people live longer,' he said, beaming.

Finn had to smile.

'What was the school like that you went to in North Boresia?'

'I didn't go to thchool,' said Camomile. 'I had my own tutor. Hith name wath Kim too.'

'Are all boys in North Boresia called Kim?' Finn asked.

'No, no, that would be thilly!' Camomile laughed. Then he stopped.

'I oneth met a boy called Pim,' he said, totally deadpan.

CHAPTER 7

SINCE FINN'S HOMESICKNESS WAS for a home he no longer had, and since Camomile was a positive soul open to most things, they agreed that they wouldn't go straight back to 18 Inkognitogate after school.

A well-trodden path through the snow led to a basketball court above the school. There was so much snow on the ground that Finn could almost reach the basket when he stood underneath it, and he wondered if that was how it felt to be really tall.

'Maybe we thould take part in the quith contetht,' Camomile said. 'I think it thoundth fun.'

'Yeah, but we need a girl on our team. And who would we get?' asked Finn.

'True. Agh. I don't have a clue when it cometh to girlth,' Camomile said with a sigh.

Finn sighed too. Finally something fun had happened, but he was too shy to ask anyone to be on their team. What a wimp he was.

'Look, thereth the man with the whithle,' said Camomile, pointing across the court.

Finn scanned the benches sticking out of the snow. One of

them had been dug free. And there he sat – Bojan, the gym teacher. Still wearing the same long-haired fur coat with the big metal whistle round his neck, like a patient basketball referee waiting for the snow to melt. He was surrounded by small birds, and Finn quickly realised why. A lunchbox lay open next to him. But instead of eating the bread himself, Bojan was breaking it into small pieces and throwing it into the snow. The birds hovered and fluttered around him, competing for every single crumb.

Bojan noticed the two boys coming closer and watched them as he prepared to throw some more bread.

'Hi,' Finn and Camomile chorused as they passed him.

Bojan's face didn't react, but his head gave the merest of nods.

The school grounds didn't extend much further back than the basketball court, and soon they came out onto a pavement. They hadn't walked far when Finn stopped. The Pocahontas girl was sitting on top of a fence across the street, legs dangling. Her long, dark hair stuck out from underneath a big, purple beanie. Finn squelched the urge to turn and flee.

'He doesn't say much, does he?' Sunniva said.

'What?' Finn asked.

She nodded in the direction of the basketball court.

'Bojan. Silent Bojan.'

'No, I suppose he doesn't,' Finn said.

'He's from Croatia. They say he fought in the war down there. That he lost his family.'

'Life can be unfair,' Finn said.

33

Sunniva cocked her head and narrowed her eyes.

'That's a good one coming from the boy who lives in the nicest house in Inkognitogate and can eat lobster and canary whenever he wants.'

'It's true though. And I don't eat lobster. And I certainly don't eat canary.'

She looked at him for a few seconds without saying anything. Then she spoke.

'I'm Sunniva.'

'I know.'

'Yes, of course you do, Finn Popps,' she said, slowly.

She turned to Camomile.

'And you're Camomile.'

The little North Boresian smiled so widely that his eyes almost disappeared.

'I'm Camomile. Camomile, yeth, that'th me.'

Sunniva smiled for the first time. Then she looked serious again and turned back to Finn.

'OK. Sorry I called your dad an idiot. There's a lot to suggest he is an idiot, but I don't really know him. So I'm sorry.'

Finn looked her in the eye to see if she really meant it. It certainly *sounded* genuine.

'That's fine,' Finn said.

'No, it's not,' Sunniva said. She let go of the fence, dropped at least two metres and ended up with snow over her knees.

'I hereby invite you back to my place for cheese toasties and hot chocolate! And we're not talking normal toasties with meagre helpings of sweaty cheese – these are Vera Vester's super crispy, super cheesy grilled sandwiches. Come on!'

She didn't wait for an answer, just clambered out of the snow and set off down the street. Finn and Camomile stood watching her for a few seconds, her dark hair and purple beanie bouncing with every step, and then followed her.

'Hot chocolate? Wouldn't it juth be thticky?' Camomile asked, confused.

CHAPTER 8

'WELL, WHAT HAVE WE GOT HERE?'

No sooner had they come through the door than they were set upon by a tiny lady. Despite her diminutive size, she held both boys so tightly that Finn wasn't entirely sure whether it was a hug or some sort of judo hold.

'It's so nice to have visitors!' exclaimed Vera Vester, finally letting them go.

Then her face fell. 'But dearie me, I've not tidied up and this place looks like a bomb's hit it. Doesn't matter though, eh, boys?'

Vera Vester laughed – a long, rippling laugh of the sort that only very small or very large mothers can do.

'It's much more important that I go and make a pile of Vera's super cheesy, super crispy toasties and a jug of hot chocolate so we can all sit down and you can tell me who you are.'

'A lot more important, Mum,' Sunniva said.

Soon they were all sitting in the little kitchen in the little flat on the top floor of the big apartment building. Even though space was limited, the rooms were stuffed full of strange objects, pictures and books, and it all put Finn at ease for the first time in ages. In the living room there were posters for films he had never heard of, in the toilet four scary African masks stared at him and in the kitchen a small mother sang as she grilled the cheese.

They ate, drank and chatted, and when Vera finally found out who the two boys were, she was astonished.

'Goodness me, this really is quite the visit! The sons of the prime minister himself in our tiny flat!'

She smiled, but Finn noticed that there were question marks hiding behind the smile.

'Er, well, yes, we are his sons,' Finn answered, still unused to Camomile coming under the heading of 'son' in the Popps family.

Vera gripped her cup of hot chocolate with both hands, leaned over the table and spoke in a low voice.

'I must admit that I didn't vote for your father in the election. This country needs someone who can get us all to think more about one other and less about ourselves,' said Vera gravely, before hurriedly adding: 'But we can talk about that some other time. And you two seem like lovely boys! Speaking of the More Party, can I interest anyone in More hot chocolate?'

Vera Vester laughed her rippling laugh again and walked over to the big hot chocolate jug. Then she turned and looked at them.

'But you should know that human brains have been boiled in this jug. I got it from an old witchdoctor I met in Papua New Guinea, and he said that they still eat people there. Tourists who get lost and the like,' Vera said, casually pouring more hot chocolate into their cups.

Camomile looked freaked out. Finn glanced over at Sunniva

to see if her mum was joking or not, but Sunniva just nodded with exaggerated solemnity.

They ended up sprawled out on the plush purple sofa in the living room, their tummies full and warm with hot chocolate. It was already dark outside, and Sunniva's mum was on the night shift at the old people's home where she worked. She left after giving both boys an even longer, tighter judo hug than the one they had been treated to when they had first arrived.

'If I'd known we were having visitors I'd have baked Vera's super chocolaty chocolate cake as well, with deep-fried monkey toes, badger testicles, a cream filling and other fun surprises. Oh well, next time!' she shouted, running down the stairs.

It was quiet in the flat after Vera left. Finn had a question on the tip of his tongue, but he couldn't quite get it to make the leap out of his mouth.

'Sunniva . . .' he started.

'Yes?'

'I was wondering . . . if maybe you . . . well . . . if we . . .'

It was as if the words just didn't want to come out. Particularly words like 'quiz' and 'be on our team'.

'It's nothing,' he said.

'What were you wondering? If I wanted to be on your quiz team?'

Finn blinked at her in surprise.

'Er, yeah.'

'Of course I do! We're gonna crush 'em!'

'Are we?' Camomile asked.

38

'Oh yes. But first we have to practise.'

Finn was taken aback by how happy he was. They had a team. They would be taking part in the quiz. And not only had they persuaded a girl to be on their team, they had persuaded a girl who was clearly determined to win.

They practised answering questions on everything under the sun. And on everything beyond the sun. They practised answering questions on distant planets and high mountains, American presidents and poisonous mushrooms, long rivers and short wars. And on a lot of other weird and wonderful topics. Camomile surprised them again and again with what he knew, and perhaps even more with what he *didn't* know. He knew, for example, that, at 6,768 metres, Huascaran was the highest mountain in Peru. But a country called *Denmark*? No, he had never heard of that. Sunniva had learned a lot from all the stories Vera was always telling. Such as that Miles Davis was a legendary jazz trumpeter from the sixties who'd had diabetes. Or that Barack Obama loved *Harry Potter* and liked to drink blackcurrant ice tea while he listened to . . . Miles Davis. Finn knew a little about a lot, and for the most part they complemented one another well.

In the end they were so tired that it felt like there were Japanese car brands and French artists coming out of their ears. Camomile's eyes grew even narrower than usual, and in the end he seemed to have hit a dead wall, answering 'The Nile' or '1955' to everything, regardless of the question.

Finn was starting to get tired too, and when Camomile answered

'1955' to *What's the longest river in Africa?* he knew it was time to call it a night.

'Adieu,' Finn said, yawning as they went out of the door. 'Which, by the way, was the name of Norway's entry in the 1982 Eurovision Song Contest.'

CHAPTER 9

FINN WOKE WITH A start. He had been right in the middle of a bad dream. It was the same nightmare he'd had since he was little, ever since Baba had read him the scariest tale he'd ever heard – *The Pied Piper of Hamelin*. The story was about a piper who lured all the children in the town away from their parents up into a mountain cave, where he kept them trapped forever. It haunted him in all sorts of ways when he slept, and tonight he had been locked in a dark basement at the palace along with hundreds of other children and Gulliksen.

Finn looked over at the alarm clock on his bedside table. It was 4:44, the middle of the night, but something or someone had woken him. He sat completely still in his bed. There it was again. A sound. It was coming from downstairs. He got out of bed and tiptoed into the corridor. He could hear snoring from his dad's bedroom, and for a moment he wondered if he should wake him. But if there was one thing his dad liked even less than stupid potholes in roads, it was being woken up when he didn't want to be.

Finn went downstairs. He stayed close to the wall because he knew the stairs were more likely to creak if he was in the middle.

He made it to the ground floor without making a noise and snuck into the kitchen. He paused there for a few seconds – he could feel his heart beating underneath his pyjama top. Then he heard it again. There's someone down here, thought Finn. The sound was coming from the big living room facing the garden. Finn held his breath. He wished he had never left his bed, but it was too late now, so he left the kitchen and walked along the hall, still hugging the wall, not stopping until he reached the door of the big living room. It was ajar. Someone had turned on the light. He tried to see inside through the narrow crack, but all he could see were the newly painted walls. Yellow ochre, just like the morning sun in Gran Canaria.

Slowly, he pushed the door open. The standard lamp was lit, and in the big green armchair sat . . .

'Camomile!' Finn stepped into the room.

'Good morning! Or ith it thtill "goodnight"?'

Camomile smiled toothily, lighting the room up even more.

'I'd almoth convinthed mythelf you were a burglar.'

You don't say, thought Finn, letting go of a breath he hadn't realised he'd been holding.

'Why are you up in the middle of the night?'

'I . . . I couldn't thleep. There'th an eight-hour time differenth between Norway and where I come from, and I thuppose my body ith thtill adjuthting to Norwegian time.'

Finn yawned.

'Oh well. But you should try to sleep, or you'll be like a zombie tomorrow.'

Then he noticed that Camomile was holding a small bottle. 'What's that?'

Camomile looked down at his hand. He seemed surprised to see it.

'Er . . . it'th olive oil. I had a thore tummy, and it helpth. And it tastth fantathtic,' Camomile said, smiling.

'You drink olive oil? Why . . . no, never mind. Goodnight, Camomile,' Finn said, heading for the stairs.

Even though he liked Camomile, Finn realised his new brother was not like other people.

'Thweet dreamth,' he heard from behind him.

Finn walked back past his dad's bedroom. He was still snoring – it sounded like he was sawing down an entire forest in there. Then he went back into his own room and gently closed the door behind him. The last thing he thought about before falling asleep was racing along on water skis on a deep blue ocean not far from the chalk-white beaches of a distant tropical island, because he had once heard that the last thing you think about at night is what you dream about.

CHAPTER 10

FOUR WHITE ANGELS FLUTTERED down towards a small, brown stable at the bottom of Gulliksen's tummy. Today's jumper appeared to be a bit itchy – he was constantly tugging at it or scratching the angels.

'Albert!'

'Here!' someone shouted from next to the window.

'Cato!'

'Yes.'

Finn leaned towards Sunniva.

'Thanks for the toasties and hot chocolate yesterday,' he whispered.

'Mum makes great hot chocolate, doesn't she? Might even be the best in town. Although I've heard the hot chocolate at Hotel Bristol is criminally good,' she whispered back.

Finn smiled. Being so new to the city, it was nice to have someone who clearly knew their way around.

'Einar!'

'Yes,' Einar said.

'Hedda!'

'Mmm . . .'

There was only one name not met by a tired 'Yes', 'Here' or 'Mmm' that morning: Big Jimmy's.

His chair was empty.

'OK then, Jim-Erik Svendson, so you're ill today,' Gulliksen murmured to himself, marking the absence on the register.

'Yeah right, done a bunk more like,' Viktor muttered grumpily.

Iver, who sat next to Viktor, laughed. Finn glanced over at them, but quickly turned away again when Viktor stared right back at him.

'Just a quick word about tomorrow's quiz,' Gulliksen began, scanning the classroom.

'The four best teams after the first round will go on to the final . . .' he started.

'Camomile, Finn and I want to sign up!' Sunniva said loudly, not even putting up her hand.

Gulliksen scratched the brown stable.

'Er, OK . . . does your team have a name?' Gulliksen asked.

Then Finn remembered that they had not agreed on a name. He sent Sunniva a hesitant look. Viktor had Iver and Junita on his team and they were called 'Viktory' – no surprises there. 'The Einsteins' and 'Liverpool 4ever' were also raring to go.

'Our team name can be "Thun Factor 50"!' Camomile cried.

The entire class turned to look at him. Finn blinked. *Thun . . . Sun Factor 50*? Camomile just grinned.

'We are going to Bora Bora, after all!'

CHAPTER 11

THEIR TIMETABLES CALLED IT 'physical education', but the rest of the world just called it 'gym'. Finn, Sunniva and Camomile walked across the playground towards the building where the gymnasium was. Camomile had had a sore tummy all morning and didn't want 'to gym', as he put it. Maybe he had drunk too much olive oil, Finn thought.

Bojan was waiting for them when they shuffled into the gymnasium after changing into their gym kit. He was wearing a red, rather tight-fitting Adidas tracksuit which reminded Finn of the Eastern European athletes he had seen in some old Olympics footage. The big whistle around Bojan's neck was covered in dents and looked home-made, but it ensured he made his fair share of noise, even though he himself had never been quieter. He waved his arms around, blew the whistle, and before they could so much as say 'dodgeball', they had been divided into two equal teams.

As with so much else, and particularly ball games, Finn was better in theory than in practice. It was as if his body adamantly refused to do what his brain so clearly wanted. He knew, for example, that in order to stay in the game it was best to throw the ball hard at knee height so that it was difficult to dodge, head or catch. But when Finn finally got hold of the uncooperative little red ball and actually had to throw it, it was usually a feeble attempt, with the ball bouncing at least three times before it was picked up by an opponent determined to do far more damage. Thankfully Finn was quite fast, and he kept his distance from the people doing the throwing. Viktor was the other team's 'king', but he rarely got Finn within range, and when he did, Finn managed to jump out of the way.

The king, or rather, the queen, in Finn's team was Sunniva. She stood at the back, yelling instructions to her teammates with fiery commitment. Dodgeball gave Finn the opportunity to see Sunniva's temper and competitiveness come to the surface – and explode. The red ball flew from her hand like a bullet, left and right, and she screamed in triumph every time it smashed into a thigh or an unprotected back. She was ruthless; Finn was quite unnerved. He was not the only one. Tiny Josefine started crying, trapped in the corner, as Sunniva prepared to let fly with the ball once more.

'No . . . p-please don't, Sunniva,' she stammered.

'Then get off the court!' Sunniva shouted, red-faced. 'I'll count to three. One . . .'

'All right, all right, just don't throw the ball . . .' sobbed Josefine as she ran away and sat next to Camomile on one of the low benches.

In the end there was only Finn and Magnus running around their own respective halves of the court, with Viktor and Sunniva as king and queen in their safe zones. Sunniva threw the ball hard at Magnus's stomach and knocked him flying.

'Yes!' she cried, punching the air as Magnus lay on the ground gasping for breath.

This meant that Viktor had to come out onto the court and pick up the ball. Finn stood as far back as he could while still moving from side to side. Viktor bounced the ball a couple of times.

'Well, well, squirt, no one to hide behind now, is there?'

'Just chuck it and we'll see,' Finn said, concentrating hard on Viktor and the ball.

Viktor took a short run up, and just as he threw the ball, Finn leapt the other way. He lay where he was for a couple of seconds, relieved not to have been hit. Weird thing was, he hadn't heard the ball whizzing past him. He finally looked up at Viktor and realised why. Viktor hadn't thrown the ball. It had been a feint. He was still standing with the ball in his hand, getting ready to throw and smiling. Finn curled up to make himself as small as possible.

'Die, you little . . .'

Finn heard the sound of the red rubber ball flying through the air and then felt a searing pain as it hit his naked thigh just below the hem of his shorts.

For a couple of seconds it was like having a red-hot poker on his skin. Finn didn't want to give Viktor the satisfaction of seeing how painful it was, so he tried to walk off the court as calmly and casually as he could, albeit with his face scrunched up. It sort of worked – he just looked as if he needed the loo.

'Are you OK? That looked really painful,' Junita said by way of comfort, looking at the glowing red round mark on his thigh.

'Yeah. Didn't feel a thing,' Finn lied.

Sunniva left her safe zone and ran to catch the ball before it went out. Now it was king vs queen – Viktor vs Sunniva. Her eyes were wild as she held the ball tightly in one hand, prowling along the halfway line. Viktor stood at the back of his half, close to the line. He swayed back and forth, maintaining a low centre of gravity, knees slightly bent, ready to jump to the side.

'Well now, reckon you can throw it all the way here?' he shouted, in a babyish voice.

'We'll just have to wait and see, won't we?' she replied calmly. 'But first . . .'

She straightened up and looked at something behind Viktor, a surprised look on her face.

'Headmaster Bentson, what are you doing here?'

Everyone followed Sunniva's gaze, looking for Bentson. Even Viktor turned to see why the head teacher had suddenly decided to pay a visit to their gym class. The problem – for Viktor at least – was that Bentson wasn't there. A split second after he had glanced at the closed door behind him, Viktor realised that he'd been duped and he seemed to know what was coming when he turned back to face Sunniva. Which he did anyway, just in time to glimpse something red before everything went black.

'Yippee ki-yay!'

The ball hit Viktor right in the face, and Sunniva later maintained that she could have thrown it a lot harder, 'but I didn't want to kill the guy'. Viktor did a kind of semi-pirouette and fell to the ground clutching his nose. The twins Morten and Magnus shouted 'He headed it, he isn't out, he headed it!', but since blood was pouring from his nose and Bojan had blown his whistle, everyone sat on the bench reasonably convinced the game was over.

CHAPTER 12

'FINN!'

The final bell had rung, and Finn was halfway across the play-ground when someone shouted his name. It was Gulliksen, jogging towards him in the chilly afternoon air with a few sheets of paper flapping in his hand.

'Could you and Camomile stop by Jim-Erik's house with his homework?' he asked, shivering and waving the stapled pages at Finn. 'I thought that since you two are new here, it'd be nice if it was you who popped by. And he lives in the same street as you, at number . . .'

'I'll go with them. And I know where he lives,' Sunniva inter-rupted, snatching the papers from Gulliksen before hurrying off.

They said goodbye to Camomile in front of Big Jimmy's house. His tummy was still so sore that he was keen to get home and rest.

Finn and Sunniva started up the driveway. At the end there was an elegant building surrounded by a garden the size of a small football pitch.

'Wow,' Finn said as they reached the entrance, ready to walk up the wonderfully majestic staircase leading to the front door.

'Wrong door. He lives there,' Sunniva said, pointing at a little door at the bottom of a flight of narrow basement steps.

'His mum works for the people who live in the main house. She cleans and looks after their kids and stuff,' she explained. 'They get to live in the basement as part of the deal.'

They rang a doorbell above a homemade sign with 'Trygve + Rita = Jim-Erik, Jon, Jens and Jenny' scrawled in a child's hand.

They hadn't been waiting long when the door opened, by a lady Finn guessed had to be Big Jimmy's mum. She looked exhausted – her eyes were red-rimmed – and a small girl who must have been seven or eight years old stood next to her. Finn recognised her – she was the girl who had run after Big Jimmy with the red winter boot he'd lost while fighting.

'Yes?'

Big Jimmy's mum stared at them blankly.

'Hi!' Finn said as cheerfully as he could. 'We're in Jim-Erik's class at school, and we've brought his homework round as he's ill.'

'Jim-Erik isn't ill,' said the woman at the door, her lip starting to wobble. 'Jim-Erik's disappeared.'

CHAPTER 13

THEY ALL SAT IN the Svendsens' small basement living room – Finn and Sunniva on the long section of a flowery corner sofa, each with their own glass of juice, and Big Jimmy's mum on the short section with Jenny next to her. Big Jimmy's dad didn't even look up when they came in; he just sat in his chair in front of the fire, staring listlessly into the flames.

The room was quite dark even though the lights were on and the fire was lit. The two windows just below ceiling level would probably have let in more light if there hadn't been so much snow on the ground.

'For some reason we all overslept today. And that's quite some-thing considering there's six of us,' explained Big Jimmy's mum. 'But when I went to wake Jimmy, he wasn't there. There was just this note.'

She pushed a small slip of paper across the table. Sunniva picked it up and read it aloud.

'I've run away. Love, Jimmy.'

Finn swallowed. Kids his age didn't run away from home, did they? Not in the middle of the winter anyway. Big Jimmy's mum shook her head sadly.

'I don't understand. Sometimes he lost it with us – he's got a temper on him, Jimmy has – and yesterday he was in a particularly bad mood.'

She nodded towards the man in the chair.

'Trygve, his dad, told him off because he went straight to his room after school instead of helping with dinner as he usually does.'

She stopped talking. Finn wanted to say something, but he wasn't sure what.

'He's a good boy, he really is,' she continued. 'I don't know why he'd just run away.'

Finn looked around. Toys and clothes lay scattered all over the floor. He noticed that all the plants had died. Must have their hands full with all those kids around, he thought.

'Have you told the police?' Sunniva asked.

'Yes, they were here this afternoon. We've looked all over the place and checked to see if he's with anyone else in the family, but no one's seen him.'

She looked up at the window.

'And it'll be dark soon too . . .'

Her voice cracked and she gripped Jenny's hand.

'I'm sure he'll be back soon,' Finn said, trying to be reassuring. 'Maybe he just fancied . . . a day off.' It was unlikely, but he felt he had to say something.

'I don't know what to think,' said Big Jimmy's mum. She took out a round box and put it on the table. Finn knew what it was. A snus box, full of little packets of tobacco which could be placed under your upper lip.

'I found this in his room too. On the floor. I don't understand, I had no idea such young boys used snus. And certainly not Jim-Erik,' she said, turning away slightly. Then she put on a brave face.

'But thank you for coming round with his homework.'

'Didn't want him to miss anything,' Finn said, taking a big gulp of his juice.

'We really should be off,' Sunniva said demurely, getting up from the sofa.

Big Jimmy's mum followed them out into the little hall. It was just as untidy there: shoes and clothes belonging to the whole family lay tangled in one big heap. She thanked them once more for stopping by.

'He never says much about school, but it's nice to know he's got friends,' she said.

'I agree with Finn. I think Jimmy will be back soon. I'm sure of it,' Sunniva said, giving a determined nod for emphasis.

Big Jimmy's mum smiled, but she still looked sad.

Finn and Sunniva walked down the driveway and into Inkognitogate without saying a word. The pavements had been cleared at some point during the day and big piles of snow lay close to the fences, but huge snowflakes were still falling around them. It was getting dark. The streetlights flickered before coming on properly.

Sunniva finally broke the silence.

'Do you really think Big Jimmy will come back tonight?'

'I don't know,' Finn said. 'I didn't know what else to say.'

'There's something fishy going on here,' Sunniva said.

'What do you mean?'

'I don't know. But no one runs away from home at our age. Just like that, in the middle of winter. And I mean, come on – snus? Big Jimmy might not be the best-behaved boy in our class, but I've never seen him use snus.'

Finn could barely picture Big Jimmy – he had only met him for the first time the day before. However, one thing had caught his attention. When they were standing in the hall with Big Jimmy's mum, Finn felt that something didn't quite add up. At first he wondered if it was something to do with the flowers on top of the chest of drawers. They hung limply over the side as if in mourning, even though there was a lot of water in the vase. But that wasn't what it was. No, there was something else he had seen, but as good as he was at remembering things, he just couldn't quite put his finger on what it was.

CHAPTER 14

FINN DIDN'T GO ROUND thinking of his family as particularly abnormal. First off, they were the only family he had. Second off, what was a 'normal family' anyway? Weren't all families a bit abnormal in their own unique way? Wasn't it, in fact, normal to be a bit abnormal? And wouldn't it be boring if everyone was the same?

That was how Finn mentally argued his case at any rate, as he showed Sunniva around his new home. And he desperately hoped Sunniva thought the same. Especially when they found Baba sitting on the worktop next to the cooker, still in her dressing gown, stirring the contents of a pot with one hand and painting her toe nails with the other, all while reading a gossip magazine and yelling excitedly.

'Oh my God, look – it's me outside the palace! Teddyyyy, there's a picture of your mother in a mag!'

Nor did it seem all that normal when they found Camomile in the prime minister's office. The door was usually locked, but now it was wide open, and Camomile was sitting on the floor with ring binders and documents strewn around him, about to take a large swig from a bottle of olive oil. When he spotted Finn and Sunniva he jumped so much that half of it came back up again.

'Fnn!' he gurgled, before pausing to swallow properly. 'I wath jutht reading about Norway. You never know what they might athk about in the quith.'

However, the biggest surprise was awaiting them in the large dining room. The prime minister of Norway had climbed onto one of the elegant, velvet-upholstered dining-room chairs and was shouting at the television on the wall half a metre away.

'You filthy, dirty, useless scuzz box! What have I ever done to you, eh?' Eh? EH?'

All things considered, for the first time in his life, Finn was grateful he had a big brother who just lay on the sofa texting, like normal big brothers do.

'Go for it, Pops, you show that telly who's boss,' Bendik mumbled.

Prime Minister Popps had insisted on having a TV in every room, in case he happened to be on. As he was now.

'Hi, Dad,' Finn said. 'This is Sunniva. She's in our class at school.'

'Hi,' Sunniva said.

But Teddy Popps was completely absorbed by the dead telly and hadn't even noticed they were watching him.

'Brand new, and do you work, you pile of junk? No, you don't! And the news will be on any minute!'

He stabbed at the remote control with his finger like a man possessed. His face was bright red and in his white shirt he looked like a fat little lighthouse.

Finn looked at the black TV screen.

'Is it really that big a deal?' he asked.

Teddy finally acknowledged his son.

'A big deal?' his dad half-asked and half-yelled. 'Today I made one of my biggest decisions to date as prime minister! I kept a promise I'd made to the voters!'

The lighthouse was pink now.

'What did you do?' Sunniva asked calmly.

The prime minister whirled around, finally realising they had a visitor.

'What did I do? I made a very important decision.'

He turned back to the telly and resumed his stabbing.

'What decision?' Sunniva asked, still calm. 'Are nurses going to get paid more? Are care homes going to get more money so that old people can get help to go to the loo and stop eating fish fingers and leftovers?'

Finn's dad abandoned his tirade against the telly for a moment and turned to look at Sunniva.

'Huh? Care homes? No, I bought the famous Maarud crisp factory. So that we can make sure packets contain more crisps and less air!'

He was proud and miffed in equal portions. And a tiny wee bit unsure about the girl asking him difficult questions in the middle of his own dining room.

Sunniva started to say something, but decided against it. Instead she looked at the remote control in his hand.

'If it's brand new, have you checked it's got batteries in it?'

59

'Of course it's got batteries in it. They're . . . they're . . . er . . .'

He opened the battery compartment.

'What the hell? Who's taken the batteries?'

He turned to Sunniva and gave a slow nod.

'Nice one, Selma. Nice one.'

'Sunniva,' Sunniva said.

'Huh?'

'My name is Sunniva.'

'Oh right, well, either way. Mum?'

Teddy's mood improved somewhat as Baba entered the room carrying a huge dish of his favourite dinner: lasagne.

Soon they were all sitting around the enormous table eating lasagne and watching the news on the brand-new flat-screen TV.

They watched Prime Minister Popps inspecting the crisp factory. He smiled and said hello to the factory workers before giving a speech from a podium. He talked about the importance of protecting the nation's values and how crisps were a national treasure. He concluded his speech by reaching into a large bag of beef and onion flavoured crinkled crisps and taking out one, which he held in the air in front of all the people he had met at the factory. Then he cleared his throat before solemnly declaring:

'Some may say this is only a crisp.'

He waved it around a bit.

'But this, I say to you, good people, this is so much more than a crisp. This is what makes life worth living! We mustn't forget the little things in life. Those precious moments. Friday evenings in front of the telly. The moments when we Norwegians kick off our shoes and relax. When we finally flop down on the sofa after a long, hard day and open a packet of beef and onion crisps and know that we have earned the right to relax!'

He looked straight into the lens of the news programme camera.

'Because we Norwegians *have* earned the right to relax! We *have* earned the right to enjoy ourselves! And we *have* earned the right to open a crisp packet which contains more crisps than air!'

Everyone cheered. Teddy Popps raised his hands to hush them, but he had to wait a few seconds before he could continue.

'That's why I have just bought Maarud crisp factory. And that's why we'll be filling the bags to the top as of tomorrow – with no increase in price!'

When the news was over, and after Baba had patted him on the head, and after he had patted himself on the head, Teddy sat there beaming. As proud as a five-year-old who had just lost his first milk tooth.

They had second helpings. Then Bendik announced that he was meeting friends, so he went out. An episode of the soap opera *Love & Langoustines* came on. Baba and Teddy were both engrossed in the comings and goings of the Huntington family. Soon their jaws dropped as they watched Mr Huntington kiss Samantha, the maid, and explain to her that he could not leave his wife, Mrs Huntington, because it was she who owned the langoustine factory and thus had all the money.

'A boy in our class went missing today,' Finn said.

No one answered. Samantha cried and said that Mr Huntington didn't need the money because he had her, and she suggested that they run away together and live on love and coconuts on a tropical island.

'Are you listening?' Finn asked.

No reaction.

Mr Huntington said yes, of course he needed the money, how else would he afford his Rolls-Royce, golf membership and electric nose hair clippers with diamond-studded handle?

'Big Jimmy's gone missing and no one knows where he is. Not even his parents.'

'Hmm . . .' Teddy sighed and gazed at Samantha.

'Hmm . . .' Baba sighed and gazed at Mr Huntington.

Finn looked at Sunniva and rolled his eyes.

'They had the police round too,' Finn said.

'Hmm, you don't say,' Baba said.

Sunniva cleared her throat.

'We also shot our teacher and ate him,' she said.

Camomile's eyes widened and he stared at Sunniva in shock. Teddy Popps shovelled in more lasagne, still glued to the screen.

'That's nice,' he said with his mouth full.

Finn shook his head in disbelief.

'And then we set fire to the school and ran away, but they sent the army after us with nuclear missiles,' he said.

Camomile's eyes were popping out.

'Well, that's how it goes sometimes,' said Prime Minister Popps, wearing the same sad expression that Samantha had worn when Mr Huntington drove off to the golf club in his Rolls-Royce.

'I think they hit the Royal Palace by mistake. I hope the king and queen were out in the garden or something,' Sunniva said, getting up. 'Thanks for dinner, it was really good.' She smiled politely at Baba before carrying her plate into the kitchen.

Baba looked round for the first time.

'Hm? Oh yes, clever girl that one, thanks for dinner, yes, quite,' she said, confused.

Finn and Camomile followed Sunniva into the kitchen.

'Wath that what they call irony?' Camomile asked as they put their plates in the dishwasher.

Finn smiled.

'Yeah, I suppose it was a kind of irony,' he said.

Camomile breathed a sigh of relief.

'Do you think they realithed?' he said, concerned.

'I don't think they were listening,' Sunniva said.

'Shall we practise for the quiz?' Finn asked.

'The anthwer is yeth!' Camomile said, perking up.

Sunniva looked out of the window. The streetlights were on, and it looked like the snow was falling from them rather than the sky.

'Question one,' Sunniva said, frowning. 'Where's Big Jimmy?'

CHAPTER 15

FINN LAY ON THE back of a polar bear, writing a letter to his mother. When he finished, he looked up at the sky and counted the stars that weren't yet hidden by clouds. He counted four plus an aeroplane that he had thought was a star until he realised it was moving slowly across the sky. That eventually disappeared behind a cloud as well.

He had taken the big polar bear skin from where Baba had stowed it in the attic. Then he had climbed up the small ladder to the roof hatch, out onto the roof and flopped down on the skin after clearing some of the snow to the side.

Even though the quiz was tomorrow, practice had been slow going. Big Jimmy's disappearance made it difficult to concentrate on skating records and historical battles, so they'd given up after an hour.

'We should get some sleep. It's important to give your brain a rest, you know,' Sunniva had said as she left.

It became lighter where Finn was lying, and he noticed that the moon had managed to find a little opening. He thought about what Sunniva had said, but he didn't want to go to bed yet. Finn had sneaked out after brushing his teeth; his dad was busy anyway.

He had been paid a visit by the man in charge of road maintenance in Norway. One of the first things Teddy Popps had done as prime minister was to fill in all potholes in all the roads in Oslo, much to the delight of the residents. But now everyone living in Bergen had heard about the new roads in Oslo, and they wanted theirs sorted out as well. Pronto. The transport minister had been very red in the face when he arrived.

'They're all hopping mad over there! And you know how grumpy and angry people living in Bergen can be. Just look how they behave when SK Brann loses a football match.'

'Okey dokey,' Teddy said. 'We'll fill in the holes there as well.'

'But then Stavanger and Ålesund and Molde will hear all about it! And then everyone in Trøndelag, down south and up north will want roads as flat as pancakes as well, and in the end the Sámi will get in on the act and demand that all the bumps are ironed out on the Finnmark plateau. Do you know how many holes we're talking? We don't have the money for this!' cried the transport minister in despair.

'Then we'll do it in secret in Bergen. At night, with workers wearing camouflage,' Teddy said. 'And if it gets expensive, we'll just pump a bit more money up from the sea.'

Pumping a bit more money up from the sea was Prime Minister Popps' answer to everything that cost money. What he meant was that they could use the money Norway earned from all the oil found in the North Sea.

The problem was, the More Party had already promised to fix so much. And the last thing Teddy wanted was to be one of those people who made promises and didn't follow through. But it cost money to fix everything. It cost a lot. There might not even be enough oil to pay for it all.

Camomile had finally adjusted to Norwegian time and was already fast asleep when Finn went to say goodnight. He was a nice brother, if a little strange, thought Finn, who kept finding him wandering around the house on his own. But he was always in a good mood and a lot nicer to have around than Bendik, who was more annoying than ever.

Finn took off his gloves and started to fold the letter to his mum into a paper aeroplane, as she had once taught him. He had written about Camomile, Sunniva, the quiz and Bora Bora. When he got to Big Jimmy, he just said that something mysterious had happened and he would tell her more about it next time. He ended the letter with: 'I miss you, but I'm not as lonely as I was before. Love from Finn.'

Finn peered carefully over the edge of the roof down into Inkognitogate before throwing the paper plane upwards as hard as he could, straight at the sky. It flew off into the night. The start was promising, a little gust of wind took it upwards, and something in Finn rose as well, a hope that it would fly straight to heaven, straight to his mother. But then it banked abruptly, and for a moment it looked like it would fly right back to him, but it passed a couple metres away from him, then spun around a couple times as if circling and looking for a good place to land. Gravity trumps faith, thought Finn, watching as the paper plane swooped past the streetlamps below. Then a large truck came round the corner from Riddervolds gate, slowly turned into Inkognitogate, and it was almost as if the plane had been waiting for it, because it straightened up and dived straight into the opening at the back. It was a kind of dustbin lorry. Finn read 'Norway Recycles Ltd' on the side. And underneath: '– we're thinking about the future'. Wow, thought Finn. What were the chances of that?

The truck maintained a low speed, stopping briefly outside 18 Inkognitogate before driving on.

CHAPTER 16

A MAN WITH A hat and a big walrus moustache was standing on the pavement smoking a fat cigar when Finn and Camomile opened the door. Behind him was the extra long, extra shiny prime minister's limousine, with the engine running. Finn and Camomile jumped in the back seat, but the passenger door opened before Miss Syversen drove off and the man with the moustache got in. Minus the cigar.

'Say hello to Maxwell Jones, boys.'

'Oh . . . hi,' Finn said, smiling at the man in the front seat. As well as the silver-grey walrus moustache he had silver-grey hair, silver-grey eyebrows and even a few long, silver-grey hairs growing out of his ears, He was old, but not as old as Miss Syversen. No one else was that old.

'Hello,' Maxwell Jones said. He had a deep voice and spoke English.

'Maxwell is an old friend of mine from England,' Miss Syversen explained.

'Nice to meet you, thir,' Camomile said in perfect English.

Finn stared at Camomile in amazement.

'Wow, you've got a knack for languages,' Maxwell said to Camomile with a sideways glance at Miss Syversen.

'Laila and I have known each other for many, many years. Since she won the European Rally Championsh . . .'

'Aghhhhhh!'

Camomile shrieked as if he had been attacked by a zombie that hadn't had his Rice Crispies yet. He pressed his entire body up against the window in terror and stared at the object lying on the back seat between him and Finn. It was a drill.

'Finn, get thith thing away from me!'

Finn looked at the drill.

'What, the drill? You want me to move the drill?'

As soon as the drill was out of sight, Camomile sat back in his seat. But he was clearly spooked, and examined the rest of the back seat with great care.

'It's gone now, Camomile, you're fine,' Finn said, but he still couldn't quite get his head round his new brother's reaction. 'How come you're so afraid of a drill?'

Camomile turned to him, eyes still darting around nervously.

'I don't know. I jutht am. I'm thcared of all thorts of toolth actually.'

They drove on in silence. Miss Syversen turned the radio on, and by the time they had reached the school, Camomile seemed to have calmed down. He was already out of the car when Finn heard something on the radio that caught his attention: '. . . in the last few days several children have run away from home in

69

the Oslo area. The police are afraid that they are running away to join criminal youth gangs . . .'

Finn thought about Big Jimmy. Criminal youth gangs? That sounded a bit far-fetched.

'Are you coming?' Camomile shouted, knocking on the car window. An icy wind chilled the air and blasted handfuls of fresh snow into Finn's face as he got out of the car.

Miss Syversen rolled down the window and leaned across Maxwell to shout at Camomile.

'Tsetnoc ziuq eht htiw kcul doog!'

Finn gave her an odd look. Had she finally lost her marbles?

But Camomile just smiled.

'Thankth! Thee you later!' he said.

Finn had no idea what was going on. He made a mental note to ask Camomile about it later. And to tell him what he'd heard on the radio.

For now they had to concentrate on not freezing into blocks of ice as they walked into the wind. Finn pulled his scarf up over his face and trudged across the playground. Perhaps it was not all that surprising that Amundsen beat Scott in the race to the South Pole in 1911, he thought – Amundsen would have been used to having snow in his face all the time. Even Camomile was looking a bit tousled when they finally fell through the door of the building where the big gymnasium was.

'Holy Motheth! No offenthe, Finn, but thometimeth I withh I'd been given to the Prime Minithter of Brathil!' he groaned.

70

CHAPTER 17

THE GYMNASIUM LOOKED QUITE different to how it had looked the day before, when it had just been a gymnasium. Twenty-seven tables had all been given their own tablecloth and a team name card, as well as paper and pencils. The long curtains were drawn so that the only light came from the ceiling lamps. An old desk had been carried onto the stage, one just like teachers had used in days gone by, and an old-fashioned leather office chair. I suppose Bentson will sit there, Finn thought, eyeing the microphone stand next to the desk.

Sunniva was already sitting at a window table near the middle of the room. When they strolled over, they discovered a card with 'Sun Factor 50' written on it. The atmosphere was formal and full of anticipation; participants murmured to each other as they gazed at the stage. Finn told the others what he had heard on the radio.

'What a load of nonsense,' Sunniva snorted.

'Criminal youth gangth?' Camomile repeated.

'Big Jimmy's not old enough for that sort of thing,' Sunniva said.

Finn looked round. They were quite young compared to many of the other teams.

'This isn't gonna be easy,' he whispered.

Sunniva whipped round and glared at him.

'Hey, what sort of an attitude is that?' she hissed. 'Just because they've been alive a year or two longer than us doesn't necessarily mean they know more. Besides, most of them aren't here because they know a lot, they're here to skive classes.'

Maybe Sunniva had a point. Some people were not looking particularly focused.

As the minute hand made a tiny jump to indicate it was five to nine, the lights dimmed and the desk on the stage was lit up by spotlights hanging from the ceiling. Bentson appeared from behind the stage curtain. He strolled towards the desk, even better dressed than he had been when he had visited their classroom. Today he was wearing a brown three-piece suit with what Finn guessed was a pocket watch on a metal chain hidden in his breast pocket.

'Dear pupils,' he started, his voice solemn. 'Welcome to the qualifying round of the National Knowledge Competition here at Uranienborg School.'

Bentson paused for dramatic effect as he looked out over the twenty-seven teams.

'The first knockout round comprises two sets of twenty-five questions. You should work together and write your answers down on a sheet of paper, which will be collected in. The four highest scoring teams will proceed to the final. At the end a winner will be selected to represent Uranienborg School at Oslo Spektrum.'

Another pause. Bentson lifted one finger into the air.

'I expect you know this already, but I'll say it again anyway. Cheating of any kind will not be tolerated.'

He lowered his finger and nodded towards the door where Bojan was standing. The huge whistle hung around his neck as always, and Finn knew what they would hear if someone broke the rules.

CHAPTER 18

A DRAMATIC FANFARE ERUPTED from the loudspeakers at precisely nine o'clock. Bentson put on his spectacles, and as the music ended, he started reading from a sheet of paper.

'Question number one,' he said, his voice loud and clear.

'What was the name of the ship that sank on 15 April 1912 with over 2,000 people on board?'

Easy as pie, thought Finn. The others just nodded in agreement when they saw what he had written. *Titanic*.

The next two questions were plain sailing as well. Finn knew that England had won the football World Cup in 1966, and all three of them knew that Mount Everest was 8,850 metres high.

But it soon got a lot harder. Question four was: 'In Greek mythology, who was the god of the sun?' Question number seven was even worse: 'Which tree grows taller – spruce or pine?' Nature was not their strong point, but Sunniva had said, leave it to her, she'd answer those questions. When Bentson then asked what the gestation period for a sow was, she just shook her head.

After question twenty-five had been asked and their time was up, Bojan blew hard on his whistle and everyone put aside pens, papers and any plans they had to sneak a couple more seconds.

Bojan, along with a few other teachers who had come along to help with marking, collected in the answers.

After fifteen minutes, Bentson announced the results of the first round. They could have done better, but they could also have done a lot worse. They were in seventh place with seventeen points, but it was close and they were only three points away from the all-important fourth spot that would secure them a place in the final. The bad news was that Viktory were in second place, five points ahead of them. Megabrain were in the lead with twenty-three points.

Bentson cleared his throat into the microphone and shuffled his papers ready for the second round. Sunniva leaned over the table.

'This isn't over by a long shot,' she whispered through gritted teeth, clenching her right fist as if she wanted to take a swing at someone. Which she probably did.

'Question number twenty-six . . .' Bentson said gravely from the podium as he tapped his papers on the edge of the desk to keep them tidy.

'. . . what is 95 multiplied by 87?'

A wave of muttering rippled through the hall and some people started protesting vociferously. This was a general knowledge quiz, not a maths test.

'Quiet!' Bentson boomed, so loudly that everyone in the room jumped, and so sternly that they all shut up.

'Maths is also knowledge,' he said in a voice leaving no room for argument.

'Eight thouthand, two hundred and thikthty-five,' Camomile whispered.

'What?' Finn and Sunniva chorused.

'The anthwer ith eight thouthand, two hundred and thikthty-five,' Camomile said, looking pleased with himself. Finn looked at him. He hadn't even picked up a pen, he had just worked it out in his head.

'Wow,' Sunniva said, hurriedly writing it down.

'Question number twenty-seven . . .' Bentson continued.

The second round went much better. Fortunately, Bentson had run out of nature questions, and Finn was able to retrieve one Post-it note after another from his memory wall. He knew, for example, that the capital of Hungary was Budapest, that Kilimanjaro was the highest mountain in Africa, that a birdie was a golfing term and that amnesia was another word for memory loss. He also knew that it was the Italian inventor Antonio Meucci who had actually invented the telephone, not Alexander Graham Bell, as many people thought.

Sun Factor 50 were feeling good when Bojan blew his whistle.

'All right, everyone. Time's up. Your answers will be collected in, and we'll meet back here in fifteen minutes,' Bentson said, rising to his feet.

Sunniva suggested they use the break to go outside and clear their heads in the chilly air. It was still pretty cold, and they were just turning to go in again when Finn saw Jenny heading towards the gate. Big Jimmy's little sister was obviously finished for the day.

'Hey, Jenny!' Finn shouted.

When Jenny heard her name she started in surprise.

'Have you heard anything from your brother?'

The small girl said nothing, just shook her head as they walked towards her.

'Oh, this is getting ridiculous,' Sunniva said under her breath and bent down to talk to Jenny.

'Can you remember anything from the night he disappeared?'

Jenny peered up at them shyly. Finn flashed her what he hoped was a friendly smile.

'Erm . . . there was one thing I thought was a bit strange,' she said.

'Oh yes?' Sunniva said, eyes lighting up.

Finn leaned towards her slightly to make sure he heard what she said.

'I had a dream. Or, well, I didn't realise it was a dream at first, because it was so real . . .'

Jenny looked down at her shoes. She seemed to be regretting she had said anything at all.

'Yes?' Sunniva prompted gently.

The girl looked up at them.

'There were two big flies. Two big flies came into my room, and they had rucksacks on. That's all I remember.'

They said nothing until they were on their way back into the gymnasium again.

'Two big flieth?' Camomile asked.

'Which flew in and kidnapped him?' Sunniva asked, scepticism written across her face.

Finn was disappointed. Even though Jenny seemed to be telling the truth, there was little doubt it had been a dream. Finn knew that the biggest fly in the world was a South American species that could grow to be six centimetres long. Which was enormous for a fly, but not big enough to buzz around wearing a rucksack and kidnapping people.

Seeing Jenny in the playground had, however, jogged his memory. Once again he had the feeling he had seen something in Big Jimmy's hall. Something that should not have been there.

CHAPTER 19

'AND NOW THE MOMENT you've all been waiting for.'

Once again Bentson's slow, solemn voice filled the loudspeakers.

It was clear many of the teams didn't think they had a chance of a place in the final, and couldn't care less about the result. Others sat chewing their lips nervously and wishing one another good luck.

'I'll read out the top ten teams,' Bentson announced.

'In tenth place, with thirty-two points . . . er . . . The Gryffindors!'

Sun Factor 50 were not ninth, eighth, seventh or sixth. They looked at each other.

'Surely we weren't eleventh?' Finn whispered.

'No chance. We did way better in the second round,' riposted Sunniva, rubbing her temples.

Even Camomile seemed nervous. He was usually so cheerful and laid back, but now he closed his eyes every time the head-master leaned towards the microphone. He had them closed so tightly now that they had all but disappeared.

If their team name was not announced next, they were in the final.

'In fifth place . . . with thirty-eight points . . .'

Bentson paused for dramatic effect, and it was the longest pause yet. Finn glanced at Sunniva, whose face was one big grimace.

'. . . The Smarties!'

'YES!'

Sunniva shrieked so loudly that the teams closest to them jumped. The Smarties, however, who had been in fourth place after the first round, didn't look so smart any more as they slumped over their table in disappointment. Finn waited for confirmation that they were among the four best teams before daring to give vent to his joy.

'And the four teams going through to the final are . . . Sun Factor 50 with thirty-nine points . . .'

They were in fourth place. They had actually come top in the second round, scoring twenty-two points. Viktory shared second place with Pride of Urra, and Megabrain held the lead. The teams would now meet in the final round starting in half an hour.

They congratulated each other. Camomile offered his hand to Sunniva, but she just batted it aside and gave him a big hug.

'Good work, Camo!'

Then Finn sensed someone standing behind him.

'Well now, isn't this nice?'

Finn turned round and was met by Viktor Krantz's sneer. Iver with the red hair was standing next to him, but their third team member, Junita, was nowhere to be seen.

'I don't know if you heard,' Viktor said, looking at Sunniva. 'But unlike yesterday, you can't cheat here.'

'I didn't cheat,' Sunniva hissed back. 'I just used the weapons at my disposal. In this particular case – your stupidity.'

Viktor's sneer flickered and died. His voice shook slightly as he spoke.

'You'd better watch yourself, Sunniva Vester. Just saying. And you,' he said, looking at Finn. 'Being the son of the prime minister won't help you here. Or of a tubby taxi driver, which is what he really is.'

Viktor glared at Finn for a few seconds before turning on his heel and departing, Iver trailing after him. Finn could feel the fury prickling under his skin. It was easy to understand why Big Jimmy had attacked him. He had to be the most obnoxious boy in the entire universe.

CHAPTER 20

'ANY IDIOT COULD HAVE made the final. This is when it gets really difficult,' Sunniva said.

They were sitting on a bench in the boys' changing room. The four teams in the final had each been allocated their own room where they could prepare in peace and quiet, and Sun Factor 50 had been given the boys' changing room.

The old door to the changing room creaked open and they heard footsteps in the little entrance hall. Then two elderly people came into view.

'Miss Syversen?' Finn exclaimed in surprise.

Miss Syversen, wearing her long black chauffeur's coat, and Maxwell Jones, her British friend, stepped in.

'Congratulations!' Maxwell Jones thundered in English, and Finn caught a glimpse of a smile under his moustache.

'We heard you made the final. Congratulations,' Miss Syversen said dryly.

'Er . . . thank you,' Finn said.

'I ran into your teacher, by the way,' Miss Syversen said. 'He said he wanted a word with you and Sunniva.'

'Why's that?' Sunniva asked.

'No idea,' Miss Syversen said, shrugging.

Finn and Sunniva left Camomile with Miss Syversen and Maxwell in the changing room and went to find Gulliksen. Sunniva was irritated.

'Maybe it's something to do with tomorrow's homework,' Finn said, jumping to Gulliksen's defence.

'Homework? Right now all I care about is types of Northern Norwegian rock,' Sunniva snarled.

They crossed the playground without their coats on. Finn wondered whether it would be worse to freeze or to sweat to death. His money was on the latter, but he wasn't sure.

They had just entered the school building when Gulliksen came down the stairs. He looked like a walking Christmas present. Today's jumper was purple and had a big red knitted bow on the stomach.

'All right, out with it! What is it you wanted to ask us?' Sunniva asked, eyes narrowing.

Gulliksen stopped in his tracks and shot her a half-questioning, half-frightened look.

'Who . . . me? What are you talking about?' he asked, disconcerted.

Finn hastened to explain.

'My dad's chauffeur said you wanted to talk to us.'

Gulliksen looked even more confused.

'Chauffeur? I don't . . . I've never met your dad's chauffeur.'

Finn and Sunniva exchanged concerned glances. Why would Miss Syversen have lied?

'Come on! Let's head back,' Sunniva said, dragging Finn with her. They left Gulliksen looking perplexed and went back out into the wintry weather.

'Why do you think . . .?' Finn started to ask, but then he was interrupted.

'There's something fishy going on,' Sunniva said. 'And who's that English bloke anyway? Is the prime minister's chauffeur allowed to have friends in the car? Aren't there rules for that sort of thing? And why did Miss Syversen tell us Gulliksen wanted to talk to us?'

Finn didn't know, but agreed that something was up. It *was* odd that Maxwell had got into the car with them. Then Finn remembered what Miss Syversen had said to Camomile when they got out of the car. What had that meant? Finn had a bad feeling about all this. They ran across the playground and into the gymnasium building.

No sooner had they opened the door to the changing room when they heard Camomile screaming.

'Nooo! Nooo!'

They stormed in, but halted abruptly at the sight that greeted them. Huge Maxwell Jones of the walrus moustache was lying on the floor holding Camomile in an iron grip, while Miss Syversen stood on the bench pulling as hard as she could . . . at Camomile's head!

'What are you doing?' Sunniva shrieked.

'Stay back,' Miss Syversen gasped.

'Help me! Heeelp!' Camomile shouted as Miss Syversen tugged at his head even harder.

Then it happened. As Finn and Sunniva rushed forward to help Camomile there was a loud bang. Old Miss Syversen lost her balance and fell headlong backwards.

At first Finn thought they had arrived just in time to save Camomile. Maxwell was still lying on the ground with his arms around him. But there was something not quite right, and it took Finn a few seconds to work out what it was. When Miss Syversen got up again he realised what was so totally and utterly wrong: Miss Syversen was holding Camomile's disembodied head in her hands.

CHAPTER 21

THERE ARE SOME MOMENTS in life that you know you will always remember. Finn knew immediately that this was one of those moments. The sight of Camomile without a head. He felt both nauseous and afraid, and he could feel his pulse throbbing throughout his entire body as if he were one huge beating heart.

Even though Camomile's head had been detached from his body, his face was still moving. Just.

'Heelp,' he said weakly. Then there was only silence as the eyes of the small, North Boresian boy finally closed.

Finn felt as if his chest were about to explode. Had they . . . had they killed Camomile?

He glanced at Sunniva. She was also in shock. She looked from Camomile's head to his body and then back again.

'What . . .?' she started, but then stopped in mid-sentence. Perhaps because she had just registered the same as Finn: there was no blood. Not a drop of it. Anywhere.

Sunniva and Finn backed away as Miss Syversen took a step towards them.

'Take it easy,' she said.

That got Sunniva's attention.

'Take it easy?' she spluttered. 'You've killed Camomile and you're asking us to take it easy? You're going to rot in prison,' she said.

Miss Syversen shook her head.

'We haven't killed Camomile.'

They stared at her and waited for her to continue.

'Camomile is . . .' Miss Syversen began. 'You weren't supposed to see this, I promise you.'

Finn studied Miss Syversen. Behind her wrinkles, she did actually look genuinely sorry. Maxwell had also got to his feet. Camomile's body was still on the floor. The tall, aged Englishman was breathing heavily. The struggle had taken a lot out of him.

Then Miss Syversen held up Camomile's head. Finn's first reaction was to avert his eyes, but something made him look. She showed them the underside of the head, and just inside the exterior layer of skin, Finn saw . . . metal?

Miss Syversen nodded, as if to confirm his observation.

'Camomile is . . . a robot,' she said.

Finn swallowed.

'Eh?' was all he could utter.

'Or to be more precise . . . he's an android,' Maxwell said. 'A robot designed to look and act like a human.'

Sunniva opened her mouth to say something, but nothing came out except an exhalation of hot air. Miss Syversen was quick to explain.

'I've been sceptical from day one. Mostly because Kim Il-Ding is an uncommonly devious leader, perhaps the most devious of them all, and he never does anything without an ulterior motive. And North Boresia has made a lot of progress in the field of . . .'

She stopped.

'Maxwell can tell you more about this than I can. But, first, let me introduce you to him properly.'

Miss Syversen carefully placed Camomile's head on the bench. Finn could not comprehend what she was saying. Camomile wasn't . . . real? Miss Syversen turned to Maxwell.

'Max is a kind of secret agent. He's worked for the British intelligence service MI6 for many, many years. His specialist field is . . . er, sophisticated devices, spying equipment and technology in general. There aren't many people in the world who know more about robots and androids than he does.'

Maxwell – or Max, as Miss Syversen called him – smiled.

'Except maybe the North Boresians,' he said. 'We suspected they were close to developing a perfect android. One almost impossible to distinguish with the naked eye from real humans,' he explained.

Finn looked at Camomile again. He had skin, hair, teeth . . . everything about him was so real.

Sunniva, who had been a lot quieter than usual, finally spoke.

'But how did you find out Camomile was a . . . a robot?'

Max looked at Miss Syversen.

'Small tell-tale signs,' she said. 'He didn't react at all when I played loud music in the car whereas everyone else tapped along. But we weren't sure until today.'

'How come?' Finn asked.

Max took a deep breath and scratched his moustache.

'What amazes me is they seem to have overcome the biggest problem . . .'

He paused for a few seconds.

'It appears that Camomile has feelings. Which means it's impossible to rewrite his programming to remove deep-seated fears. And if there's one thing real androids are afraid of, it's being dismantled.'

Tools, Finn thought. That's why Camomile was so afraid of tools.

'I put a drill on the back seat today, and you saw how he reacted,' Max said, looking at Finn.

Then Finn remembered what Miss Syversen had said to Camomile that morning.

'Did what you said to him this morning when we got out of the car have anything to do with this?'

Miss Syversen smiled.

'It's all the same to him whether we speak forwards or backwards. I had practised saying the sentence beforehand, and he didn't even notice it was backwards. He knew what I'd said straight away and answered without any surprise.'

Max shrugged apologetically.

'We wanted to do some more tests, but we weren't as careful as we could have been, so he became suspicious. And he clearly knew some sort of self-defence. I had to use my old judo skills,' Max explained.

Finn had a flashback to when Camomile had held Big Jimmy's arm in the playground.

'So we had no option but to . . . switch him off, if I can put it like that. We didn't want North Boresia to know they'd been rumbled,' Miss Syversen said.

Finn did a double take.

'Didn't want North Boresia to know? What do you mean?'

He stared at Miss Syversen, his mouth agape. Then he realised what she meant. He knew before she said anything, and felt a chill run down his spine.

'Camomile was presumably given to your father to spy on him.'

As she spoke, the changing-room door creaked open again.

'Hello?'

There was no mistaking Bentson's voice or the sound of his stick hitting the floor. Finn looked from Camomile's body on the floor to his head on the bench in panic. What would happen if Bentson saw one of his pupils was in two pieces?

CHAPTER 22

'QUICK, GET HIM UP!' Max whispered.

Together, they lifted Camomile's body onto the bench. Miss Syversen positioned the head against the neck so that it looked as if Camomile was still in one piece, like a real human. They had just managed to manoeuvre him into a sort of sleeping position when Bentson hove into view, his stick in his right hand. He banged it on the floor once more.

'How's it all going in here?' he asked in that brusque manner of his.

'Shhhh,' Miss Syversen whispered, stroking Camomile's hair. 'He suddenly felt unwell, so he's taking a nap.'

Bentson looked at Camomile and nodded mutely.

'Ah. I see. Well, I just wanted to tell you we're starting in five minutes,' he said quietly.

Everyone nodded. Bentson registered all the nodding with some surprise before turning and limping out again.

Finn shut his eyes and took deep breaths after the door closed. That had been a close call. He felt dizzy, and leaned against the wall before sliding to the floor and putting his head in his hands.

Camomile, a spy? It was unbelievable. Yet he knew it was true.

That was why Camomile spent so much time wandering around the house. That was why Finn had found him awake in the living room that night. And that was why he and Sunniva had found him sitting on the floor in the prime minister's office with all those documents spread out around him. On reflection, he had not been a particularly good spy. Of all the conflicting emotions in his head, sadness was still dominating. He had come to appreciate his new brother.

It was as if Maxwell had read his mind.

'Before you get angry or sad and start thinking about how Camomile fooled you . . . it's not really his fault. It's all part of his programming.'

'What do you mean?' Finn asked.

'Well, even though Camomile has feelings and is really somewhere between being human and a robot, he's still programmed to spy. He can't help it. He has to do it, in a way it's in his nature.'

Then he dropped another bombshell.

'He probably doesn't even know he's a robot,' he said.

'What?' Sunniva asked in disbelief.

'Yup. He thinks he's human just like you and me,' Max said, scratching at his moustache.

They heard the fanfare from the gymnasium. Finn staggered to his feet. The room swayed for a few seconds before returning to normal.

'What now?' he asked, nodding towards where Camomile lay on the bench.

Miss Syversen raised her hands.

'Relax. There's a good chance he'll be fine.'

Some of the tension in Finn's chest eased.

'Really?'

'We hope so,' Max said.

'But what about the spying? The prime minister can't have a spy wandering about his house,' Sunniva said.

Miss Syversen looked at Max.

'We've been giving it some thought, haven't we, Max?'

The huge Englishman scratched his moustache with such force it sounded like twigs breaking.

'I'll try to reprogram him. To . . . to be loyal to you and not Kim Il-Ding.'

'You can do that?' Sunniva enquired.

'Yes, I think so. But I'll need a little time with him. I need to take him back to the hotel with me. Is that OK?'

He looked at Finn, who in turn looked at Camomile. What choice did they have? He couldn't stay here in the changing room. In two parts.

'Erm . . . yeah, all right,' Finn said.

'We need to go back,' Sunniva said.

Finn looked at her. Sun Factor 50 was just the two of them now. It had been hard enough when there were three of them, but now Camomile had quite literally lost his head before the final.

'Come on,' Sunniva said calmly. 'You and I will go in and win this thing.'

And then she marched out of the changing room.

CHAPTER 23

FINN STILL FELT DIZZY. His head, which ought to have been lucid enough to allow access to all the knowledge he had accumulated throughout his life, was a chaotic whirl of questions. The last thing he needed was even more questions from Bentson. He didn't think he would be able to answer any of them. He was in shock, and upset to boot. He felt as if he had lost a brother, even though he now knew his brother had not been what he seemed.

He had to think about something else, and looked around. The gymnasium had been rearranged again. All the team tables had been tidied away and replaced by chairs for the audience. The light was even dimmer than before, and there were spotlights shining on each table on the stage. One of them was on Finn and Sunniva, who sat at the table on the far right, painfully aware of Camomile's empty chair. On each of the four tables there was a score pad which the teams had to flip over to show the audience how many points they had.

The same fanfare they had heard earlier was sounded again, and the room, which was jam-packed with pupils and teachers, quietened down. Bentson stepped out onto the stage and positioned himself behind a small table off to the side. Finn felt like he was on some sort of TV show when the fifth spotlight came on, illuminating Bentson in a perfect circle of light.

'Welcome, everyone, to Uranienborg's final qualifying round for the National General Knowledge Competition!'

The audience applauded enthusiastically, some shouting for the name of the team they were rooting for. Bentson banged his stick on the floor and the cheering subsided.

'There will be forty questions, and the four finalists are . . . Megabrain, Viktory, Pride of Urra and Sun Factor 50!'

Bentson paused and took a sip of water, just as a real presenter would. Then, in a serious voice, he started reading:

'Question number one: What is the name of the device used for decapitating people during the French Revolution?'

Finn gaped at Bentson. The last thing he needed at this precise moment in time was more mental images of people losing their heads. His thoughts wandered back to Camomile. Camomile, who wasn't human but a robot. Or . . . what was it Max had called it . . . an android, halfway between a human and a robot, because he had emotions? Who was programmed by Kim Il-Ding to spy on them.

'I know what it is, but I can't remember what it's called,' Sunniva whispered frantically, burying her face in her hands. Finn had already forgotten the question. His thoughts were a jumbled mess of spies in hats and long coats watching people through eyeholes cut in newspapers, R2D2 from Star Wars trundling through the desert on a strange planet and a headless North Boresian boy.

'Sorry,' Finn said, sighing as Bentson announced the correct answer.

He had known very well it was called a guillotine. Four questions later they were in last place with only one point. Sunniva rubbed her face harder and harder, clearly frustrated by Finn's inability to answer any questions. Finn scanned the hall. It was difficult to make out any faces; he was blinded by the spotlight and could only see a restless mass of silhouettes and shadows. Which was maybe just as well considering how foolish he was feeling; he didn't really want to look anyone in the eye. Least of all Sunniva. He resolved to pull himself together.

After unpinning 'Rome', 'Munch', 'Fridtjof Nansen' and 'George Washington' from his memory wall, they were back in the running. They answered question number twenty correctly – What's the largest lake in the world? The Caspian Sea – which put them in second place, three points behind Viktory. With one question left, they were tied in first place.

'Come on now, focus, focus! We CANNN do this!' Sunniva whispered through gritted teeth, punching Finn on the thigh under the table.

Bentson cleared his throat and leaned towards the microphone.

'And the final question: In which year was Uranienborg School built?'

Finn looked at Sunniva. He had no idea; he had only just started at Urra. Sunniva started rubbing her face again, this time so hard she seemed to be making a serious attempt to remove the skin.

'It was . . . it's on the wall somewhere outside . . . 18 . . . 81 . . . or something,' she mumbled.

They really needed Camomile for questions like this, Finn mused. He was a whizz with numbers and dates.

A whizz with numbers? Finn's stomach twisted as he realised. They had done something terrible.

They had cheated.

They'd had a robot on their team. Even though Max said that Camomile had emotions, he was still a machine programmed to remember things. And those who cheat have smelly feet, Baba always used to tell him when they played cards. They're always found out.

They had reached the final with Camomile's help. They couldn't win. Finn didn't want to win.

He knew he had no hope of explaining this to Sunniva. Not at this precise moment. Her face was bright red, partly because she kept rubbing it and partly because she was so determined to beat Viktor.

'1886,' Sunniva muttered to herself, nodding. 'I think it's 1886,' she repeated.

'No. It's not 1886, it's 1884,' Finn whispered.

'What?'

'I'm certain. 1884,' Finn said.

'Are you sure?'

Bentson leaned towards the microphone again.

'Time's up. Your answer sheets, please.'

When Bentson reached their table, Finn gave him the sheet of paper.

'What did you write?' Sunniva asked, her face puce.

'1884,' Finn said.

'I hope you know what you're doing,' Sunniva said, shaking her head.

Bentson was back at his table.

'We'll start with Pride of Urra.'

'1884,' said a tall boy with glasses.

Sunniva's face lit up and she looked at Finn, hope shining through the madness in her eyes.

'Megabrain?'

'We're going for 1886,' said a girl with red Pippi Longstocking plaits. Sunniva grimaced.

'And Viktory?'

'We say 1886,' Viktor said, sounding confident.

Bentson looked at them.

'And last but not least, Sun Factor 50?'

'We think 1884,' Finn said.

It was so quiet in the hall that when Bentson tapped his papers on the table right in front of the microphone it sounded like a thunderclap. He let a few seconds tick by.

'Well, ladies and gentlemen, this is the final question,' he said solemnly, as if the entire audience had not been paying attention.

'And the correct answer, the year in which our wonderful school opened, is . . . the autumn of 1886!'

'NOOOO!' Sunniva howled, but no one heard her over the celebratory whoops of Viktory and the cheering from the audience.

Finn closed his eyes. His stomach hurt. This was just too much

to deal with after everything else they had been through today –
all of the preparation, all of the questions, the drama in the
changing room, Camomile in two pieces and now this . . .

And he still had to tell Sunniva why he had given the wrong
answer.

The opportunity didn't take long to present itself. Finn and
Sunniva stood in silence in the playground as the other participants and the audience headed home. Bojan was sitting on the
bench by the basketball court with his packed lunch, as usual.
Finn knew that Sunniva was so disappointed she was unable to
speak.

'Sunniva?'

'Mmm?'

'I gave the wrong answer . . .'

'I know . . .' Sunniva said gently. 'You did your best. It's just
. . . ugh,' she said, kicking a block of ice, which bounced off in
the direction of the climbing frame.

'No, I didn't. I didn't do my best. I gave the wrong answer
deliberately,' Finn said.

Sunniva turned to look at him.

'You did what?'

Her voice was not so gentle now.

'Listen,' Finn said. 'I suddenly realised that having Camomile
on our team . . . was . . . was as good as cheating.'

'What?'

'Well, he's a robot, isn't he?'

Finn watched Sunniva's face redden.

99

'Are you having a laugh? We worked our butts off to learn everything under the sun, and you gave the wrong answer deliberately? Are you a complete moron?'

She took a step towards him. Finn looked around, hoping someone might intervene and help him persuade her he had done the right thing.

'But, Sunniva, he's a machine! He's programmed to remember things! He . . .'

He got no further.

'I can't believe this! We're a team! And Camomile's as good as human, just think of all the things he *doesn't* know! Just like a human!'

Her eyes narrowed. Finn retreated.

'We were so close to crushing that slimeball Viktor Krantz. We could've done it, I know we could! We could've won the whole thing! And you ruined everything!'

She took a run-up, and for a split second he was afraid she was going to hit him, but she just kicked another block of ice. This time so hard that her boot flew into the air, landing at least fifteen metres away in a snowdrift. She hopped after it, muttering darkly. She turned halfway, still standing on one leg.

'Goodbye, Finn Popps,' she said. And hopped off.

Finn didn't know what to say. He just stared at the boot in the snow.

Then he realised what he had seen in the hallway at Big Jimmy's house. Finn bit his lip. The evidence was beginning to suggest that Big Jimmy had not left the house voluntarily.

CHAPTER 24

FINN LAY IN BED trying to sleep. But it was a bit like trying to stuff a huge brass band, a whistling steam locomotive and a herd of pink elephants into a small closet, close the door and pretend nothing had ever happened.

There was too much going on in his head. He was particularly preoccupied by what had happened that afternoon. When Sunniva had kicked her boot into the snow, he had suddenly remembered how Big Jimmy had lost his red boot while fighting with Viktor, and how Jenny had run after him with it. It was one of a pair of boots that he had seen in the hall at the Svendsen's house – *after* Big Jimmy had disappeared. And since Finn was fairly sure that the Svendsen family only had one pair of winter boots each, there was one obvious question:

Who would run away from home barefoot?

So Finn had dropped in to see Rita Svendsen on the way home. She had dark rings around her eyes and was clearly distraught that her son had now been missing for two full days.

'It's odd you ask me that,' she said. 'Because you're right, we noticed his boots were still here too. And he doesn't have another pair.'

'Did you tell the police?'

'Yes.'

Rita Svendsen paused for a few seconds.

'But they're so busy. I'm starting to think we'll have to find him ourselves.'

Finn felt sorry for Big Jimmy's mum. But that was not the only reason he couldn't sleep. Camomile had lost his head, Sun Factor 50 had lost the quiz and Finn was afraid he had lost a new friend. All of this was keeping him awake.

The day had not got any better when he returned home either. Baba had a sore back and was lying on the sofa complaining. His dad was in a rare bad mood. The latest popularity polls made for bleak reading if you were called Teddy Popps. And his dad was. Trondheim had discovered that workers in camouflage gear had repaired all the roads in Bergen at night, and that this had happened *before* Trondheim had had so much as one measly hole filled in. And now every town with bad roads, which was every single town in Norway, was angry. Even Jevnaker was angry, and they weren't technically speaking a town. Everyone wanted better roads, and they wanted them now. Because that was what Teddy Popps had promised them.

Teddy was pacing around the living room with his arms behind his back like a worried speed skater who couldn't see the finishing line. Finn hadn't seen him this stressed and harassed in a long time.

'If only they knew how many holes there are! Arghhh,' he groaned, his arms behind his back, walking round and round. If, on top of this, Finn had informed his dad that his new son was a spy, there would have been no telling what he might have done. Finn decided it was best not to say anything and hope that Max would be able to fix Camomile.

To make this catastrophically miserable day even more catastrophic and miserable, Baba announced between bouts of grumbling that Teddy had also invited the entire Krantz family to dinner the next day.

'Perfect,' Finn said. And went upstairs to bed.

And there he lay. Listening to the wind howling as it blew snow up the walls of the house. It was almost a song, the tones fluctuating in volume as if someone were playing the flute in the distance.

He wondered where Big Jimmy was. During breaks from the quiz he had heard the rumours sweeping the school. Some said Big Jimmy had joined the tough Maja gang who hung out in Majorstua. Others maintained he had been recruited as an errand boy for the Hells Angels biker gang or he had travelled to Italy to train as an assassin for the Italian mafia. Sunniva had lost her temper and told them to get a grip. He remembered how narrow her eyes had been, how angry she had been when she had left him in the playground. He had been so sure that he was making the right decision when he gave the wrong answer. He hadn't wanted to cheat. But when he had seen how angry she was, he wasn't so sure any more. And now he just wished he could start the day all over again.

The wind was blowing harder than ever. Finn pulled the duvet more tightly around his ears.

He wondered whether Sunniva would talk to him tomorrow. He hoped so. Either way he would have to tell her what Big Jimmy's mum had said as he was leaving.

'The weirdest thing isn't the shoes though,' she said.

'It isn't?'

'No. The weirdest thing is we're actually missing a pair of boots.'

There were tears in her eyes.

'Jon's boots went missing that night. His brother's boots. But they're much too small for Jim-Erik.'

CHAPTER 25

Maybe there was a meteor shower going on. Maybe the moon was yellower than usual. Maybe they were having a disco on Mars. No one in Oslo would have noticed, not with the dark, heavy clouds blanketing the city. Even more snow fell from them now as most people lay asleep in their beds.

A big vehicle pulled into the kerb and a man wearing a red cap put his face to the window. He peered into the dark to see what the street sign said.

'Damn. It's not this one either.'

Vulture swore, hunched over the steering wheel and drove on. Red-Cap glanced over at him.

'I thought you knew this town inside out. I told you we should've brought a map,' he sneered.

'Oh, button it,' Vulture said. 'I know it's around here somewhere.'

Vulture looked once more at the address he had written down on the back of an envelope. Red-Cap tipped back his cap and scratched his forehead, as he always did when he was thinking about something.

'Why do *we* always have to do all the dirty work?' he asked after a few seconds.

Vulture glanced over at him.

'That's just how it is. Some people are thinkers, and some people have to do what the thinkers think.'

Red-Cap said nothing, so Vulture continued.

'In our case, the Colonel's the thinker, and we're the ones who implement his plans,' Vulture said.

'But I don't understand *how* he thinks. Sometimes this just seems nuts.'

'Be patient. These kids are . . . how should I put it . . . guinea pigs. It'll step up a notch soon. Several notches.'

Vulture hit the brakes. Red-Cap sent him a questioning look.

'It's here. We're here,' Vulture said. He opened the envelope and took out a sheet of paper, which he then put in his pocket.

'Have you got the masks?' he asked.

'Yeah,' Red-Cap answered, taking off his cap.

Vulture grabbed a little round plastic box from between their seats.

'You should wear yours more often, it's an improvement,' he said, laughing.

Then he opened the box and stuck a new packet of tobacco under his top lip.

'ow ow ow, IT's like a little devil's got his fork stuck in my back and he's trying to eat me! This blasted arthritis is going to kill me, Teddy! Are you listening to me, Teddy? Teddy, where are you? You're not just going to leave me here, are you?'

Teddy could hear her. They could all hear her. Baba was lying on the sofa in the living room, but her rasping filled the entire house, including the kitchen where Finn and Teddy were having breakfast. Teddy had already called Dr Breyholtz so that he would come before his mother's back got even worse and she drove him mad. Finn was running late. He had a second piece of toast between his teeth and was tying his shoes in the hall.

'Get well soon, Baba!' he called through a mouthful of bread and pâté.

'Oh, don't worry about me,' said the sandpaper voice from the living room. 'I only have to tidy the house, clean up and make dinner for seven people.'

Finn knew that Baba was even more stressed because the Krantz family were coming for dinner – Ernst, Viktor and Viktor's mother, who was called Jeanette Marielle.

'But that's just how it is when everyone else is more important than your sick old mother,' Baba shouted.

'Mum, I have to go to work, I'm the prime minister!' shouted Teddy in exasperation. 'And I've ordered in caterers. You don't need to do anything!'

Finn went out of the door, having already heard this conversation multiple times. But he had only just placed his foot on the top step when the sound of another familiar voice caught his attention.

'Sorry.'

It came from the pavement. Sunniva looked as if she were in prison where she stood clinging to the iron gate with her gloved hands, gazing at Finn. The prime minister's limousine and Miss Syversen stood waiting behind her.

'Hi, Sunniva . . . what did you say?'

'I said I'm sorry. And it's not one of my favourite words, so I hope twice is enough,' she said solemnly.

The cold, painful sensation he'd had in his stomach since he last saw her melted away instantly.

'Yes, of course it is. Sorry for what, anyway?' Finn said, walking towards her.

'You like to rub it in, don't you?' she said. But he glimpsed a smile in her eyes.

'You did the right thing,' she continued. 'It would've been cheating to win with a robot on our team. Completely . . . dishonest. I talked to Mum about it, and she thought it was . . . well, *wonderful* that you gave the wrong answer on purpose.'

'Oh. Thanks,' Finn said. The pain had not only disappeared but had been replaced by something light and fluffy.

'But that's enough about that. I have something else to tell you, something much more important. Hedda's mum rang us earlier this morning. She wondered if we'd seen her.'

'Really? Why?'

Sunniva let go of the gate.

'Because Hedda's run away from home.'

The light, fluffy feeling evaporated.

'What?'

'Hedda's missing. And there was a note, just like with Big Jimmy. "I've run away. But don't worry, I'll be OK" it said.'

Finn shuddered. One missing child was strange. Two was just creepy. Something was seriously wrong, and Sunniva thought the same.

'Children are disappearing, Finn, and in exactly the same way. And you know what? The police didn't even have time to go and speak to her mum. No one's doing anything, Finn. No one cares.'

He saw the determined expression on her face and knew what she was going to say.

'So we have to do something.'

In the distance they heard the Uranienborg School bell ring. It was half past eight. Gulliksen was probably standing at the front of the classroom, register in hand.

Miss Syversen rolled down the tinted passenger-side window.

'Come on, you two chatterboxes. Time for school,' she said.

Sunniva turned towards the open window.

'Can you keep a secret, Miss Syversen?'

'I wouldn't have this job if I couldn't keep a secret,' Miss Syversen said dryly.

'Good,' Sunniva said, opening the rear door and jumping in. 'We're not going to school.'

CHAPTER 27

FINN HAD NEVER SKIPPED school before. It was something else to add to the list of new experiences he'd had in the last week. But he agreed with Sunniva. Someone had to do something.

'Well spotted, Finn,' Sunniva said when he told her about Big Jimmy's boots and how they had been left behind in the hall.

'But why would Big Jimmy take his brother's boots if they didn't fit?' he asked.

'Because he didn't,' Sunniva said.

'What do you mean?'

'I'm not sure what I mean. The only thing I'm sure of is that neither Big Jimmy nor Hedda ran away,' Sunniva said.

They had Miss Syversen and the prime minister's limousine at their disposal for the entire morning. Teddy Popps was in crisis talks about the potholes-in-the-roads situation and wouldn't need his chauffeur until later. Sunniva asked Miss Syversen to drive them to Briskebyveien, where Hedda lived. Or had lived until last night. While they were driving, Miss Syversen updated them on Camomile.

'Max says he's never seen such an advanced robot before. But he won't give up. He wants you to go and see him at the hotel tomorrow. He hopes he'll have Camomile ready by then,' she said.

'Oh, good,' Finn said. He missed his new brother, robot or no robot.

Hedda's flat was a dodgeball throw from the school, a bit further up the road. Miss Syversen stayed in the car while Finn and Sunniva went into their classmate's apartment building.

'I know she talks a lot and can be quite disruptive in class, but Hedda's the nicest person in the world,' Sunniva said as they jogged up the stairs.

When they reached the first floor, an old man wearing pyjamas came out onto the landing.

'Keep it down, will you! It's impossible to get any sleep around here,' he said grumpily.

'Sorry,' Finn and Sunniva chorused, grinding to a halt.

'As if it wasn't enough with all the loud music and dustbin lorries in the middle of the night. Do you have to clatter up and down the stairs just when I've finally managed to nod off?'

'Sorry,' Finn said again. They tiptoed past the old man and scuttled up to the third floor as quietly as they could.

Even though Finn was getting used to talking to distraught mothers, he still didn't like it. Luckily, Sunniva knew Hedda's mum because she had been invited round a few times.

'We had such a nice evening yesterday. We played games and had tacos for dinner,' Hedda's mum said, gripping Sunniva's hand.

They sat in the kitchen of the spacious flat. Hedda's dad was working abroad, but he had booked a seat on the first plane home as soon as his wife had called to tell him what had happened. And what had happened was very similar to what had happened to Big Jimmy. Hedda's mum hadn't heard the alarm clock go off, and when she had finally woken up, Hedda had vanished. Finn wasted no time asking if Hedda's shoes were still there.

'No, of course not. She'd have needed her shoes,' Hedda's mum said, looking at Finn as if he had just grown an extra head. Finn felt a bit foolish.

'But for some reason, she took my coat.'

Finn and Sunniva exchanged glances.

'And you didn't hear anything last night? No noises or anything?' Sunniva asked.

Hedda's mum thought for a few seconds before slowly shaking her head.

'No. I was out for the count.'

Sunniva got up.

'Do you know if she's been hanging out with Jim-Erik from school recently?'

'The boy that ran away? Hedda told me about him.'

Sunniva nodded.

'No, I don't think so,' she said.

'Thought not. We'll spend the day looking for her,' Sunniva said.

'Thank you. That's so sweet of you,' Hedda's mum said, burying her face in her hands. After a few seconds she got up and walked over to the window. There were two wilted plants in pots on the windowsill.

'Dearie me, look at these,' she sighed and carried them over to the kitchen worktop.

Then she turned.

'It's odd, I do remember that I had . . . a nightmare. I dreamt there were people here last night.'

Finn leaned forward.

'How do you mean?' he asked.

'Well, I mean it was only a silly dream . . . I dreamt that I saw people in my bedroom.'

'Really? What did they look like?' Sunniva asked.

'That's what makes it seem so stupid. They were like two . . . insects,' she said, flashing them a weak smile.

Finn and Sunniva exchanged another glance, remembering what Jenny had told them in the school playground.

'Like . . . two flies?' Finn ventured.

'Yes, exactly. Like two flies,' Hedda's mum said, staring at him in amazement. 'How did you know that?'

Finn gave a tentative smile.

'I . . . I was just guessing.'

CHAPTER 28

ANYONE TRACKING THE MOVEMENTS of the extra long, extra shiny prime minister's limousine as it drove around Oslo all morning would have been forgiven for wondering whether the prime minister had too much time on his hands. What they *wouldn't* have known was that there were actually two children inside on the lookout for their missing classmates.

'OK, so people oversleep and wake up to discover their children are missing. And our chief suspects are two *flies*,' Sunniva groaned.

'Yeah, it sounds completely crazy. But if Camomile's a robot, who knows, maybe flies can kidnap children,' Finn suggested.

'No, they can't,' Sunniva said dryly.

Finn didn't believe it either. But it was very curious that Jenny and Hedda's mum had had the same dream. That said, it had been a weird few weeks with all sorts of weird things happening every day. He rested his forehead against the car window as they drove past a group of young people standing outside a 7-Eleven. Finn tried to see if Big Jimmy or Hedda were among them.

'It's like looking for two needles in a sewing factory,' Sunniva said.

'What?' Finn asked. Camomile with all his North Boresian

sayings was one thing, but Sunniva had her own unique twist on the Norwegian ones.

'Just imagine how many needles there are in a sewing factory! And we need to find two specific needles.'

'Oh. Right. I get it.'

Sunniva was right – it was hopeless. They had driven up and down streets, trawled parks and shopping centres, eyeballed homeless people and beggars and spied on anything even vaguely resembling a youth gang, even though neither of them really knew what a criminal youth gang looked like.

All without finding sewing needles, Big Jimmy or Hedda.

'At the very least we should tell the police what we know,' Finn said when they were back in the car.

'Don't you know the chief constable? You could call him using that,' Sunniva said, pointing to a wireless phone attached to the seat in front.

To say he *knew* Chief Constable Malthe was something of an exaggeration. He had really only watched while the huge man had systematically devoured a small mountain of food at the palace. But it was worth a try. He got through after Miss Syversen told the switchboard that it was the prime minister's office calling.

'Malthe,' came a growl from the other end.

Finn gave his name and tried to explain as best he could. About the snus box in Big Jimmy's room, the boots that didn't fit, Hedda's mum's coat, parents oversleeping and two people having the same dream about two massive flies breaking into their houses. About how they were sure the children hadn't left their homes voluntarily.

116

Malthe said nothing while he spoke, and remained silent for several seconds after Finn had finished.

'So, Popps Junior, you think two flies have taken your classmates? With all due respect, I don't have time for this.'

Then the chief constable hung up. Finn regretted calling immediately; he felt like a complete idiot. Sunniva looked at him.

'Sooo . . . he's not going to issue a red alert telling Europe to keep their eyes peeled for two giant flies with snus boxes and badly fitting shoes?'

Sunniva was unable to suppress a snigger. Finn turned away from her. Sometimes she could be unbelievably irritating.

CHAPTER 29

'FINN POPPS!'

Baba was standing at the bottom of the stairs. Dr Breyholtz had given her a selection of colourful painkillers, and she was almost back to her old exuberant self. Finn wondered if she had perhaps taken too many tablets, because she was *very* stressed and shouting *much* louder that she usually did.

'Yes, I'm coming,' he called from his room.

'Put on a nice shirt and a different pair of trousers,' she shouted, just as loudly. 'The Krantzes are coming, you know.'

Last night no one had noticed that Camomile was missing. It was only now as Baba laid the table that she thought to ask about him. Finn hated lying, but 'He's staying with a friend' was almost true and, fortunately, enough to ensure that no one asked any more questions.

Dinner started better than Finn had dared imagine. Even Viktor was being relatively pleasant.

'I must say, you've got really good taste,' he said, smiling at Baba.

'Oh my, listen to him, Teddy,' Baba said, still a bit too loudly, feigning embarrassment and fanning herself.

118

Finn seriously doubted Viktor's sincerity, but at least he was steering clear of his usual rude, arrogant self.

'I browsed through interior design magazines and used colours from Gran Canaria. I was there in 1989, you see,' Baba continued, now directing her comments at Jeanette Marielle.

'Were you now?' Jeanette Marielle asked, giving the meat on her plate a dubious poke.

Ernst and Teddy wasted no time getting on to the subject of the unfavourable opinion polls.

'It's completely hopeless, Ernst! Here I am doing my best from dawn till dusk, and this is the thanks I get!'

Teddy was waving his fork so vehemently that Finn was worried his roast pork would fly across the table and hit someone.

'Relax, Teddy,' Ernst said. He also had his eyes on the fork. 'What you need is a diversion.'

'A what?' Teddy asked, looking interested.

'You need something to draw everyone's attention away from all the holes in the roads. Something that will make people happy.'

'Happy people is good, I get that,' Teddy said, his curiosity piqued. 'But what kind of deviation?'

'Diversion,' Ernst said, looking left and right as if to check that no one except those present was listening.

'I have a few ideas, but we can discuss them later.'

The assurance that Ernst had 'a few ideas' was enough to placate Teddy for the time being, and soon the conversation turned to other topics. Topics such as that no one could remember when it had last snowed so much, and that it was now you really wanted to be on a sunny beach with an umbrella drink in your hand. Viktor alternated between talking to the adults and Bendik, ignoring Finn.

'And how about you, Finn, how are you getting on at your new school?' Jeanette Marielle asked out of nowhere.

But before he had a chance to answer, she continued.

'Viktor's doing sooo well, and I think you're quite popular too, aren't you, Vik darling, especially with the girls, isn't that right?'

Jeanette Marielle chuckled as Viktor glared at her. Then his expression did an about-turn and he smiled at the rest of the table.

'It really *is* a good class. Some people are a bit immature and unruly, but that's to be expected,' he said.

What a big-headed ninny, Finn thought, feeling himself getting irritated.

'It's just a shame that students are disappearing,' Finn said without a second thought. Everyone turned to look at him in surprise.

'What do you mean?' Ernst leaned across the table.

Finn hesitated for a moment before continuing.

'Well, erm . . . two people in our class have gone missing,' he said, not enjoying being the centre of attention.

'We heard about that . . . that they'd run away,' Ernst said.

'But that's just it! They didn't run away. Someone took them.'

'Come on now, you're just being silly . . .' Jeanette Marielle started to say, looking round the table to see if anyone actually believed him.

'Missing children? I haven't heard anything about that,' Teddy said, laughing nervously as well.

'And how do you know so much about it?' Ernst asked calmly, fixing Finn with his beady eyes.

'Er . . . I just do. I . . . I've been asking around . . .'

Finn didn't like the way Ernst was looking at him, and didn't want to say anything else.

Teddy clapped his hands together.

'Oh well, children will be children. They get some strange ideas,' he said, and Finn wasn't sure whether he was referring to the missing children or him.

'Time for coffee and cake, don't you think? Maybe I could give you the grand tour while my mother sorts things out in the kitchen?'

Finn regretted having said anything at all. He just felt stupid now. He opted out of the tour of the house. He helped Baba to clear the table instead.

'What's up with her?' Baba asked, holding a full plate of roast pork and potatoes in front of Finn's nose.

'She didn't touch her food. What do you reckon, not good enough for Her Nibs?'

'It was really good, Baba,' Finn said hurriedly, afraid that Jeanette Marielle would hear them.

Finn crept upstairs to his room. From there he could hear his dad wandering from room to room with the Krantz family in tow as if he were a guide showing people round Tutankhamun's tomb in Egypt. Teddy knew he had the best house. He was no longer just a taxi driver with a comb-over and beer belly, a normal man living in the shadow of people like Ernst Krantz. No, he was Prime Minister Teddy Popps, the man who *did something about it*, the everyday hero who made a difference to people's lives, who bedecked the front pages of newspapers and magazines and dominated the top stories in news broadcasts. Despite the continued existence of the comb-over and beer belly.

Finn hid under his duvet as they got closer.

'And this is Finn's room,' Teddy said as the whole flock ambled in.

'I chose a kind of southern sunrise theme for this room,' came a rasping voice. Baba had joined the sheep.

'I was in Gran Canaria in 1989, and I remember . . .'

'Yes, you said,' Jeanette Marielle interrupted, yawning.

Through an opening in his duvet cocoon, Finn saw Baba's mouth tighten. He knew her well enough to know she hated being interrupted, especially when she was talking about Gran Canaria.

'And Camomile's room is next door,' Teddy said quickly, leading them onwards.

Finally they all went downstairs again. Or at least Finn assumed they had all gone downstairs when everything went quiet. But then he heard a low voice right outside his door. He was still under his duvet, but he made the opening bigger so he could hear.

'I think I'm gonna puke. Why is that fat, bald idiot strutting around like he rules the world?'

It was Viktor.

'Calm down, Viktor, not so loud,' answered a deeper voice.

That was Ernst.

'You're way smarter than him. Just like I'm way smarter than that little suck-up Finn. You have no idea how satisfying it was to beat him in the quiz,' Viktor said.

Finn clenched his fists under his duvet.

'I can imagine,' Ernst said.

'He's so irritating. He thinks he's special because he gets to live in the prime minister's residence. Why aren't we living here, Dad?' Viktor said.

Ernst lowered his voice, and Finn stuck his head out from underneath the duvet to hear.

'Relax, Viktor. I've got a . . . I suppose you might call it a plan. Before long you'll be shot of Finn for good, I can tell you that much,' Ernst said.

CHAPTER 30

FINN LAY UNDER HIS duvet going hot and cold as he went over what he had just heard. "Before long you'll be shot of Finn for good"? What had Ernst meant by that? He hardly dared breathe. It was only when he heard the steps creak that he pushed the duvet aside and gulped down fresh air, trying to clear his thoughts.

He was still struggling when Baba's rasping voice trumpeted through the house.

'Finn Popps! Come down here! Time for cake!'

Teddy had ordered Napoleons from a bakery in Frogner. He was now pouring champagne for the adults and green pop for the children as Jeanette Marielle talked about what they were doing for Christmas.

'I think the Canary Islands are a bit tacky now. We were thinking of going to Hawaii.'

Finn looked at Baba. She had just taken a bite, but looked as if she had got Napoleon himself stuck in her throat. She reached for her champagne glass and took a big gulp to wash it down. She drained the glass with the next gulp and glared daggers at Jeanette Marielle, doubtless imagining four types of quick death.

Jeanette Marielle declined cake, patting her flat stomach and saying it had been years since she had 'indulged in calorie bombs like that', then continued to prattle on about Hawaii and its sooper long beaches, sooper leafy palm trees and sooper high surfing waves. She also showed them photos of the sooper huge house they had rented. Baba said nothing, but Finn noticed that she barely glanced at the photo, she just poured herself a sooper big glass of champagne.

Then Teddy and Ernst went into the study to discuss how they might divert attention from the holes in the roads to something that would make Trondheim & Co. happy again.

Bendik put on an old James Bond film in the TV room, and the three boys sat drinking lemonade as they watched the British secret agent jump out of moving cars, beat up Russian henchmen and turn his charm on scantily clad women – sometimes all at once. Finn thought about Max and how he had worked for MI6 and wondered if being a secret agent really involved cameras that shot laser beams or key rings that exploded if you whistled a certain tune.

'I hear you crushed Finn in the school quiz,' Bendik said to Viktor.

Finn looked at Bendik, wishing he had a key ring big enough to zap annoying older brothers.

'Didn't take much.' Viktor grinned.

'He thinks he's so smart. Nice to bring him back down to earth every so often.' Bendik grinned back.

Finn was about to respond when they heard loud voices from the living room. Or, to be more precise, one loud, rasping voice.

'Now I think you should take your sooper scrawny arse and surf right out of this house!'

The combination of a sore back, painkillers, champagne and Jeanette Marielle Krantz had finally become too much for Baba. Jeanette Marielle appeared in the doorway to the TV room, her face crimson.

'Viktor, we're leaving. Now!'

The entire Krantz family were gone in less than two minutes. Baba took the remaining Napoleons into the living room where she sat alternately eating and talking to herself.

'Never seen anything like it. What a know-it-all, ungrateful cow,' she huffed between mouthfuls of cake.

Finn and Bendik stayed in the TV room drinking lemonade and watching James Bond fighting and kissing a lady spy who was both beautiful and scary all at once. They hadn't been watching long when Teddy bounded into the room looking rather cheerful despite the explosive end to the dinner party.

'Boys, listen to this,' he said excitedly.

Bendik hit the pause button just as James Bond put his hand on the terrifyingly beautiful lady spy's bum. Finn turned away from the screen in embarrassment and gave his dad his full attention.

'Right . . . before Baba chucked out the Krantzes,' he started, nodding in the direction of the living room.

'What a cow!' they heard Baba shout.

Teddy rolled his eyes before continuing.

'Anyway . . . Ernst and I have thought up a great way of . . .

diverting people's attention so that they forget about all the stupid holes in the roads for a while. It'll make me popular all over the country again! Good, eh?'

He made a sort of 'ta-dah!' gesture and smiled, obviously waiting for a reaction.

'Sounds good, but how?' Bendik asked.

Teddy adjusted his comb-over with three judicious moves.

'OK, well, it's winter and snowing like no one's business, right?'

Finn and Bendik nodded.

'There are perfect snow conditions all over Norway and everyone's out making the most of it. There's just one thing missing. What do you think that is?'

He looked from Finn to Bendik, smiling as if it were the most obvious thing in the world.

'Christmas spirit?' Bendik ventured.

Teddy snorted.

'No, no, no – Kvikk Lunsj chocolate bars. The perfect accompaniment to any outdoor trip! And Norwegians don't ski anywhere without it! I've decided to hand out free Kvikk Lunsj bars all this weekend!'

He ta-dahed again.

'Five per family! Good, isn't it? They're going to love me, don't you think?'

Teddy nodded more maniacally than ever, as if answering his own question.

Bendik grinned.

'Clever. Good plan, Pops,' he said, impressed.

Finn didn't quite know what to say. It wasn't that he didn't think free chocolate bars were a good idea, he just wasn't entirely sure it was the best way to solve the road problem. Teddy gleefully clapped his hands.

'Yup. It's such a good plan we're putting it into action tomorrow. I'm holding a press conference at one o'clock to announce the good news,' he said before wandering off again.

Is this politics? Finn wondered. The people in charge try to make everyone happy while those not in charge try to make everyone unhappy? He reflected for another couple of seconds, but then the bum on TV started moving again and James Bond asked the lady spy whether it might not make more sense for them to spy on each other in the bedroom.

CHAPTER 31

FINN WOKE UP NEEDING the loo. The alarm clock on his bedside table showed 3:28. He stumbled to the bathroom and back in a dream, and was on the cusp of sleep again when he heard noises coming from downstairs. At first he assumed it was just Camomile wandering around. Then he remembered Camomile wasn't even in the house.

Dad's probably fixing himself a late-night snack, he told himself, pulling the duvet tighter around him and closing his eyes.

But what were those strange hissing sounds his dad was making? It sounded like a dragon breathing through its nose in small pants. Did his dad have a cold? Finn stuck his head out from under the duvet and sniffed the air. And what was that slightly bitter smell?

Finn got out of bed again feeling irritable and shuffled to the top of the stairs to see what his dad was up to.

Then he saw them.

The flies.

Little Jenny hadn't been dreaming. Two men in black with gas masks on stood in the hall downstairs. The masks made them look like two giant insects, or to be more exact, two flies. On their backs they were wearing what looked like rucksacks, with a fat hose coming from each of them, which they held in their hands.

They're gassing us, Finn thought, panic-stricken. He could feel his heart pounding wildly. But the men hadn't seen him. He crept back the way he had come until he was hidden from view. Then he heard one of them put his foot on the first step. They were coming towards him! He cast around for a place to hide. Where could he hide? A large wardrobe, currently homeless, had been left a little further along the landing. He hurried over to it, slipped between the clothes hanging inside and closed the door behind him. Again he heard the stairs creak. He tried to think clearly, but it was difficult with his heart trying to escape through his mouth. What was going on?

The hissing came closer. They're using gas to send us off to sleep, Finn thought. So that no one wakes up when they kidnap the children. That's why the families had overslept! He guessed the flies were already up the stairs and on the landing now, and he could hear the gas being pumped out in short bursts. For the time being he couldn't smell it – the wardrobe functioned as an airtight room. He stood perfectly still for what felt like an hour but was actually only a minute or two as the men went from room to room. Eventually they met right outside the wardrobe.

'He's not here,' said a voice. It sounded strange and muffled because of the mask.

'He *has* to be here,' said the other. 'We *know* he's here. We saw him through the window, and no one's left the house.'

Finn held his breath. They were after *him*! He held a woollen

130

garment in front of his mouth so that he wouldn't make a sound. Then he realised whose clothes they were. His mum's. It was her old wardrobe. His dad obviously hadn't known what to do with it. Finn could smell her as he breathed through what felt like a thin jumper. Finn started to feel giddy. He could still hear the gas being pumped through the hoses. It probably wouldn't be long before it filtered into the wardrobe as well. He would have to hold his breath. Finn took one last deep breath and closed his mouth.

'That foreign kid's not here either,' said the first voice.

'We're not looking for him,' the other answered. 'Remember what the Colonel said. Only Finn. We need to get him to Angelica down at the harbour. The Colonel's going to visit her tomorrow.'

'Yes, I know. But where *is* the little brat?'

'No idea. Ground floor maybe. Or top. Come on, we'll check downstairs first. Maybe he's sleeping on the sofa or somethin'.'

They headed for the staircase and Finn let go of his breath. What now? He had to get out of the wardrobe – the gas was already seeping in. And it was much stronger in the rest of the house. But how? Then it hit him: the roof! He had to get up onto the roof. He took another deep breath, hoping the air in the wardrobe was still pure enough for him not to be affected. Then he carefully opened the door and snuck out. The gas made his eyes sting as if invisible glass dust were rubbing against his corneas. He tiptoed barefoot upstairs as quickly as possible and into the attic. His eyes were streaming now, making it difficult to see, and he tried to wipe away the tears with the back of his hand. Finn knew he would have to breathe soon, so he had to be fast. Not only that, he could hear the men coming back upstairs. He shinned up the ladder and opened the hatch to the roof. They were on the first floor now and heading towards the stairs to the second. He swung open the roof hatch until it hit the snow, then clambered up the last couple rungs of the ladder. The ice-cold air hit him like a hammer, and he took a long-awaited deep breath before the next question occurred to him: where could he hide? There was a good chance they would check up here too. And his footprints would give him away. It was a detached house, so he couldn't climb onto another roof, and even though there had never been so much snow, jumping would mean an almost certain death.

The polar bear skin! It was out here somewhere, under all the snow. He felt around with his hand and soon found something furry. He carefully closed the roof hatch behind him. Then he stood on the hatch as he erased his footprints from the snow. He lifted the skin carefully so none of the snow would fall off, just enough for him to crawl underneath. He curled into a ball, fear keeping him warm for the time being, even though he was only wearing pyjama trousers and a T-shirt. With any luck they wouldn't even check the roof.

Seconds ticked by. A minute maybe. Then, through the snow and the roof, he heard sounds from the attic beneath him. Someone was coming up the ladder. His body quivered with every step. He heard the roof hatch open. He could hear the man breathing through his gas mask – it was like listening to Darth Vader. Finn stopped breathing.

'Is he there?' asked a voice from below.

The man close to Finn waited for a few seconds. He's seen me, Finn thought. He'll reach out a hand in a minute. Reach out and grab me by the hair and drag me from underneath the skin and the snow, down from the roof and out into the street and away from 18 Inkognitogate.

Finn squeezed his eyes shut and waited for the hand.

But it never came.

'No. He's not here either,' said the man with the Darth Vader breath before climbing back down the ladder again.

'Goddamn pesky kid,' was the last thing Finn heard before the roof hatch closed again.

Finn lay with his eyes closed, listening intently in case the men came back. But he could feel his fear melting away bit by bit as he became more and more convinced they would *not* check the roof again. The more he relaxed, the colder he became. It started in his toes. He had the bearskin over him, but he was still lying on the freezing snow. His little toe was the first to go numb, and then the cold spread up his legs to his tummy, chest, along his arms and all the way up to his head and ears. He knew he couldn't stay there long. He crawled out from underneath the skin, carefully shook off the snow and sat on top of it. He massaged his toes to get them warm again while he waited.

After what seemed like an age, he finally heard sounds from down by the front door. He heard the men walking down the driveway and out of the gate, and then he heard two car doors open and close. Finn crawled over to the edge of the roof to look down. He heard an engine start, a rattle and a rumble. It had to be a big vehicle. As it drove off he peeped over the edge, just in time to know he had seen it before. It said 'Norway Recycles Ltd' on the side of the vehicle. The dustbin lorry. He remembered what Hedda's grumpy neighbour had said, the man who had complained about all the noise: '. . . and dustbin lorries in the middle of the night . . .' That was how they were transporting the children!

The lorry drove down Inkognitogate. There were no other vehicles or people in sight, and gradually the rumble of the engine grew fainter and fainter until it was replaced by an all-consuming silence. It was snowing. Finn was already soaking wet, but still felt every snowflake that landed on him: cold, soft and gentle.

Nothing is as quiet as December, he thought, standing in just his pyjamas on the roof of 18 Inkognitogate watching thousands of snowflakes swirling around him in total silence.

He was cold and exhausted, too cold and too exhausted to think about what had actually taken place. All he knew for certain was that he wouldn't survive if he stayed on the roof. He had to get inside before he froze to death. It didn't help that the house was full of gas. He was fairly sure however that it wasn't deadly. Frozen stiff and without any clear plan, he opened the hatch and climbed down. The gas stung his eyes now more than ever. Don't breathe, he thought, but before he had even reached the first floor, Finn could feel that something was happening to him. It felt like a heavy fog was seeping into his head. It got in through the corners of his eyes, his nostrils and ears and settled in his head and body like invisible liquid cement, making him feel languid and heavy. It didn't hurt. Quite the opposite in fact – it was a pleasant heaviness, as if his entire body just wanted him to lie down and rest. He tried to fight it, holding tightly to the banister as he took the stairs one at a time. By the time he reached the first floor, Finn realised he had neither the strength nor the will to continue. He sank slowly to the floor and passed out.

CHAPTER 32

FINN WAS WALKING THROUGH a forest. Tall, green trees stood arm in arm around him. Only a few rays of bright sunlight permeated the foliage above him. At first, he didn't know where he was going or what he was leaving behind. Then he heard a melody. Beautiful music wafted towards him from somewhere far away. The faster he walked, the closer it came, borne by the wind. Maybe it was just the wind playing its own unique song? The same trilled notes again and again, a melody that started low, then rose higher and higher and ended far above the trees in the brilliant sunshine. He sped up as he approached the crest of a hill, the melody was much clearer now and he knew he would soon find out where it was coming from. A big beech tree stood at the top of the hill, and he stopped underneath it. The forest was spread out below him like a meadow of tall grass and flowers upon which the sun bore down unimpeded. In the middle of the meadow was a path, and it was there he saw them. Walking in a long, long line.

All the children.

Big Jimmy, Hedda and many, many more. They were walking towards him, and it was as if they were sleepwalking, as if they had succumbed to the melody and would follow it no matter where it led. But it wasn't the wind that was making the music. It was a man. He was at the head of the line and the children were following him as he played his flute. The man was wearing a long, dark cloak with a hood, but Finn knew who it was straight away. It was Ernst Krantz. Finn knew that he had to take the flute off him so that the children would wake up. He looked around the hilltop for an object he could attack Ernst with. A stick, a stone or anything at all. He found nothing, so he grabbed one of the branches of a beech tree and tried to break it off. The children were coming straight towards him now. Ernst had spotted him, but continued to play, although it was no longer a tune but one note – one intense, piercing note he played again and again as he came closer and closer.

Finn woke with a start. But the note he had heard in his dream persisted. It took him a few seconds to work out what it was. The doorbell. Someone was at the door. He blinked and rubbed his eyes. He was lying on the first-floor landing. Although his head was still fuzzy, slowly but surely the events of the night all came back to him. For a few seconds he wondered if the whole thing had been a dream. Men wearing gas masks had broken in and tried to kidnap him . . . no, surely not. But he knew that this had actually happened, just as he knew the dream he'd had about Ernst in the forest was indeed that: a dream. And he knew this was how the other children had been kidnapped, sedated with gas and carried out of their houses in the middle of the night. Another bout of intense doorbell ringing got Finn to his feet, and he went downstairs to open the door. It was unlocked.

'What kept you, slowpoke? It's eleven o'clock. I've been out here ringing the bell for ages.'

Sunniva was standing on the step with her arms crossed and an irritated expression on her face. Finn was unable to speak at first, he just stood gaping at her. Then it all came out at once.

'The flies were here, Sunniva. After me. Well, they weren't flies, they were men wearing gas masks spraying gas from rucksacks to put us all to sleep, but I hid behind my mum's clothes in the wardrobe and on the roof under the bearskin . . .'

Finn had to repeat himself several times. It was only after the third time that Sunniva had the story straight and was sure Finn was telling the truth. When Finn had finally finished, they sat looking at each other in silence. Sunniva shook her head slowly.

'This is not good, Finn. Not good at all,' she said.

'I know,' he said quietly.

Then he noticed that the tulips the Krantzes had brought round the evening before, which Baba had put in a vase on a table in the hall, had wilted.

'Look at the flowers,' he said.

'They're dead,' Sunniva said.

He was suddenly reminded of the dead plants on the windowsill at Hedda's and the flowers at Big Jimmy's. Of course.

'The gas killed them,' Finn said, prodding one of the withered tulips. Then he remembered that the rest of his family were probably still asleep.

'I need to wake the others,' he said, hurrying upstairs.

Half an hour later they were all sitting around the breakfast table. They were all amazed that they had slept in for so long, and the prime minister was stressed because he only had an hour before his press conference. But, to Finn's despair, no one was the least bit prepared to believe him.

'Men wearing gas masks? Codswallop,' Baba said. Her voice was raspier than ever, and she was wearing a red beanie. Finn knew she had an ice pack underneath it. She always did that when she had a headache.

'You have some weird dreams, Finn my lad, I'll give you that,' Teddy said with his mouth full.

'I wasn't dreaming. It actually happened! They sprayed the whole house with gas, and that's why we all overslept!' Finn shouted in exasperation.

'Or maybe you've finally gone round the twist. We all saw it coming,' Bendik sneered.

Sunniva leaned towards Finn.

'Give up, there's no point,' she murmured.

But Finn couldn't let go.

'That's so typical!' he said, banging the table with both fists.

Teddy, who had just stuffed his mouth full of food, stopped chewing and looked at his son. Baba grimaced and held onto her hat.

'You never listen to me. You're not listening now and you never ever do!' Finn continued, glaring at his father. 'All you think about is yourselves! You wouldn't even notice if I disappeared! And I nearly did last night!'

Teddy looked from Finn to the others, his expression a mixture of surprise and uncertainty. He wasn't used to his youngest son talking to him in this way.

'But . . . Finn my lad . . .' he smiled nervously. 'All I'm saying is we were all out for the count, and so it's not unusual to have . . . er . . . strange dreams.'

Finn looked at him and opened his mouth to shout once again that it hadn't been a dream. But he knew this was a waste of time. He got up from his chair and marched out of the kitchen painted the same colour as the sea around Gran Canaria.

CHAPTER 33

'WHAT IS IT WITH grown-ups?' Finn sighed.

He was walking so fast that Sunniva had to jog to keep up.

'With all due respect, Finn, your dad's not a typical grown-up. And even a normal dad would've had a hard time believing your story. You've got to admit it's a tough ask,' Sunniva said.

Finn was fully aware he didn't have a normal dad, but still. He was getting irritated with Sunniva as well, even though he knew she was right.

'They'd believe me if I was a grown-up,' he grumbled.

'Hm, maybe.'

'And there's no way I'm calling the police again,' Finn said.

Sunniva thought about that for a few seconds before firmly shaking her head.

'No. Not yet,' Sunniva said. 'We haven't got any proof, just what you saw and some dead flowers. And they're not going to take your word against the prime minister's,' she said.

'And it really does sound like a dream,' she said. 'A really bad dream.'

Finn sighed. He knew she was right. Again.

'Here we are.'

Sunniva nodded in the direction of an old building across the street. H-O-T-E-L B-R-I-S-T-O-L, Finn read, looking at the sign above the entrance. A line of suitcases stood outside. This was where Camomile had spent the last few days.

'I think we should tell Max and Miss Syversen. Hopefully they've seen and experienced enough in their lives to believe us,' Sunniva said.

They crossed the road and walked up to the heavy hotel door. Sunniva pulled it open and held it for Finn, but he had hardly reacted before a well-dressed businessman came through, clearly in a hurry, and Finn had to jump to the side to avoid being trampled underfoot.

'I almost forgot,' Finn said as they entered the hotel lobby. 'Something happened while the Krankies were here yesterday. Something that might explain the events of last night.'

He told her what Ernst Krantz had said to Viktor outside his room the previous evening. That Viktor wouldn't be seeing a lot more of Finn. Just a few hours before he had almost been kidnapped.

'And on top of that Ernst was the only person who took me seriously at dinner when I told them about the children who'd gone missing. He was genuinely interested and wondered how I knew so much,' Finn said.

'Mystifistic.'

'Eh?' Finn asked.

'Nothing, Mum always says mystifistic when something's . . . well, mystifistic. And there's definitely something mystifistic about this Ernst Krantz. Maybe he's the Colonel?'

'Maybe. What about this Angelica person they mentioned?' Finn asked. 'And what do they do with the children they kidnap anyway?'

There was no end to the questions. However, the question that worried Finn the most right now was whether he would ever see Camomile again.

The answer came eighteen minutes later.

'I thwear, I've never felt better!' chirruped the little North Boresian, with a loud laugh. Finn had to smile. Not only was Camomile back to his old self, he was quite possibly happier than he had been before they had pulled off his head.

Max, Finn, Sunniva and Camomile were sitting in the lobby of Hotel Bristol. Camomile had just finished a bottle of Coke, and Finn and Sunniva were drinking the hotel's famous hot chocolate. The rumours were true, it *was* criminally good.

Miss Syversen was working, which at that precise moment meant she was driving Prime Minister Teddy Popps to the Kvikk Lunsj press conference.

After two Cokes, Camomile needed the loo, providing Max with the ideal opportunity to tell them what he had been up to since they had last seen him. When Camomile's head had been re-attached and he had woken up, he hadn't had a clue what was going on. Max had told him that he had slipped in a pool of water in the changing rooms and hit his head on the hard floor tiles. And slept for two days.

'Not the best lie, but luckily he's quite trusting,' Max said, smiling at Finn and Sunniva.

'Yes, he is,' Finn said.

Max glanced to his left and right before leaning over the table.

'It's not been easy, but I think I've cracked it. Camomile's good as new,' he said, smiling proudly. 'His eyes work like a kind of video camera. Everything he sees is stored in his head, so any secret information he had on the prime minister was automatically sent to North Boresia. But I've re-programmed him to send only boring and not-so-secret information, like the number of reindeer hit by trains every year. Or how much toilet paper is left in the downstairs loo.'

Max laughed so much the cups shook on the table. Finn and Sunniva laughed too, Finn mostly because he was so relieved that Camomile was both well and whole again.

'And I've also made sure he'll be loyal to you rather than Kim Il-Ding, Finn. So now you've really got a brother for life.'

Finn smiled. Something relaxed in his chest, deep down where he had been sure he had lost Camomile forever.

'Thank you. He still doesn't know he's a robot then?' Finn asked.

'No. He didn't even know he was a spy, or that everything he saw was being sent to North Boresia. He just acted instinctively,' Max said.

'One thing still bothers me,' Finn said. 'Why did he drink so much olive oil?'

Max laughed again.

'Camomile's a kind of machine, and drinking olive oil was kind of . . . er, a way of lubricating the machine, as it were,' he said, smiling.

*   *   *

144

Just after Camomile came back from the loo, Miss Syversen arrived as well. Teddy had been right: the prospect of free Kvikk Lunsj bars had gone down a storm.

'They almost raised the roof. And as soon as it was over they all ran to the nearest shop,' she told them drily. 'We can only hope the prime minister made sure there was a big enough supply. If they run out he'll be in trouble for that as well,' she said.

Finn cleared his throat.

'While we're on the subject of people in trouble,' he said. 'I have something to tell you.'

Finn took a big gulp of his hot chocolate before continuing. This time he calmly explained what had happened, and he told the whole story from the beginning. About Big Jimmy, and how he hadn't come to school, about Big Jimmy's mum, who thought he had run away from home, about Hedda, who was also missing, about the families oversleeping, about the notes left on pillows, about the missing shoes and the wilted plants. He finished by telling them what had happened in Inkognitogate the night before, about the fly men who had scoured the house for him, and the roof, where he was hiding. He also told them about that morning, about how his family hadn't believed him and about his suspicions regarding Ernst Krantz.

After he had finished, they all sat for a few seconds without saying anything. In the end, it was Camomile who broke the silence.

'Nithely done, Finn,' he said, imprethed.

Max nodded.

'Yes. Most people would have panicked in that situation, but you kept your head,' he said.

'So you believe me?' Finn asked.

'Of course we believe you,' said Miss Syversen, every wrinkle in her forehead expressing concern.

'But this is serious,' Max said. 'And even though Ernst Krantz is clearly a man who knows what he wants . . . why on earth would he kidnap innocent children in the middle of the night?'

Miss Syversen raised both her hands.

'Now, now. Let's not get ahead of ourselves. We know there's something off about this fellow, but we don't know *for certain* that he's behind this,' she said. 'And in any case we don't have enough on him to go to the police. I agree that they're much more likely to believe the prime minister than you, Finn.'

'I suppose so,' Finn sighed.

'But what are we going to do?' Sunniva asked.

'We're going to do a bit of old-fashioned spying,' Miss Syversen said, as if it were the simplest thing in the world.

'Ooh, yeth! Thpying ith fun,' Camomile intoned enthusiastically.

Finn and Max exchanged glances.

CHAPTER 34

A SLIPPERY ESTATE AGENT might have asserted that the Krantzes' huge mansion was located a mere stone's throw from Uranienborg School. But it would have been a throw of more than 350 metres, and if an estate agent could throw a stone that far, they would be better served quitting their job and taking up athletics. But apart from that they would not have had to lie at all, because the house at the end of Uranienborg Terrasse was truly majestic. It was set back from the road and had a big garden surrounded by a high fence with a cast-iron gate that served as an effective deterrent to anyone who might fancy wandering in uninvited.

A black Alfa Romeo Giulietta with 235 highly trained horses under the bonnet was parked close to the pavement forty metres further along the road. Inside sat a very old woman and three young people. So far, life as a spy was far less glamorous and exciting than the James Bond films suggested. Of course, Finn knew that films were films and reality was reality, but after two long hours up the road from the mansion in Uranienborg Terrasse without anything more exciting happening than an old man falling flat on his face in the snow, Finn was getting seriously bored. They had caught a glimpse of Ernst through a first-floor window an hour ago, but since then nothing had happened to change their view that spying on people was more about waiting than having fun.

'Anyone want to play a game?' he asked.

'Yeth! Or we could have a quith!' Camomile said.

'No games or quizzes now,' Miss Syversen said, even more sternly than usual.

Just for once Miss Syversen did not have her long, dark chauffeur's coat on. She was wearing a dark leather jacket, and the fingers drumming lightly on the steering wheel were encased in matching black leather gloves. Finn thought she was quite stylish for someone over a hundred years old.

They were making do without the expert spy. Max had had to stay at the hotel and work. He had a lot to catch up on after spending two full days working on Camomile.

They waited in silence for another fifteen minutes. Finn saw at least two families on their way home from skiing trips and wondered if they knew about the free Kvikk Lunsj.

'Here he comes,' Sunniva said suddenly.

Ernst, dressed in a dark winter coat and fur hat, was walking in the direction of his car. He brushed the snow from the silver Range Rover, climbed in and drove towards the tall cast-iron gate, which opened automatically as he approached.

They followed at a safe distance, and Finn marvelled at the elegant way in which Miss Syversen manoeuvred between the lines of traffic, hid behind other cars and made sure they crossed junctions within the same light sequence as Ernst. All without being seen. She was a professional, and it all rather made Finn feel like they were in a James Bond film after all.

Ernst was driving towards the centre of town, and soon he disappeared into the Ibsen Tunnel.

'He's on his way to the harbour,' Sunniva said, filled with hope.

She was right. Ernst was heading for where the big cargo ships docked.

'Yes, I knew it!' Sunniva beamed. 'They said the Colonel was going to the harbour to meet Angelica!'

Ernst parked next to a small wooden building. A crooked sign showed 'Oslo Fish Hall', and a poster on the wall of the building proudly proclaimed 'A Cold is healthy – all year round!' Someone had obviously thought it would be funny to add an 'A' and insert an 'l'.

They parked a short distance from the Range Rover and watched from the car as Ernst walked over to the fish hall.

'What's he doing in there?' Finn asked as Ernst went inside.

'We won't find out sitting here,' Sunniva said, opening the door.

'Wait!' Miss Syversen said, but it was too late. Sunniva had pulled her green beanie down over her ears and was already climbing out.

'I'm going with her,' Finn said, turning to Camomile. 'Stay here with Miss Syversen. Follow him if we're not back when he leaves.'

'OK. But don't go in. And don't let them see you!' Miss Syversen called after him.

Finn jogged to catch up with Sunniva.

'We'll just walk past and try to see what he's doing in there,' Sunniva said.

Finn was no fish expert, but he thought he spotted a couple of big cod in the window. However, he was more interested in what was going on further inside. They had to go right up to the window to see anything, but even then all they could see was an empty shop. There wasn't even anyone behind the counter.

'He knows who *you* are, but he doesn't know me so well. Wait round the back,' Sunniva said, pulling her beanie down even further and heading for the door.

'No, no!' Finn hissed, but he knew it was no use. Sunniva opened the door and a little bell rang to announce her presence.

Finn went round the back of the building. The last thing he needed was for Ernst to see him. He just hoped Sunniva would be careful and not do anything stupid. And that Ernst wouldn't recognise her. Finn looked around. It was quiet here at weekends. Especially in December. A huge cargo ship cast a shadow over a few cars parked down by the quayside.

Then he saw the dustbin lorry. He moved closer. Yes, that was it. Or at least one exactly the same. It said 'Norway Recycles Ltd' on the side in big letters. There was no one in sight. The steady hum of traffic from the town centre was only occasionally interrupted by the sound of metal on metal elsewhere in the harbour. Must be doing repairs on one of the ships, Finn thought. He went over to the lorry, checked no one was sitting inside and looked around once more to check that the coast was – quite literally – clear before climbing up onto the step on the driver's side. He looked in the window and his suspicions were immediately confirmed. There was a gas mask on the passenger seat. He tried the door handle, but it wouldn't budge. He tried once more, this time with both hands. He heard a loud click and the door opened. Finn wobbled and almost fell over backwards. He grabbed hold of the doorframe at the last minute and steadied himself. He climbed in quickly and checked that the quayside was still deserted and no one was running towards him. The driver's cab looked as if it had seen a lot of sitting around and waiting as well. Empty pop bottles and crisp packets were strewn across the floor and between the seats. There was something white under the gas mask. Finn moved it aside and saw four or five envelopes with days of the week written on them. He picked up the one marked 'Monday'. The envelope wasn't sealed. Finn opened it and took out a sheet of paper. 'I've run away. Don't worry, I'll be fine. Einar.'

Finn felt a flush of excitement. There were a lot of Einars out there, and apparently one of them could expect a visit some time soon. A movement in the corner of his eye made him look up. Two men were coming along the quayside towards the dustbin lorry. His heart started pounding. He ducked down, put the envelope back with the others, replaced the gas mask and inched open the door. He crept out of the lorry, but didn't dare close the door properly behind him. It would make too much noise. He jumped down and moved quickly and resolutely towards the fish hall, making sure the dustbin lorry was always between him and the two men.

About halfway he spotted Sunniva coming towards him. She waved impatiently at him with one hand. Her other hand was holding something. Finn set off at a run, and when he reached her, he saw it was a huge fish wrapped in newspaper.

'What are you doing? Ernst just drove off,' Sunniva said, irritated.

Then Finn heard an engine starting up behind him. He turned just in time to see the dustbin lorry trundling out of the harbour area.

'See that?' he asked.

Sunniva looked at the lorry, but it took a couple seconds for her to work out what he was getting at.

'Norway Recyc— is it the same one?'

'Same lorry. Or one almost identical, maybe they've got a few. There was a gas mask in the driver's cab.'

Sunniva gaped at him.

'You were inside it?'

He told her about the envelope he had found. And about the note inside.

'Damn,' was all Sunniva said.

'What about you? What happened in there?' he said, nodding at the fish she was carrying.

It looked heavy.

'There was no one in sight, but then I heard Ernst and the woman who works there talking. After a while she came back and, well, I had to buy *something*. She was so grumpy. Say hello to Carl the Cod.'

She lifted the fish for Finn to inspect.

'I was busy paying when I realised Ernst was driving off. He must have gone out another door. Miss Syversen and Camomile followed him, but I wanted to find you first.'

'Was the fish lady Angelica?'

'I don't know. She was blonde. Angelica sounds more like a brunette. And there was something about the way she spoke to him. I heard her say "Yes, OK, see what you can find". It sounded like they knew each other.'

They stood in silence for a few seconds.

'Come on,' Sunniva said. We'll go and ask her what her name is.'

'Just like that?' Finn asked, hesitant.

'Just like that,' Sunniva said.

They walked around the building and into the shop. A woman in her forties stood behind the counter reading a magazine. She had bleached her hair blonde, maybe in an attempt to look younger than she was. Mostly she looked grumpy. She didn't look any happier when she spotted them either.

'Sorry, no returns. Bought is bought,' she said, going back to her magazine.

'I haven't come to return it. It's great,' Sunniva said, running a hand over her fish.

The woman peered suspiciously at the little girl petting her dead fish.

'What do you want then? Another one?'

'No,' Sunniva said. 'I was just wondering what your name was.

So I can tell my mum who to see when she wants the best fish in town.'

Finn thought he saw the flicker of a smile pass over the fish lady's face.

'Oh . . . I'm Randi. Randi Knutsen,' she said, with some uncertainty in her voice.

'Not Angelica?' Sunniva retorted.

'What?' said the woman whose name was not Angelica.

'Nothing,' Sunniva said. 'Thanks for your help, Randi Knutsen. And for the fish,' she said, opening the door.

Finn hurried out after her.

'Well improvised,' he said to Sunniva. 'I think she was telling the truth, too. I don't think she's Angelica. But what now?'

'Let's have a look around the harbour. Maybe we'll find something else,' Sunniva said after a few seconds.

They wandered around the dock area for a while, but all they saw were huge ships completely still in their moorings and some men talking and laughing as they made for town. Maybe sailors on shore leave, Finn thought.

Even though it was the middle of the day, it was as if someone had fiddled with the dimmer switch up there. The sky grew dark and they decided to trudge homewards. Finn wanted to find out where Ernst had gone. And whether the dustbin lorry had gone the same way.

It was a long walk through the city. Mostly thanks to the enormous cod, which went from fresh to frozen in minutes and seemed to get heavier with every step they took.

CHAPTER 35

THE THREE SPIES SAT around the rather small kitchen table in Sunniva's rather small flat eating the only visible result of the day's cloak and dagger activities. Vera had gutted and cooked the cod, and served it with potatoes, carrots, bacon and melted butter.

'Cod ith a lot better than I thought it'd be! Jutht like thpying ith a lot more boring,' Camomile said, spearing a large chunk of fish with his fork.

Vera was sitting in the living room trying to comfort Hedda's mum, who had popped round for a visit. It wasn't that difficult to hear what they were talking about.

'I just can't get my head round it,' Hedda's mum said, sniffing. 'I mean, we argued occasionally, but it was never anything serious, and we were so close . . .' she said, bursting into tears again.

'There, there, honey, I know. I can't imagine how horrible it must be, but I can see you're devastated. Listen to me now. I'm sure you'll have her back very, very soon,' Vera said.

'I hope so,' Hedda's mum sniffled.

Finn, Sunniva and Camomile exchanged looks across the table. It would do more harm than good to reveal what they knew: that it was highly unlikely Hedda would be home very, very soon.

Ernst hadn't led Miss Syversen and Camomile to either suspicious men or a basement full of kidnapped children. He had driven straight home to his house in Uranienborg Terrasse, and that was where Finn and Sunniva had found the Alfa Romeo on their weary way home. The only thing of note they'd had to report was that Ernst had been carrying a white box when he came out of the fish hall, which he had put in the garage before entering the house.

After sitting in the car for half an hour discussing whether they should climb over the gate and sneak into the garage, they decided it was too risky. There was a good chance of getting caught, and if they were, that would ruin everything. Ernst might even panic and do something rash to ensure that the other children were never seen again.

In the end, the car had started to stink of fish and they decided to drive to Sunniva's for dinner. Miss Syversen had had to leave again to drive the prime minister to the television studios, where he was to be a guest on a chat show later in the evening.

Hedda's mum put on her coat and left at the same time as Vera, who was on night shift again. Finn called Baba to ask if it was OK for him and Camomile to spend the night at Sunniva's. After what had happened the night before, he didn't want to sleep at home, just in case the men came back.

No sooner had Finn said he was at Sunniva's than Baba's voice shot out of the receiver, spraying words like machine gun bullets straight at his right eardrum.

'Finn, have you heard?' Baba asked.

He hadn't.

'They want me to go on TV. Your wrinkly old grandmother's going to be on the telly! You know that really popular chat show on NRK on Saturdays with that handsome young man? They're going to interview your father, and they want me along too! Just think, Baba Popps on telly! At first I thought I was going to faint, I get so nervous, you know, what if I say something stupid and the entire country sees it, or Margot from the bingo, oh my God, can you imagine, but anyway, I've been to Mrs Hermansen, and she's done my hair up a treat, I've bought a new blouse, bright yellow, you know how I love yellow, same colour as the upstairs bathroom . . .'

Finn hung up after a while, guessing it would take Baba a while to realise he had gone, if she realised at all.

A few hours later, Finn and Sunniva were lying at opposite ends of the plush sofa while Camomile was curled up in a soft armchair. Vera's little TV was on, and Teddy Popps was in his element. He leaned back casually in the guest chair with the air of a man in complete control before repeating the glad tidings: Kvikk Lunsj bars were free to all and sundry.

'Just help yourselves and I'll pick up the tab!' he laughed as the audience burst into wild applause. Finn tried to follow what his dad was saying, but it was difficult with another interview going on in his head where questions were fighting for attention. Who were the men who had been at his house? Was Ernst behind the kidnappings? Who was helping him? What had happened to the children they had taken? Were they alive? What was in the white box Ernst had picked up from the harbour? And who was Angelica, if she wasn't the lady in the fish shop?

The lack of answers and sleep made him tired, and soon he could feel his eyelids getting heavy. Not even when Baba appeared on TV in a completely luminous yellow blouse could he keep his eyes open. Slowly he sank into a warm, soft sleep as he listened to the faraway voice of his grandmother talking about how blooming sore her knee had been that morning until Dr Breyholtz had given her some pills, which – thank God – had helped to soothe the pain now.

CHAPTER 36

LATER THE SAME NIGHT, IN A WOOD CABIN, IN A FOREST.

'It's sheer negligence and I won't tolerate it!'

Everyone was looking at them. Vulture bowed his head and his back. If he had been stooped to start with, he was almost folded in half now, his head was hanging so low with shame that he looked like the Hunchback of Notre-Dame. The man standing next to him wasn't looking so chipper either, wringing his cap in his hand like a disgraced schoolboy. They were standing next to the fireplace, a laughing stock to everyone sitting around the long dining table.

'Look at me when I'm talking to you!' the Colonel yelled.

Vulture tried to straighten up and meet the eyes of the man standing on the other side of the table shouting at him. It looked as if it hurt in more ways than one.

'The boy was there somewhere, and you . . . *couldn't find him?*'

'Sorry . . .' Vulture started.

'Shut up! I don't want any more excuses. One more mistake and you're out. Not just out of GAG but . . . well, trust me, you really don't want to know what "out" means!'

159

Vulture said nothing. For a few seconds it was deathly quiet in the spacious cabin, apart from the crackle of the logs as resin pockets inside them caught fire. Then a large man to the Colonel's right spoke up.

'I agree it was a hash-up. Very poor. But I think that all of us in GAG are pleased with how they've acquitted themselves so far. The other kids were snatched without a hitch. And it's not the easiest job in the world.'

The Colonel snorted.

'They drive around in a refuse vehicle in the middle of the night. They have the world's best sleeping gas. How hard can it be?'

A woman raised her hands in an attempt to placate them.

'Settle down now. We have a new plan for the prime minister's boy now anyway, don't we?'

'Yes, we do.'

'How much does he really know?'

The Colonel's eyes grew distant.

'I don't know. Something.'

He turned to the window and looked out at the forest.

'That boy knows something.'

CHAPTER 37

'up and at 'em, sleepyhead!'

Finn rubbed his eyes. When he opened them, he saw Sunniva and Camomile fully dressed in front of him. He looked at his watch. He had slept until half past eleven.

'He who thleeps where he lieth hath a peathful heart,' Camomile said.

'Let me guess, another North Boresian saying?' Finn mumbled with a yawn.

'Yeth. But now itth time to get your thoes on!' Camomile lithped cheerfully.

'We need to go home too. I'm not sure Baba grasped that we were staying over,' Finn said. 'They might be worried,' he added, although he was fairly sure they wouldn't even have noticed they weren't there.

'Cool, then let's head to yours,' Sunniva said.

They took the lift down from Sunniva's flat on the fourth floor, and soon they were out on the street.

'Look out!' Sunniva said, grabbing Finn's arm and pointing at the ground.

Finn froze on the spot. He had been about to stand in a huge pile of brown dog poo in the middle of the pavement.

They hadn't walked much further when they spotted another pile glistening in the snow in front of them.

'Dogs may not have any manners, but their owners should know better,' Sunniva said with a grimace.

There were obviously a lot of ill-mannered owners out walking their dogs that afternoon. The pavement was an obstacle course of brown traps.

Finn noticed a family of four on their way home after a day's skiing. Doesn't look like it was a very successful day out, Finn thought. The children, two small boys of maybe five and seven, were crying as they walked along the pavement. But that wasn't the main reason they had caught Finn's eye.

'Why are they walking tho thtrangely?' Camomile whispered, and with good reason. The children and their parents were staggering forward with their legs wide apart as if they hadn't decided whether to practise the splits or walk.

They stepped over more and more dog mess, and a few hundred metres later they met two more skiers. Some very short skiing trips today, Finn thought. This time it was a young couple, each carrying cross-country skis. They were also walking strangely. And either the girl had a cold or she was crying, because she sniffled with every step she took.

Closer to Inkognitogate, they passed the 7-Eleven on Riddervolds plass just beside Uranienborg School. There was a long queue outside. People were eager to collect their free Kvikk Lunsj bars.

'He'll be popular again soon, your dad will,' Sunniva said dryly.

'Itth jutht a thame that tho many people are throwing them away without finithing them,' Camomile said. And he was right. It wasn't just dogs making a mess on the snow-covered roads today. A little further on they saw half-eaten Kvikk Lunsj bars on the ground.

'That's what it's like when you get something for nothing. People help themselves even when they're not really interested,' Sunniva said.

It was only five minutes later, when they reached 18 Inkognitogate, that they realised how wrong Sunniva was. How very wrong. The half-eaten Kvikk Lunsj bars weren't strewn all over town because they were free. The actual explanation was far worse. And it also explained why the streets were covered with disgusting dog mess and why all the tearful skiers had funny walks.

CHAPTER 38

THE FIRST THING THEY heard when they came through the door was a plaintive whimper from the downstairs loo, followed by a squeaky voice.

'I'm finished. It's all over for me, I'm done for, ruined, finito, kaputt,' it moaned.

Finn hardly recognised his dad's voice; it was falsetto. Finn, Sunniva and Camomile exchanged glances, hung up their coats and kicked off their shoes before heading into the living room where the TV was blaring out and flashing "Urgent News Bulletin" in the top right-hand corner. Baba was sitting on the sofa with her hands in front of her mouth.

It took them a while to work out what had happened. When they finally twigged, everything made sense. His dad's boundless despair, why he was sitting on the loo and what they had seen on the way to the house.

People all over the country were outdoors making the most of the wonderful sunny weather and crapping in their pants.

Or in the forest. Or on the pavement. Or in their cars. Or on the tram. Wherever people were, they felt a sudden urge to commune with nature. And they couldn't hold it in for another metre. And on a lovely day like this, a lot of people found themselves an alarming distance away from a toilet.

'The whole of the hiking area north of Oslo smells of shit,' said a man in a sports shirt being interviewed next to Lake Sognsvann, before sprinting off as the camera zoomed in on a suspiciously dark stain on the seat of his trousers.

Back in the newsroom they had conjured up a professor of medicine. He frowned as he spoke about the nationwide outbreak of diarrhoea. He had never experienced anything like it. The only similar case he could recall was when billions of locust larvae had crawled up from the sewer and poisoned the Mongolian rice crops in 1971, resulting in every single Mongolian having to sit on the toilet for a week. Similarly, millions of Norwegians were now squatting alongside ski trails and pavements to avoid filling their pants.

'But why?' Sunniva asked.

It was as if the newsreader had heard her.

'Let me repeat once more so that no one else will be affected. The Kvikk Lunsj bars being given out for free from kiosks and supermarkets contain a strain of salmonella. This bacterium causes acute stomach problems and a sudden, uncontrollable need to defaecate,' he said, pausing for a moment as he looked straight into the camera with an expression of the utmost gravity.

'*Do not, under any circumstances, eat Kvikk Lunsj.*'

They heard Teddy moan from the loo again.

'Turn it off, I don't want to hear any more,' the prime minister shouted, his voice followed by some other noises which made it quite clear that he had also indulged in the popular hiker's chocolate.

165

Finn closed his eyes for a moment. A few bods in Trøndelag county getting angry with his father because of some potholes in the roads was one thing. The whole nation filling their pants because of him was something else entirely. He picked up the half-eaten Kvikk Lunsj on the table and gave it a sniff. At first, all he could smell was chocolate, but after a few seconds there was something else as well, a strong smell that wasn't very Kvikk Lunsj-like.

'I take back what I said about your dad becoming popular again,' Sunniva murmured.

With good reason. The special news bulletin was followed by a host of extra-special news reports. And as the day progressed they grew more and more concerned with who was – quite literally – to blame for all the crap. There was no doubt as to which way the finger was pointing.

'Teddy Popps has to go,' they all said. Some of them said it in the street, some of them said it in the studio, and others said it on the telephone because they were still on the loo.

'He's poisoned the entire population. And who knows, perhaps he did it on purpose? What if he's really trying to kill us?' said a woman with a purple shawl and huge earrings.

'He might be good at finding his way through the traffic, but a taxi driver can't run the country,' said the leader of one of the other political parties.

And so it went on. Teddy Popps was about as popular as a hedgehog in a sleeping bag.

*   *   *

Teddy's toilet visits became less frequent over the course of the afternoon, and he took instead to sitting on the sofa, utterly alone, watching the news reports through unseeing eyes. Baba had gone upstairs to rest. Finn had rarely seen her so off-colour, and she hadn't even eaten any Kvikk Lunsj.

As it grew darker outside the window, Teddy's mood also darkened. His wispy hair hung limply over his right shoulder and he didn't even try to reposition it, which Finn found very worrying indeed. He felt sorry for his father, because he knew he had meant well. Nevertheless, all the evidence seemed to suggest he would be back driving a taxi before long.

'And here with us we have Ernst Krantz, deputy leader of the More Party,' the newsreader announced.

'Well, what are *your* thoughts on what's happened today?'

Ernst Krantz sat in the studio wearing a stylish, dark suit and a white shirt. He shook his head apologetically before tilting it to the side as if to emphasise how sorry he was.

'What has happened today is very unfortunate. I just hope the voters can distinguish between the decisions of one individual and the rest of the More Party,' Ernst said.

'What do you mean?' the newsreader asked with interest.

'It's no secret that this free Kvikk Lunsj campaign was Prime Minister Popps' decision. The rest of us were very sceptical, we felt it was a populist and overly hasty decision to make. And everything seems to indicate we were right.'

Teddy sat bolt upright on the sofa. At first he was unable to speak, it was as if he couldn't even breathe as he sat there, mouth agape, listening to Ernst stabbing him in the back. In the end, the air in his lungs did manage to surface and transport the words that already lay on his tongue.

'But it was your idea, you snake in the grass!' Teddy shouted, adjusting his hair with a lightning-quick flick of his hand. 'You conniving weasel, you cowardly dog, you spineless worm, you . . .'

Teddy waved his arms around, not stopping until he had used at least half the animal kingdom to describe Ernst Krantz's despicable behaviour. Finally he slumped back against the sofa, exhausted. It almost seemed as though he would never get up again, ever.

CHAPTER 39

EVEN THOUGH IT WAS still afternoon, the sun had already set, disappointed after another day's completely wasted journey over Oslo and obscured behind thick, dark clouds. It was probably looking forward to climbing into a clear blue sky above another city in a much hotter country and in a much hotter part of the world. But the capital of Norway wasn't completely dark. Predictably, it was only when the sun had set that the clouds had a break and allowed the moon to peep through. Now it reflected the rays of sunshine meant for sunbathers on velvety white beaches in Brazil.

In fact it was so light it was easy to see that Ernst Krantz's car wasn't where it usually was, and so light that Finn, Sunniva and Camomile had to be extra careful in order to avoid being seen.

'The garage ith thut, maybe the car'th in there,' Camomile said.

'But the house is dark. I don't think anyone's home. And he was on TV earlier, so he's probably got a load of other interviews to do as well, especially on a day like today,' Sunniva said.

Finn looked up at the mansion and its dark windows. Sunniva was right. It seemed empty.

'We can't climb over the fence from the road. That'd be a bit obvious,' Finn said.

'Let's go up their neighbour's driveway and sneak over the fence from there,' Sunniva said.

'Thoundth good,' Camomile said.

They walked up the path to the house next door, which was actually a block of flats. If anyone sees us they'll just think we're visiting someone, Finn thought. But instead of ringing one of the buzzers, they continued past the door and ducked behind a shed right next to the fence around the Krantz's property.

'Let's climb over here,' Sunniva said.

Finn and Sunniva went first and managed without incident. But just as Camomile was about to swing over the top and climb down, he lost his grip on the shed roof and fell all the way to the ground. Finn remembered what Max had said about Camomile being full of delicate mechanisms, and for a moment he worried that his brother would be damaged. But the soft snow had broken Camomile's fall, and he quickly got to his feet.

'Are you OK?' Finn whispered.

'Abtholutely fine,' Camomile said with a smile.

The moonlight and the white snow created a magical atmosphere; once again Finn felt as if he were in a film. This feeling did not diminish as they crept over to the garage: he knew what they were doing could be dangerous. If Ernst really was behind all this and he saw them, he wouldn't hesitate to capture them as well. He had already tried to kidnap Finn after all. Sunniva tried to lift the garage door. As expected, it was locked. Finn suspected that it could only be opened using a remote control, which Finn guessed Ernst kept in his car. There was a normal door next to the garage, but that was locked as well.

They walked round to the other side of the garage. There was a small window ajar.

'If I climb onto your shoulders, I think I could get through there,' Finn said.

Sunniva and Camomile squatted down so that Finn could climb onto their shoulders, one foot on Sunniva's and one on Camomile's. He grabbed hold of the window frame and pulled himself up as Sunniva and Camomile straightened. Then he opened the window completely and wriggled through. Luckily, he found a shelf inside that he was able to use to climb down instead of just falling and hoping for the best. It was pitch black inside. Finn felt his way along the wall. He found a light switch next to the door. Finn jumped. The Range Rover was there. Was Ernst at home after all? He unlocked the door to let the others in.

'Nithe work, Finn,' Camomile said after he and Sunniva had come in and closed the door behind them.

They looked round. It was a big garage with enough room for another car in addition to the Range Rover. It also contained a lot of tools and garden equipment, which was unsurprising considering they lived in a stately mansion with a big garden in Uranienborg Terrasse.

'OK, let's get this show on the road,' Sunniva said. 'Find the white box.'

They searched everywhere. They moved things around, looked

under flowerpots and opened an old ski box, but they couldn't find it anywhere. In fact, they couldn't find anything particularly suspicious or that didn't belong in a garage.

'We can't stay here much longer,' Finn said.

'What about the car?' Sunniva asked.

'It'll be locked,' Finn said.

'Letth thee,' Camomile said, walking over to it.

The car was unlocked. And that wasn't all.

'The keyth are thtill in the ignithon,' Camomile said, climbing into the driver's seat.

'I s'pose he didn't think anyone would get in here,' Sunniva said.

'Cool car. Lotth of nithe buttonth,' Camomile said, before reaching up to hold his nose.

'Forget the buttons and find the box,' Sunniva said sharply.

'It thmells of fart,' Camomile said, climbing down.

He was right. A pong followed him out of the car.

'Focus, Camomile. We should check the boot,' Sunniva said, even more sharply.

Finn opened the boot. And there it was. A white polystyrene box.

'It's here!' he said eagerly.

Sunniva and Camomile hurried over. Finn had no idea what he expected to find inside it, but right now the white box was all they had to go on. He picked it up. The first thing he realised was that this had to be where the smell was coming from. The second was how light it was. To Finn's disappointment, it weighed almost nothing. He lifted it out of the boot and put it on the floor.

'I think we're too late. It feels empty,' he said.

He took off the lid. The box was full of . . . a terrible stench. The smell hit him like death and putrefaction wrapped in a fist. And death and putrefaction was exactly what it was. The box was empty, but there were still traces of blood and small scraps of meat.

'Ith that . . .?' Camomile started.

'Rotten fish,' Sunniva said coldly.

Finn remembered where Ernst had got the box.

'Fish that's gone off, rotten. My uncle used to work on a fishing boat. I recognise that smell from the nets that hadn't been cleaned properly,' Sunniva added.

The smell reminded Finn of something as well, but he hurried to replace the lid. They all took a deep breath of fresh air. The disappointment grew in his tummy like a horrible little balloon filled with nothing. This was all they had. Nothing. Ernst had picked up some fish at the shop on the harbour. Not exactly a major crime.

'All that effort . . . for nothing,' he sighed.

'Shit,' Sunniva said.

'Yeth, thit,' Camomile said.

They stood in silence for a few seconds. Finn backed away from the car to escape the smell still assaulting his nostrils. What had he expected? That the answer they were looking for would be in the white box? That three ordinary children would solve the

173

mystery themselves and find out what had happened to the others? What idiots they were. What an idiot he was. This was a case for the police. Maybe they should try talking to Malthe again. After all, Finn could now explain why people thought they had seen two giant flies before they blacked out. Maybe even his dad would believe him if he told him the whole story? Finn felt a stab of guilt when he thought about his dad. He regretted getting so cross with him. The future wasn't so bright for Teddy Popps now. Finn was afraid the transition from running the country to driving a taxi again wouldn't suit him much.

Especially not if that slippery slimeball Ernst Krantz took over as prime minister.

'But what did he want the rotten fish for?' Sunniva wondered aloud.

'That wath two dayth ago. It might have gone rotten thinth then,' Camomile said.

'Maybe, but I doubt it. That fish smells like it died ages ago,' Sunniva said.

Then Finn remembered where he recognised the smell from and a thought struck him that was both totally obvious and utterly unbelievable. He let it brew for a few seconds to check it could really be true. Yes. It could be. He turned to Camomile.

'Did you say the keys were in the ignition?' he asked.

He didn't wait for Camomile to answer; he just opened the door and climbed into the car. To his delight, but not surprise, he saw that Ernst had satnav in the Range Rover. He found the key and turned it. Not all the way round so that the car started, but enough to supply power to the dashboard and electronics. Sometimes it helps to have a dad who used to be a taxi driver, Finn thought.

'What are you doing?' Sunniva asked.

'I just need to check something,' Finn said.

The satnav wasn't the same as the one his dad had in his taxi, but similar enough for him to know how to find what he was looking for. And he found it.

'Yes!' he whooped.

Sunniva cleared her throat as quietly as she could.

'Yes, what?' she asked.

Finn looked at Camomile and Sunniva with a contented smile. He wasn't sure he was right, but for the time being there was nothing to tell him he was wrong.

'Ernst Krantz has had a busy day . . . and night.'

Sunniva's eyes narrowed.

'Can we drop the riddles, Sherlock?' she asked as calmly as she could, but Finn could see she was starting to get annoyed.

'Sorry, let me explain. I'm not sure Ernst has anything to do with the children going missing.'

'No?'

'But I think he has a lot to do with the imminent fall of a prime minister. I think Ernst Krantz collected rotten fish from the harbour to make Kvikk Lunsj bars.'

'But there thouldn't be any rotten fith in Kvikk Lunth,' Camomile said.

'Right. He contaminated them. I think Ernst Krantz mixed rotten fish into the vats at the chocolate factory.'

'What'th the point of that?' Camomile asked.

Sunniva looked a bit less confused now.

'Because he knew the prime minister would get the blame,' she said.

'Exactly,' Finn said.

'I don't doubt that Ernst is devious enough to do something like that. But saying we saw him collecting rotten fish from the harbour isn't going to convince anyone that he tried to poison the whole country,' Sunniva said.

'No, but we also know he drove to the chocolate factory at half past one last night,' Finn said.

He grabbed the wheel and pretended to drive the Range Rover.

'Satnav,' he said with satisfaction, 'doesn't just help you find your way, it also records where you've been.'

Then a sound from the doorway made them all whirl around.

'I knew I should've deleted that journey straight away. But thanks for reminding me,' said the dark silhouette as it stepped into the garage and blinded them with a huge torch.

CHAPTER 40

FINN WASN'T EVEN ABLE to let go of the steering wheel. It was as if the open door had let in an ice-cold wind that had frozen him to it.

Ernst Krantz switched off the torch and stepped out of the shadows into the cone of light from the ceiling lamp. He was wearing his dark winter coat with only a shirt underneath, and his shoelaces were undone. Finn supposed he must have seen the light under the garage door and thrown some clothes on.

'You just couldn't help yourselves, could you?' Ernst said, beaming.

'How long have you been standing there?' Sunniva snarled.

'Long enough to work out what you're up to,' he snapped back. 'And I must say it's quite something. I underestimated you, Finn Popps. You're not as stupid as I thought,' he said, taking another step closer.

Finn's shock was immediately replaced by intense fury. He got out of the car and stood next to Camomile and Sunniva.

'I underestimated you too. You're even . . . worse than I thought possible,' he said.

'Now, now, young man. I'm not so bad, I'm just good at being, how should I put it . . . in the right place at the right time.'

'Like when you mixed rotten fish into the Kvikk Lunsj chocolate at the factory last night?'

'For example. And like now, finding you here. Or like how I'm deputy leader in a party whose awful leader is about to be fired because he's given the entire country diarrhoea.'

Ernst Krantz laughed. It wasn't the evil, maniacal laughter of villains in films, where they lean back and laugh louder and louder and with more and more malice, but it wasn't far off either, Finn thought.

'What are you laughing at, you troll? You'll never get away with this,' Sunniva said.

'Of course I will. You can't prove anything. Thanks to Finn, I'll even remember to delete that car journey from the satnav,' Ernst said.

Finn knew that Ernst was right. They had broken into his garage and all they had found was a foul-smelling, empty box. Ernst Krantz had all the cards.

'When you were round for dinner, you told Viktor he wouldn't have to put up with me much longer. Was that anything to do with this? Because you knew we'd have to leave the prime minister's residence soon?' Finn asked.

Now it was Ernst's turn to be surprised.

'Goodness me, so you heard that too, you little snoop. But, yes, as soon as I get rid of your irritating taxi-twerp of a father, I imagine you'll all ship out into the countryside again, the whole lot of you. And I must say, I'm looking forward to that,' he said.

'It's not going to happen,' Sunniva said.

Ernst looked at her again, but without a smile this time.

'Oh, yes it is. And quicker than you think. Just like you meddling little brats are going to get out of this garage now before I call the police and report a break-in,' he said. His tone was sharper now.

Finn was both furious and desperate at the same time. He was furious with the man who was trying to ruin his dad's life. Teddy Popps might not be the world's best prime minister, but if he was going to fall flat on his face, he would do so through his own actions, not because Ernst Krantz had tripped him.

And Finn was desperate because he didn't know how to stop it happening.

Ernst walked over to the door and pressed a switch on the wall. The garage door opened slowly.

'Thanks for stopping by. Hope never to see you again. I won't be as forgiving next time,' Ernst said.

Finn hesitated for a moment.

'So you're not going to kidnap us?'

Ernst tut-tutted as he walked towards Finn.

'Finn Popps, Finn Popps. Just when I was starting to think you had a brain. I heard your crazy theory during dinner. First of all, children aren't going missing. Secondly, I've got more than enough on my plate getting rid of your father.'

To Finn's great disappointment, it seemed Ernst was telling the truth. So he really wasn't behind the kidnappings?

'And now I'd really quite like you all out of my sight, so cheerio!'

Ernst Krantz swatted the air as if trying to get rid of a few wasps flying too close.

CHAPTER 41

'IT'S LIKE LYING ON a sunbed in Bora Bora,' Sunniva said.

Finn and Camomile sent her a questioning look. It was only an hour since they had been thrown out of Ernst's garage, and now they were sitting on Bojan's bench opposite the school. The basketball court was surrounded by four big lampposts which cast overlapping circles of light onto the ground. They sat at the far edge of one of them. The atmosphere was somewhat morose, and Finn couldn't imagine how it was anything like lying on a sunbed in Bora Bora.

'Wait a second, I'm not finished,' Sunniva said, noticing their bemused expressions.

'So you're lying there and everything's tiptop totally amazing. There are colourful tropical fish swimming around in the turquoise water and you've got an ice-cold, fresh pineapple juice in your hand, and life is sweet. But then a huge mosquito lands on your arm, a real monster, a bloodthirsty creature that starts sucking your blood.'

She mimed the blood-sucking antics of the giant mosquito with great gusto.

'But here's the thing, *you can't swat it*. Or rather, you're not *allowed* to swat it, no matter how much you want to. It drinks and drinks until you're almost out of blood, until you can hardly stand any more. It's going to change everything from tiptop totally amazing to bottom of the barrel in no time at all, and you can't touch it. You can't do anything but watch as it gets fatter and fatter at your expense.'

Now they understood what she meant. Finn nodded.

'Yeah, that's how it feels. We can't prove a thing. We can't do anything,' Finn said.

'Yeth. All we can do ith watch ath that mothquito Krantth ruinth everything,' Camomile sighed.

'Exactly,' Sunniva said, pleased that they had finally grasped what she meant.

And even though Finn's new life wasn't exactly like lying on a sunbed in Bora Bora, it was starting to grow on him. He had got back his new brother and new best friend, and he was starting to like Oslo, the house and his new school.

But now Ernst Krantz was trying to ruin everything with his evil plans. It was, to put it mildly, frustrating.

'But . . . you wouldn't move away again, would you? You'd have to move house, sure, but you don't have to leave town?'

Sunniva stood in front of them looking forlorn.

'Would we have to, Finn?' Camomile asked, looking at him.

'I don't know,' Finn said, shrugging.

He was lying. He *knew* that his dad would never stay here. It would just be a daily reminder of everything he had lost.

Finn didn't want to move again, back to the old house or back to an existence where his dad was bitter and angry about everything, as he had been before. And he definitely didn't want to move because of Ernst Krantz.

Sunniva must have been thinking roughly the same.

'I can't bear the thought that that weasel might ruin everything,' she said, kicking a chunk of ice. It didn't budge a millimetre. It was frozen to the ground. Finn winced at the thought of how much that must have hurt, but Sunniva just turned away without saying anything.

'But we know itth him. Dethpicable man,' Camomile said after a few seconds. 'He thtood there and thaid it thraight to my fathe.'

It took a few seconds, but then it struck Finn like a snowball to the head. Except that it didn't hurt at all; on the contrary, it exploded in the way only unadulterated joy can.

He suddenly knew how to deal with Ernst. He knew how to prove what he had done, that he alone was to blame for half of Norway wandering around crapping their pants. He wasn't entirely sure it would work, but it was certainly worth a shot. And they had no time to lose.

There was just one problem.

He couldn't tell the other two what his plan was.

Or at least one of them.

CHAPTER 42

THE HUGE MOON OVER the Palace Gardens hung as if from an invisible thread, illuminating the snow-laden branches of the trees. Even the trunks were covered in snow, making the trees as a whole look like overgrown cauliflowers in an overgrown vegetable garden behind an overgrown, yellow house.

Three children ran through the trees, one in front and two behind. The two behind didn't know why they were running. They had no choice but to trust the boy in front of them and hope he had a very good reason to run.

They passed two snow-covered guards standing to attention in front of their tiny sentry boxes, and the boy running ahead shook his head in disbelief as he thought about how it had only been a week since he had been having dinner with the king inside the huge palace. He also thought a little about everything that had happened since.

But most of all he thought about what was going to happen now.

Or, to be more precise, what he hoped was going to happen.

Finn, Sunniva and Camomile were covered in sweat when they finally reached Hotel Bristol less than ten minutes after they had been sitting on Bojan's bench and Finn had said 'Come on, we need to see Max!' He knew that Sunniva was very annoyed that he wouldn't give her an explanation. He had been very secretive of late, she said, and then on top of that he had insisted on them running here.

'Wait here, I need to talk to him alone first, OK?' Finn said, charging upstairs before they could answer.

He was back again very soon. Sunniva was quietly fuming now.

'Camomile, Max wants to talk to you,' Finn said.

'To me? Jutht me?'

'Yes,' Finn said.

Finn waited until Camomile was out of sight. He knew Sunniva was affronted and angry, but he wasn't sure which one had precedence.

'Sorry, Sunniva, I couldn't say anything . . .' he started.

'Harrumph,' she said, looking in another direction.

'I couldn't say anything in front of Camomile. I couldn't let him hear my idea.'

She eyed him, this time with a touch less annoyance. It obviously made a difference that it was Camomile and not her who had to be kept in the dark.

'What do you mean?' she asked.

'Because Camomile . . . *is* my idea,' Finn said.

Finn explained. They knew they couldn't prove what Ernst had done even though they knew so much. But when Camomile had made a comment about Ernst confessing everything straight to his face, Finn had realised that they did in fact have proof. And that it was inside Camomile.

'His eyes are like a video camera. He films everything, you know,' he said, smiling.

Within a few seconds the look on Sunniva's face was transformed from one of utter confusion to one of pure delight.

'Finn, you're . . . you're a genius! Of course!'

Sunniva started laughing, first at a respectable volume and then louder and louder until Finn briefly speculated whether she was about to lose her head as well. But he knew she was just really happy, and it wasn't long before her laughter rubbed off on him and he joined in. After everything that had happened, it was liberating. It had been ages since laughter had filled his entire body and freed up all the worries that had taken root inside him.

They both sat in deep leather armchairs in the lobby as they waited for Max to find out whether Camomile had recorded the episode in the garage. During the previous 'head-off' operation Max had had enough foresight to think he might need to examine Camomile at a later date as well. So he had made sure he could switch Camomile off by sending a signal from his computer, thereby avoiding the necessity of removing his head. Finn and Sunniva had no particular desire to see Camomile headless again, so they ordered hot chocolate and waited.

Twenty minutes later, Max came downstairs. And when Finn saw his wide walrus smile, he knew everything had gone well.

'Everything's there on film. Every word. What a dastardly man,' Max said.

Finn breathed a sigh of relief, while Sunniva jumped out of

185

her chair and punched the air as if she had just single-handedly won the World Cup with a spectacular volley in extra time.

'Yes, yes, yes!' she cried in ecstasy.

The waiter at the next table turned towards her, but did no more than raise his eyebrows before continuing to pour wine into glasses for two American tourists.

'Good,' Finn said, getting up as well. 'Then it's time to ring some old friends of ours.'

'And who would that be?' Sunniva asked.

'The nice people at the police station,' he replied.

CHAPTER 43

THE BIG FAT MAN took up almost the entire sofa at 18 Inkognitogate. The impatient drumming of his fingers on his right thigh suggested he was anything but pleased. Finn had disturbed Chief Constable Malthe in the middle of the Sunday evening film and, as it had been a western, Finn had been forced to exert his finest powers of persuasion to get him to switch it off. That is, he had just said: 'The prime minister of Norway will never forgive you.' Malthe might well have been among those who thought that the prime minister wasn't going to be prime minister for very much longer, but, luckily, he hadn't risked failing to make an appearance.

As for the prime minister himself, he was oblivious of the dereliction of duty which he might have eternally held against Chief Constable Malthe. Teddy was at this moment sitting in an armchair looking deeply depressed. Baba sat in another armchair, unusually quiet for once. Sunniva agitatedly paced the room while Camomile slept in his room. He had been in a daze when they left the hotel, with no idea why, and didn't protest when Finn suggested he lay down as soon as they got home. He had fallen asleep as soon as his tired head hit the pillow, at which point Finn had gone downstairs to get ready for the little evening performance.

'Well, here we are. And now you'd better be about to tell me smartish why it was so damn important that I come here so late on a Sunday evening,' Malthe grunted irritably.

Finn stood in the middle of the room, suddenly feeling quite nervous. He wasn't used to being the centre of attention, especially not in situations involving such vital matters which would have consequences for whoever was running the country. And what if the recording they had was of no use? After all, they had broken into a man's garage and snooped around his car. And filmed him without his knowledge . . . were they allowed to do that?

He tried to ignore these negative thoughts as he walked over to the TV. He switched it on, picked up the remote control and turned to the others.

'Er . . . Sunniva and I have something we think you should see. Something which would perhaps explain what happened today. Or, actually, not *perhaps*; it *will* explain everything.'

He pressed the play button on the remote control. For a few seconds the screen was just grey, long enough for Finn to think something had gone wrong and the whole film had been erased, but then the figure of Ernst Krantz appeared. And even though most of what he said in the video was directed at Finn, he did look at Camomile now and then, in other words straight into the camera. Both the picture and the sound were of surprisingly good quality, and for the first time ever, Finn expressed silent gratitude to a certain dictator.

Teddy squinted at the screen, not because his eyesight was poor but because he couldn't quite believe what he was seeing. But as the conversation in the garage unfolded, and particularly after Ernst Krantz admitted that he was responsible for tipping rotten fish into the chocolate vats, Theodor Bjørnstjerne Popps became more and more animated.

'Looklook!' he shouted, pointing at Ernst.

'Looklooklooklook!' he continued, shocked, jumping up and down and still pointing at the TV.

Evidently, he can't say anything more articulate just now, Finn thought. Baba, however, exploded.

'What a disgusting, pathetic excuse of a man! If he were here now I'd give him what for, I'd wring his neck, I'd have his guts for garters. No, actually, you know what? I'd tie him to one of the nice leather seats in that shiny car of his and force-feed him Kvikk Lunsj until he crapped it to bits . . .'

Baba seemed to have completely forgotten that the chief constable was sitting right behind her. But Malthe didn't seem perturbed.

Finn stopped the film just before he asked Ernst about the missing children. At that moment he was hoisted off his feet and swivelled round so that his dad could plant a big, wet kiss on his forehead.

'You're a star, Finn my lad! I don't know how you managed it, but it's amazing!' he said. 'And you, Sonja! Thank you so, so much!' he said, walking towards Sunniva. But she held up an admonitory hand and sent him such a fierce glare that he stopped in his tracks.

'You're not kissing me. And my name's Sunniva,' she barked. But Finn thought he could see the hint of a smile in her eyes.

The sofa creaked as a hundred and forty kilograms of chief constable vacated it.

'I can see why you phoned, Finn,' Malthe said once he was upright. 'I'll call some of the boys and we'll get this Krantz in for a little interview at the station.'

Baba clenched her fist and punched the air as if fighting an invisible boxer.

'Great stuff, Chief Constable! And don't you be too namby-pamby with him now. You must have loads of old instruments of torture tucked away somewhere you could dust off?'

'I don't think that'll be quite necessary, madam,' Malthe said. 'He said more than enough in the film we just saw.'

Finn and Sunniva stopped Malthe in the hall as he was getting ready to leave. Teddy was already on the phone, busy resuming his duties as leader of the country. Baba, for her part, was equally busy settling her nerves with a glass of sherry in the living room.

'Chief Constable, there was one more thing we wanted to discuss with you,' Finn said.

'Oh yes? Spit it out, then,' boomed the huge man as he wrestled with his coat.

Finn told him what had happened the night the men with the gas masks had tried to kidnap him. He told him how he had hidden in the wardrobe and on the roof, and about the Norway Recycles Ltd dustbin lorry. And how he was sure that was what had happened to the other children, except that they hadn't escaped. He described the two men, how they resembled giant

190

flies, just as Jenny and Hedda's mum had said. Malthe's face remained impassive while Finn spoke, and he stood thinking for a few seconds after he had finished. In the end, the big policeman squatted down in front of Finn. The floorboards creaked.

'Two men came to kidnap you on Saturday night, and you hid on the roof? You should have told me this before, Finn,' he said in a stern voice.

Finn felt guilty. He knew Malthe was right.

'Sorry. But you wouldn't listen to me on Friday,' he said.

'True,' Malthe said. 'Well, if what you're telling me now is true, this is a very grave matter.'

He scratched his head with his enormous hand and then straightened up.

'I'll circulate a description of the dustbin lorry you mentioned. And I'll tell the people working on the case what you've told me. But don't tell anyone else what you know. It'll only spread panic and make it more difficult to find the children.'

Malthe had such authority that Finn and Sunniva could only nod in response.

'But first I'm going to have a chat with a certain gentleman called Krantz. Goodbye,' Malthe said, and left. He only just managed to squeeze through the doorframe.

191

CHAPTER 44

FINN FLEW UP THE stairs. He knew he had to reach the roof before the flies got him. Maybe they had already seen him. They were certainly hot on his heels, he could hear their voices coming closer as they came up the stairs. He was on the second floor, but there was another flight of stairs. He had to be near the roof now . . . and since when had the prime minister's residence had a third floor? He took the stairs two at a time and finally arrived at the top . . . only to discover that he was in the school gymnasium! And one of the huge flies was waiting for him, and it really was an insect, not a man wearing a gas mask but an enormous, greasy fly making loud buzzing sounds, and Finn turned back, intending to run back down the stairs, but they had disappeared without a trace, and the fly was coming closer and closer, but it wasn't a fly any more, it was a huge bear with long, shaggy fur . . .

Finn woke with a start and his eyes opened.

'Shh, shh, Finn my lad. I didn't mean to wake you. Were you dreaming?'

His father was sitting on the edge of the bed.

'Er . . . yes, I think so,' Finn said, still not sure whether he was awake or not. He sat up in bed. 'What time is it?' he asked.

192

'It's late,' Teddy said.

They sat in silence for a while. At length Teddy spoke.

'I . . . I just wanted to say I'm proud of you. And . . . well, grateful for what you've done. Even though you could have got into real trouble.'

Teddy ruffled Finn's hair.

'No problem, Dad. I'm glad you'll still be prime minister. You will, won't you? I don't want to move again.'

Teddy nodded.

'Malthe called. Ernst had his poker face on when they first arrived at his house. Flatly denied everything. But when Malthe showed him the film he started blubbering like a baby. And when they led him to the police car, he shouted "It's not fair, I should be prime minister!"' Teddy said, imitating Ernst's affected voice.

They both laughed.

'That's good,' Finn said.

'That *is* good,' Teddy said.

They sat in silence for another few seconds.

'I know things haven't been easy for you, Finn,' Teddy said eventually. 'What with your mum and everything, and me wanting to be prime minister and all that . . . and then me becoming prime minister. It's all a bit mad, isn't it?'

Teddy laughed again.

'Yes, it really is,' Finn said.

'It's amazing what you can do if you put your mind to it,' Teddy said, before going quiet again. After a while he got up and walked over to the window.

193

'I miss your mum too,' he said, looking out into the darkness. 'And maybe all of this has something to do with her. I was on my way to becoming a bitter old man who thought everything was wrong and everyone was an idiot.'

He turned to Finn.

'I had to try and do something about it,' he said with a sad smile.

Finn looked at his dad, suddenly feeling sorry for him.

'I'd say you did pretty well,' Finn said with a yawn.

Teddy looked at him.

'Hm. It almost all went down the pan today, quite literally. It would have, if it hadn't been for you, Camomile and . . . and . . .'

Teddy frowned, and Finn could tell that he was trying really hard to remember.

'. . . and Sunniva,' Teddy said finally.

Finn smiled.

'Yes, Sunniva,' he said, nodding.

Teddy smiled and left the room, closing the door carefully behind him. Finn could hear him quietly repeating her name on the landing, as if practising for their next meeting.

'Sunniva, Sunniva, Sunniva.'

CHAPTER 45

LATER THE SAME NIGHT, OUTSIDE A FIVE-STOREY BLOCK OF FLATS.

The man with the red cap groaned. He peered out of the car window and up at the tall building.

'Hope there's a lift,' he said, sighing.

'Lazy sod,' Vulture mumbled, looking for the right envelope. 'OK, ready to go?' he asked, opening the door without waiting for an answer.

The man with the red cap took it off and grabbed their gear: the bags and the masks.

They walked to the front door, which was locked to keep intruders out of the building. Intruders like them. Vulture had his picklock ready, and the door was open in less than ten seconds. He looked up at his accomplice.

'Where's the bin? Go and get it, man!'

Red-Cap hurried back to the car. A few seconds later he returned with a large wheelie bin.

'It's a big block. Lots of people to hear us,' Red-Cap said in a worried voice as they trundled the bin into the hall. His face lit up when he saw the lift.

'Relax. And remember to pick up the right shoes this time. The ones you took that first night didn't even fit the boy,' Vulture sneered.

Red-Cap snorted and hit the button for the lift. The number above them told them it was on the top floor.

'Seriously though, we can't mess up this time. Not like we did at the prime minister's house,' Vulture said.

'I know, I know, but we couldn't find him, could we?' Red-Cap said.

Vulture eyed him.

'Know what I heard?' Vulture said, shooting an impatient glance at the lift.

Second floor now.

'What?'

'He hid on the roof. Under the snow.'

'You're joking.'

'Nope. Smart little brat, that one,' Vulture said.

Ping.

The lift doors opened.

'But this one . . . she won't get away,' Red-Cap said, pulling his gas mask over his face.

CHAPTER 46

FINN SAT AT HIS desk feeling nauseous. Not because it was unpleasant being at school after everything that had happened at the weekend. Nor because there was something absurdly normal about Gulliksen – currently wearing a jumper depicting pork ribs, sauerkraut and potatoes – asking them to turn to page sixty-eight in their maths textbooks. No, Finn was feeling ill for another reason entirely.

He had actually been in an unusually good mood this morning. He had even whistled in the limo on the way to school although they were late; cold, wet snow was falling and Oslo was still wrapped in gloomy early morning darkness. He whistled a song his father had been singing all through breakfast, a song he had sung with particular relish after the radio newsreader announced: 'The deputy leader of the More Party, Ernst Krantz, has been arrested after confessing to adding rotten fish to the Kvikk Lunsj chocolate vat in an attempt to frame Prime Minister Teddy Popps.' Finn had felt light as air as he and Camomile crossed the playground, even though the bell had already rung. It felt good to have told Chief Constable Malthe everything the night before, not least because Finn was sure that he believed him and was going to do his best to find out what was really going on. He had felt so good that he bounded up the stairs and almost did a jig along the corridor to the classroom door.

It had been a wonderful morning.

Until he opened the door and walked over to his desk. Until he noticed the empty chair next to him.

'Sunniva!'

Gulliksen glanced at her empty chair and made a note in the register. He raised his eyebrows questioningly at Finn, but he just gazed back blankly, it was hard enough sitting still as a thousand nasty thoughts swirled around his head.

But maybe . . . Finn thought, *maybe* she was just exhausted after everything that had happened over the weekend and had overslept? Maybe Vera was working nights and hadn't been around to wake her up? It wasn't entirely implausible, Finn thought, trying to reassure himself as he chewed the end of his pen with such vehemence that the plastic came off in big chunks. He could feel concern spreading through his system like poison, making him feel more and more nauseous.

After three half-eaten pens and seven hundred and fifty-eight glances at the door in the fervent hope that Sunniva would come bounding through it, the nausea was well on its way to becoming desperation. I'll stick it out until lunchtime and then I'm off, he said to himself.

When there were only two minutes of the maths double period before lunch remaining, Gulliksen erased all the numbers from the blackboard. Then he turned to face the class, the wet sponge in his hand dripping chalky droplets onto his black clogs.

'There's been a lucky dip for those of you wanting to be part of the audience for the National General Knowledge Competition at Oslo Spektrum tomorrow,' he started.

'And the lucky . . . er, spectators are . . .' he said, pausing for dramatic effect, then read out eight names. Everyone cheered loudly. Finn was glad he wouldn't have to watch Viktor showing off in the final. He also felt a small stab of jealousy, as he would have liked to be in it himself. He looked over at Viktor, who had been unusually quiet all morning. Not surprising, Finn thought, after what had happened to his dad last night.

Then the old Uranienborg School bell rang and most of the class charged out of the door for the lunch break. Finn hurried to pack away his things. He was rummaging in the bottom of his bag when he became aware of Gulliksen and Viktor standing in front of him.

'Finn, I've got some good news for you. Very good news,' Gulliksen said, as Viktor stood fidgeting next to him, clearly uncomfortable about something.

'Oh yes?' Finn said. There was only one piece of good news he was particularly interested in right now, and that concerned the well-being of the black-haired girl who usually sat next to him.

'Yes. You may have noticed that Iver's not here today,' Gulliksen said.

Finn turned to look at Iver's empty chair a couple of rows behind him. Had he been kidnapped too?

'According to the rules someone from the team that came second can take his place,' Gulliksen continued. 'So since Sunniva's not here and Camomile didn't participate in the final heat, that's you.'

Gulliksen pushed his glasses up his nose and put on a big smile. Finn fought a wave of dizziness as yet another thought joined the tumult in his head. Was *he* going to be on the same team as *Viktor*? Viktor, who couldn't stand the sight of him? Were they supposed to work *together*?

On the other hand, he had wanted to be in the final at Oslo Spektrum. He stared at Viktor with question marks in his eyes.

'I don't know what's happened, but Iver's parents called this morning and said that he . . . he's run away as well,' Viktor mumbled.

'OK . . . OK,' was all Finn managed to utter.

'Great,' Gulliksen said, visibly pleased, before hurrying out of the room.

'Stupid rules,' Viktor grumbled, following in his wake.

Finn slung his bag over his shoulder and looked at Camomile.

'I'm going to see why Sunniva's not here. Want to come?' he asked.

Camomile's eyes widened slowly, and he took a step back.

'Oh, no. Thurely you don't think . . .' Camomile started, but he already knew the answer, and twenty seconds later they were out of the building.

CHAPTER 47

SOMEONE HAD REPLACED SUNNIVA'S tiny, affectionate, bubbly mother with a much older, much tinier and completely heartbroken version.

They went into the living room and Vera started to tell them what had happened. Finn could have told the story for her, it was all getting so predictable now. A look around the room confirmed as much: the green plants were yellowing, their leaves hanging mournfully over the edges of the pots.

'I don't understand. Run away? She . . . we're like friends,' Vera said, and burst into tears.

Finn waited for her to regain composure.

'Have you called the police?' he asked eventually.

'Yes, they said they'd stop by.'

Finn looked at the note Sunniva had left. Or rather, the note that *someone* had left.

'What's so awful is that it doesn't even look like her handwriting,' Vera said.

He looked at the petite woman before him and knew he couldn't tell her what he knew. Not now. After a while Vera accompanied them both to the door and gave them both a long hug before they got into the lift. Someone had spat some tobacco on the floor. Maybe it was them, Finn thought, remembering the snus box that Big Jimmy's mum had found. He was angry, and stamped on it. He knew what it was like to lose someone. What he didn't understand was how anyone could kidnap someone – how could anyone kidnap innocent children and destroy whole families?

Yesterday they had proved that, despite being children, they could deal with grown-up issues. But this was different. The police were investigating the case now, and they had told Malthe everything. All they could do now was trust him.

They went home. Baba was lying on the sofa with a blanket over her, completely absorbed by the TV on the wall. The news still mostly comprised features about Ernst's chocolate scam. As more and more people finally emerged from their toilets, a huge wave of sympathy poured over Prime Minister Popps, and new opinion polls showed that he was more popular than ever. Finn and Camomile watched as their dad went from interview to interview smiling gratefully for all the support, apologising for employing such a scumbag as deputy leader and announcing that toilet roll would be half price all week.

'Maybe you thould practithe a bit for the quith tomorrow,' Camomile suggested.

They were sitting in armchairs in the library. The walls were covered with portraits of old, worried-looking prime ministers, and Finn couldn't help but feel old and worried himself. The quiz final was in the far recesses of his mind. But he knew that he should really revise some of what they had practised the week before.

'OK,' he said.

Camomile borrowed Teddy's laptop and found some quiz sites online. Then he fired away with questions about African capital cities, philosophers, new world records, famous inventors and birdlife in the mountains and along the fjords.

Finn couldn't answer any of them. His head didn't want to go to Egypt, Kenya or Namibia. It seemed completely meaningless to try and remember which bird family the bullfinch belonged to. He couldn't even remember which football team had won the European Cup in 2012.

'Sorry, Camomile. I can't do this,' he said after a while.

'No, I can tell your heart ithn't really in it,' Camomile said.

Finn brought a fist down on the arm of the chair.

'I'll call Malthe,' he said. 'Maybe he'll know more now. Maybe something happened today. Can you look up the number for me?'

Camomile found the police station number online and Finn wrote it on an envelope lying on a little table next to his chair. Then he went to find one of their wireless house phones.

'Ah, is that our detective? What've you got for me now, then?'

Malthe sounded exhausted, and for a moment Finn regretted ringing.

'Nothing new. The same question . . . whether you've found out anything else about the kidnappings.'

He paused before continuing.

'Sunniva was kidnapped. Last night,' he said.

Finn could hear Malthe's heavy breathing at the other end of the line.

'I'm sorry to hear that, Finn. I knew that more children had gone missing over the weekend, but I didn't know Sunniva was one of them. I've passed on what you told me, and we're looking into the possibility that they were kidnapped.'

Finn's fist closed tightly around the envelope he was still carrying as Malthe's words sank in.

'*The possibility that* . . . but I saw them, they tried to kidnap me!' he interrupted angrily.

'Now, now, young man. You know I believe you, Finn, but it's hard to convince people that men with gas masks are breaking into people's homes at night to kidnap their children. It sounds like something that would happen in a Hollywood film,' Malthe said.

Finn had a sudden feeling that Malthe didn't believe him any more. Maybe he was just pretending to believe him to get him off his back. Grown-ups could be a real pain sometimes.

'You have to take this seriously. You have to believe me. You have to do something!' he shouted.

'Come on now, Finn. Take it easy. I know you're upset, but you have to let the police do their job. You have to trust us,' Malthe said firmly.

Finn could feel the anger spreading through his body from the head down through his chest to the ends of his arms and legs.

The hand holding the phone was shaking, and he had to force himself to breathe normally.

'I know,' he said eventually, with as much control as he could muster.

'I know you do, deep down. You're a smart boy,' Malthe said, then hung up.

Finn stood for a few seconds clutching the telephone. He fought the urge to hurl it right into the face of one of the prime ministers hanging on the wall, as if it were all their fault.

'What did he thay? Do they know anything elthe? Any new leadth?' Camomile asked excitedly.

Finn shook his head slowly, staring into space.

'They've got nothing,' he said.

Then he remembered the crushed envelope in his other hand. With the police station telephone number scribbled on the back. An idea occurred to him.

'But *we* might have.'

CHAPTER 48

FINN AND CAMOMILE WALKED though the streets. It was eerily quiet and there was no one around. Nor any stars or the moon for that matter. Everyone and everything was asleep at one o'clock in the morning. It was snowing again, but there were only a few scattered flakes, which were so light and thin that it almost seemed as if they wished they hadn't bothered and were floating back up, as if they knew they wouldn't survive the landing. Finn and Camomile had crept out of 18 Inkognitogate after everyone else had gone to bed; they had wrapped themselves up warm in thermal underwear, woolly socks and thick jumpers under their bubble jackets. They both wore dark jackets, and Finn had dug out some dark hats and gloves for them as well. They walked along Uranienborg Terrasse. Finn's head was buzzing with their plan. A plan thinner and more crumbly than crispbread, but a plan nonetheless.

They passed the Krantzes' house. Which wasn't their destination this time. The windows were dark. Finn spared a thought for Viktor and Jeanette Marielle, who now lived all alone in the huge mansion. They said on the news that Ernst Krantz probably wouldn't receive as severe a punishment as people were demanding.

After all, the whole nation couldn't continue to soil their pants indefinitely. Although it was a bit more serious that he had tried to lever the prime minister out of a job at the same time.

Finn and Camomile turned into the next street, Professor Dahls gate, and Finn soon found the right house number.

'We can't stand here,' Finn said. 'We have to hide.'

He looked around. Down at the end of the street he spotted some big, snow-covered bushes. They looked like a good place to wait. Because if there was one thing Finn was sure of, it was that they would be waiting a while.

Finn looked at his watch. It was almost three o'clock. Soon they would have been waiting for two hours, and two layers of wool weren't quite preventing the cold from getting in. They took turns to keep watch while one of them jogged up and down Uranienborg Terrasse.

'Anything?' Finn asked breathlessly when he came back from yet another jog.

'Not a thauthage,' Camomile said, shaking his head so hard that white snowflakes flew off in all directions.

Again Finn glanced up at the flat where Einar from their class lived. He knew this was a shot in the dark. But the note in the envelope he had found in the dustbin lorry at the harbour had indicated that someone called Einar was going to be kidnapped on 'Monday', which was tonight. Well, it was technically Tuesday now, but Einar had been at school today, so he hoped 'Monday' meant the early hours of Tuesday morning.

If indeed they had the right Einar. He had been optimistic when they had left 18 Inkognitogate. It felt good to have a little hope to cling to. Maybe they could find out something that would lead them to Sunniva and the others. But as the minutes turned into hours and he ran up and down Uranienborg Terrasse for what felt like the hundredth time, Finn started to wonder if they were wasting their time and energy. Every so often they would hear the sound of a vehicle approaching, and every time Finn felt a shiver of excitement. Only to be disappointed when it turned out to be a normal car that drove right on past. By half past three, Camomile was having doubts as well.

'Finn, I don't think they're coming. And you thould really get thome thleep. You're in the final tomorrow, remember,' he said.

Finn shook his head. Not because he disagreed, but out of frustration.

'Yes, I know. Sorry for dragging you out in the middle of the night, Camomile. I thought they might come here.'

'No worrieth. I thtill think it wath a good plan.'

They set off for home. What now? Finn thought despondently, looking up at the sky as if hoping for a miracle.

When they had walked about a hundred metres they heard a deep, rumbling noise in the far distance. It was gradually coming closer, but then everything went quiet again. Finn stopped.

'Did you hear that?' he asked.

'What?' Camomile asked, his hat pulled down over his ears. Everything was quiet.

'Come on!' Finn said, running back towards Majorstua.

They didn't stop until they reached the bushes where they had spent the last couple of hours. Then they saw it. Outside Einar's block there was a big dustbin lorry with Norway Recycles Ltd written on the side.

CHAPTER 49

THE WHOLE STREET LOOKED as if it had been repainted. It was so cold that snowflakes had settled in a thin, white layer over the old snow and parked cars. Advent candles and stars twinkled in the windows, reminding Finn that no matter what happened, Christmas would come this year as well, and it was not far off.

But maybe not for Einar. Not if the two men standing with rucksacks and evil plans outside the front door had their way. Finn could see one of them holding two gas masks, one in each hand, while the other pushed a large wheelie bin, just like the ones most people in Oslo had in their backyards.

'Oh no!' Camomile said.

'Shh!' Finn hissed.

He pressed up against the bush until the gaps between the branches were wide enough to give him a good view. One of the men seemed to be picking the lock, at any rate it was taking him a lot longer than if he had a key. Finally he managed to open the door, and they went in.

'At latht they came, Finn! At latht!' Camomile whispered nervously.

'Yes, at last.'

Finn was surprised by how calm he was. The fear from the last time he had seen the two men was gone. All he wanted was to find out what had happened to Sunniva. And to all the others. Right now he wasn't even sure they were the same men. It was hard to know how many people were involved.

'What thould we do now?'

'What we've been doing all night. We wait.'

'But what thould we do after that?'

Finn had only told Camomile that they were going to wait outside Einar's flat in case the dustbin lorry showed up. He hadn't told him what he intended to do if it actually came.

'You can't be therious,' Camomile said after hearing phase two of Finn's half-baked plan.

'Deadly serious. But I'll understand if you don't want to come,' Finn said.

Camomile thought about it for about a second.

'Of courthe I'll come,' he said.

Minutes passed. They saw a shadow in one of the flat windows for a second before it disappeared again. Then the front door opened. The two men came out wearing overalls just like normal bin men would wear, pushing the wheelie bin between them. It all looked rather innocent. But Finn strongly suspected there was a classmate in the bin, not rubbish.

The men climbed onto the step at the back of the lorry, then lifted the entire bin into the opening. Then they jumped down again and walked towards the driver's cab. The engine started and the back of the lorry closed with a mechanical clunk.

'Get ready,' Finn whispered to Camomile.

'I'm ready,' his brother whispered back.

The lorry drove towards them, but Finn knew it would have to slow down at the junction with Bogstadsveien near where they were hiding. They waited for the lorry to pass them.

'Come on!' Finn said, starting to run.

They tucked in behind the lorry so that they wouldn't be seen in the wing mirrors. They weren't far behind the lorry, but instead of stopping, the lorry drove straight into Bogstadsveien and took a sharp left. Finn and Camomile raced after it as fast as they could.

'We'll never make it! They're going too fatht!' Camomile shouted in desperation. Although it was a cold night, Finn was now regretting wearing so many clothes, as they made running more difficult. The lorry was moving further and further away from them, and Finn started to panic. If it got away now, they would lose the only lead they had on Sunniva – that's if the driver didn't see them first. Their sole chance was if the lorry had to stop at the next set of traffic lights. But to his frustration, Finn saw the lights were amber, which meant the lorry was fine to keep going. We're going to lose it, Finn thought.

But then it ground to a sudden halt. Finn realised why a second later as a lone black taxi came from the right along Sporveisgata and crossed the junction, which meant the lorry had to give way. Finn recited a silent prayer of gratitude to the taxi driver.

'Go for it, Cammy!' he said, getting closer to the lorry. Just as the lorry pulled away again, they both jumped up onto the step at the back and grabbed an iron handle. They had made it.

'I hope we're not doing thomething thtupid here,' Camomile said.

Finn said nothing, but ventured a smile. There was no doubt in his mind that what they were doing was stupid. And, above all, dangerous. But they really didn't have much choice if they wanted to find out who was behind all the kidnappings.

The lorry started to accelerate. Finn watched their surroundings whizz past, trying not to think about how they would survive a fall at this speed. For a while he was scared a car would come up behind them and start honking to warn the men, but luckily the streets were more or less empty of people and cars.

Finn soon realised they were on their way out of town. Blocks of flats became detached houses, and at a junction he saw a sign pointing towards Maridalen, just north of Oslo. Far behind them he could just glimpse the fjord.

'Doesn't look like we're going to the harbour anyway,' he said to Camomile.

The darkness made it difficult to see very far, but the streetlights showed them they were in a forested area, broken only by meadows and cultivated fields. It's a long walk home, Finn thought. He had no idea how they were going to get back. Maybe we won't ever get back, he thought, wishing he had left a note explaining what they were doing.

The lorry finally turned off the main road and into a side road through the forest. It was going a lot slower now, but it was even more difficult to hold on because the large vehicle wasn't designed to drive on terrain like this. Finn felt the impact of every bump shoot up his spine. Both his arms ached and it was becoming increasingly difficult to hold onto the handle.

'Cammy?'

'Yeth?'

'As soon as the lorry stops we have to jump off quickly and hide.'

Camomile gave a solemn nod.

'Right.'

Ten minutes of rugged woodland road later, the lorry slowed down. It was pitch black behind them, but when Finn stuck his head around the side of the lorry he could see light coming from a cabin a couple of hundred metres ahead of them on a ridge.

'I think we're there now,' he said.

The lorry was still going faster than Finn appreciated, but he was afraid they would be seen if they held on until it stopped.

'Let's jump now, OK? On the count of three.'

'OK.'

They both took one hand off the handle and braced themselves.

'One . . . two . . . three!'

Camomile and Finn let go together and jumped off the lorry. Neither of them was able to stay on his feet when they landed. Finn managed to break his fall with his hands, then rolled forwards and sideways. Once he had finally struggled to his feet, Camomile was nowhere to be seen. Then he remembered. Yet again he had forgotten that his brother was an android full of sensitive machinery and fragile electronics and not designed to jump off the back of moving lorries. But he couldn't have disappeared into thin air. Finn looked around. Then he spotted Camomile in a snow drift. Or part of him.

There were two legs sticking up out of the snow, and they weren't moving.

CHAPTER 50

FINN WASN'T SURE WHAT fate would have awaited Camomile if they had sent him back to North Boresia after unmasking him as a spy. He doubted he would have had a life of luxury to look forward to. The completely insane Kim Il-Ding had only pretended Camomile was his son, so the question was whether he would have ended up on some conveyor belt in some factory or in one of North Boresia's many coal mines. Or maybe he would have been sent on another, much more dangerous spying mission.

But that might still have been preferable to having his head removed time and time again, seeing his friends kidnapped and, last but not least, jumping off a moving lorry and ending his life in some snow drift in Maridalen.

Finn looked at Camomile, semi-interred in the soft snow and showing no signs of life. He pulled him out. Finn knew first aid, but he was fairly sure chest compressions and mouth-to-mouth resuscitation wouldn't work on an android. He opened Camomile's bubble jacket and took off his scarf. He could see a little crack in his neck. A little opening between his head and the rest of his body, with some metal showing through. Maybe his head was getting a bit loose after being removed so often, he thought. Finn sat down on Camomile and held him in position with his knees, then gripped his head and pressed it down as hard as he could.

Click.

'Aaaaagh . . .' Camomile shouted, but Finn put a gloved hand over his mouth and shushed him.

'We jumped off the back of the lorry and you fainted. Don't you remember?' he asked.

Camomile gazed at his brother in a stupor. Then he remembered.

'Yeth. Everything jutht went black.'

He looked around.

'Or white,' he laughed.

Finn smiled. Camomile was back. Again.

They both got up. The dustbin lorry had parked, and they could see that the two men had almost reached the cabin now. The bin containing Einar must still be in the lorry, Finn thought.

'They're here. I know they are,' Finn whispered.

It was a big cabin. But was it big enough to house all the children? Finn wasn't sure. Maybe there were more buildings nearby. Or rooms underground. Finn imagined subterranean galleries full of kidnapped children. Was Sunniva here somewhere?

'Let's follow them,' he whispered to Camomile.

They hid behind the cars parked along the road leading up to the cabin. Finn counted at least fifteen. Were there that many people involved in this? The road ended in a turning area, with the cabin a little further on, perched on a ridge with a view over the forest. A well-trodden path through the snow revealed where people had walked, and now that it was dark it was safe to follow the path without being seen. Only twenty metres away from the cabin, they could hear noises and voices. Finn could see smoke coming from the chimney, and at least two of the windows were open.

'We need to get clother,' Camomile whispered.

Finn nodded. He wanted a quick look through the window so they could see who was there.

They crouched down and scrambled closer using their hands like monkeys, out of the darkness and into the light from the cabin. The cold air had frozen the top layer of snow into a crust that stopped them from sinking. Finn knew they were visible from the road now, but decided it was worth the risk. They would hear any cars coming. It was much more important that no one saw them from the windows, so they kept a wary eye on the door in case someone suddenly opened it. As they got closer, Finn pointed to the back of the cabin, Camomile nodded and they scampered around the side, thus ensuring they were hidden from the road as well. There was another window open here. They pressed up against the wall of the cabin.

'. . . but we didn't have time to deliver him before the meeting started. So we brought him with us. He's out in the lorry. But he'll be out for hours yet. We'll deliver him to Angelica long before he wakes up,' said a man's voice.

Finn realised they were talking about Einar and this wasn't where he was going to end up. Which meant this wasn't where they kept all the children. And there was that name again. Angelica. Who was she?

'OK. I think we should start this GAG meeting even though the Colonel's not here yet,' rumbled another man's voice.

Finn jumped. He knew that voice. And what was GAG?

'But he's coming, isn't he? He should really be here. Especially with what's happening tomorrow.'

A woman's voice this time.

'Relax. He sent a message saying he's been held up.'

There was that voice again. Then Finn realised who it was. He clamped a hand over his mouth to stop himself from crying out or throwing up. His stomach lurched. It couldn't be true. He had to have a look inside to check if he was right.

'As most of you are well aware, we've had a few troublesome kids after us. But we got the girl the night before last. She's with all the others now. And you all know we have a plan for Finn Popps tomorrow, and I'm sure he won't be able to throw a spanner in the works before then . . .'

A chill crept up Finn's spine as his name was mentioned, and he saw Camomile's wince of concern. Finn took a step back from the wall of the cabin to look inside, but all he could see were the backs of heads. They all seemed to be sitting around a long table. He took another step back and managed to glimpse a couple of faces across the table. They looked older, but he didn't recognise any of them.

'. . . so Operation Purge is going as planned.'

The man talking was obviously walking around the table where everyone else was sitting.

Finn stepped close to the wall of the cabin and ducked down;

perhaps it was this movement that made the man swivel round. There was no longer any doubt.

The man in the window was Chief Constable Malthe.

CHAPTER 51

MALTHE PEERED INTO THE forest behind them. Finn was crouching down under the window, not moving a muscle. Don't see me, he willed. Don't see me. He closed his eyes as if that might make him invisible. It worked. Malthe resumed his talk, and when Finn looked up he was staring straight into the policeman's broad back again.

This changed everything. No wonder the police weren't prioritising the investigation or making any headway if their boss was one of the villains. Finn closed his eyes again. What a catastrophic mistake it had been to tell Malthe everything they knew. That was obviously why Sunniva had been kidnapped the same night. And now they had a plan for him as well.

'So are there any questions? This is an important day and I want everyone to be as well prepared as possible,' Malthe continued.

Another man spoke up.

'This isn't a question as such, but in my region a lot of the children's parents are very dissatisfied with the police investigation. I've heard rumours that they're going to go to the media . . . I'm sure we can all imagine what a nightmare it would be if they discovered the truth . . .'

Chief Constable Malthe interrupted him.

'They won't. As you know, phase two of our plan is being implemented later today. If all goes well, we won't have to worry about them.'

There was silence for a few seconds.

'If all goes well today, we'll all have a better future ahead of us,' Malthe said, sounding pleased with himself.

'All of us except the children,' said someone else. Everyone laughed. There had to be at least twenty people in there, Finn thought.

'Now, the Colonel will be here any minute, so we'll keep going for five minutes, then take a break . . .'

Finn turned to Camomile. They were going to take a break. That meant some of them were bound to come outside. He signalled to his brother that they should move, nodding in the direction of the forest behind the cabin. They were about to move when they heard a noise behind them.

They whirled round and looked up into the face of the person they perhaps least expected to see.

Two metres away stood a tall, broad-shouldered man in a long fur coat.

Bojan.

'Aaaagh!'

This time Finn didn't manage to put a hand over Camomile's mouth, who, as well as shouting, fell backwards against the cabin with a crash. It was as if the world stood still for a second. All Finn knew was they had to get away. Now. He pulled Camomile out of the snow, dragged him away from Bojan and fled blindly into the darkness.

There was a loud commotion in the cabin. People jumped up from their chairs and ran for the door. Bojan took up the chase, and Finn could hear the whole pack of wolves in pursuit.

'Ruuuuuun!'

It was more of a roar than a shout. Finn glanced over his shoulder. He could have sworn it was Bojan who had shouted. He stood with his hands cupped around his mouth as other figures emerged from the back of the cabin behind him.

Silent Bojan wasn't so silent after all, it seemed.

A new thought struck Finn despite the blind panic-wreaking havoc on his system. Bojan was the Colonel!

Finn made a beeline for the forest behind the cabin with Camomile hot on his heels. They were less likely to be caught in the darkness of the forest, and they already had a slight head start. Being a child was an advantage for once, as he and Camomile didn't weigh enough to break the snow crust they were running on.

But Finn was well aware that if there had been some younger men in the cabin, they wouldn't have stood a chance. Luckily, everyone Finn had glimpsed through the window had been quite elderly.

He could hear them now, and risked another backward glance. Some of the shadowy silhouettes had surrounded Bojan, and others were running towards the forest – and them.

'Come on, Camomile! Run!'

They fled deeper into the gloom, almost having to feel their way forwards as they ran. Tall trees flashed by them. After almost five minutes of flat-out, non-stop running, Finn shouted to Camomile to slow down. It had been a while since he had heard anyone behind them. They stopped, and it was only now that Finn noticed the sweat soaking through his clothes. The forest was silent apart from the sound of their own ragged breathing. No one was following them.

'They're not coming. They must have given up,' Finn said when he was able to speak again.

'Thuper,' Camomile said between gasps.

Well, what do you know, even androids get out of breath, Finn thought.

'Tho what now?' Camomile asked.

'Dunno. Well, I guess we should find our way back to the main road.'

Finn peered into the gloom. They were surrounded by trees.

'But I don't know which direction.'

Camomile closed his eyes for a few seconds.

'I think I know where it ith. Follow me,' he said at length.

Camomile walked off to the left. It struck Finn that a sense of direction was probably one of his brother's many skills. What luck if he had an in-built GPS system. It was bitterly cold, and if they stood still for too long their sweat would freeze. They had to keep moving.

And following Camomile was clearly the right thing to do. Within half an hour they were back on the main road. The bad news was that Finn was beginning to shiver and struggling to retain his body heat. Everything ached. Finally it hit him how exhausted he was. It was a long walk back to town, and there wasn't a car in sight. Finn tried to collect his thoughts, but it was almost impossible – he needed some sleep before he could process all this new information. Then they heard the sound of a car behind them. Soon they could see lights as well, and not just headlights but a roof light as well. It was a taxi. Finn stumbled into the middle of the road without a moment's hesitation. When it stopped, it suddenly occurred to him that the driver might be one of the GAG people from the cabin. But then a worried Indian taxi driver jumped out and hurried to the boot to get a couple of woollen blankets. Finn made up some cock-and-bull story about getting lost on a school trip and asked politely if the driver could drive them back to 18 Inkognitogate, even though they didn't have any money.

'No problem, my friend,' said the man.

CHAPTER 52

FINN WOKE UP TO someone shining an enormous torch in his eyes. Only after blinking a few times and rubbing his eyes did he realise that the source of the light was actually a good deal further away. 149,600,000 kilometres away, to be precise. The sun had finally broken through the snow-laden clouds, and the strong rays were launching an attack on Finn's bed. He looked at the alarm clock on his bedside table. It was 10:28. The final of the quiz started at Oslo Spektrum in half an hour!

After getting dressed and having a slice of toast and salami thrust into his hand by Baba, he peered out of the window. Ramesh, the taxi driver from the night before, was already waiting for him. Finn had to be extra careful now that Bojan had seen them. So for once it made sense to be driven from door to door. He also felt he would be safer at Oslo Spektrum with thousands of other people than at home with Baba. And as he knew that Miss Syversen was busy driving Teddy around at this time of day, he had asked Ramesh to wait for him outside the house at around half past ten. Finn went out into the piercing December light and looked around, but there was no sign that anyone was following him. He had let Camomile sleep. His brother hadn't been selected to be a member of the audience, so before they had gone to bed they had agreed to meet outside Spektrum when the final was over.

It was a really beautiful day. The snow was glittering everywhere, so much so that it felt as if they were driving in the bottom of an enormous treasure chest full of small, white jewels. Finn was Ramesh's last customer of the day, but he chattered and laughed just as he had several hours earlier. Before they had even reached the Palace Gardens he was extolling the virtues of the new prime minister for filling the potholes in Oslo's streets. Driving a taxi had never been better. Finn smiled. Ramesh had no idea it was his dad he was talking about. He looked out of the window at the people moving cautiously along the slippery pavements, getting on with what for them was a completely new and normal day. There are people among us who kidnap children, Finn thought. And no one is doing anything about it. He almost wanted to scream out of the window: did they know what was happening? But who would believe him now? And if even Chief Constable Malthe was involved, who could they trust? He fought back a wave of nausea as he thought of Bojan. How could the gym teacher be in on all of this? But then, if Bojan had fought in a war, who knew what his role had been. And why did he always sit on that bench next to the basketball court? Was it so that he could select the children that he wanted kidnapped? Maybe he was spying on other schools as well . . .?

But why had he shouted 'Run!', when he did finally say something, rather than 'Get them!' or something like that?

Questions pinged around in his head like popcorn in a pan.

What was GAG? And what was their plan for today? What was the phase two they had mentioned back at the cabin?

The cabin. There was one thing he could do. And he would have to do it now while he was still in the taxi.

'Ramesh? Have you got a phone I can use?'

Miss Syversen picked up on first ring. She told him she had just driven his father to the airport. He was going to Trondheim to inspect the roads and reassure the people there that all the potholes would be filled in. He wouldn't be back until this afternoon, which meant that Miss Syversen had a few hours to kill.

'I was wondering if you could check something for me,' Finn said.

'Oh?'

He was a bit worried that Ramesh would hear him, so he just gave her the edited highlights of what had happened the previous night. He didn't mention Bojan or Malthe. There was something else he wanted her to help him with. Finn wanted Miss Syversen to locate the cabin.

'You are insane. Do you realise that?' Miss Syversen said calmly when he had finished.

Finn had never felt particularly insane, but he could see that she might have had a point as far as what had happened after the dustbin lorry had appeared in Einar's street.

'The problem is I'm not entirely sure where the cabin is. But hold on a moment and I'll pass you over to someone who can explain it a bit better.'

227

Finn asked Ramesh to explain where he had picked them up. Then Finn tried to describe where the cabin was in relation to where they had met Ramesh. He could hear from his own voice that it was a near-impossible task.

'Hm,' she said when he had finished. 'I'll take Max along and we'll see what we can do.'

Finn could tell she wasn't convinced she would find it. He wasn't sure either. And even if they were lucky enough to find it, Malthe & Co. might have removed any evidence of their ever having been there. But he knew he couldn't let the matter drop. Finn was still pondering what else he could do when Ramesh pulled up outside the main entrance to Oslo Spektrum. Then he had something else to think about. He had never seen such chaos.

CHAPTER 53

THOUSANDS OF SCHOOLCHILDREN WERE swarming outside the entrance. They were making a terrible racket, shouting and singing, running and playing, bickering and shoving as everyone jostled their way inside. Finn thanked Ramesh. This time he even managed to pay. Then he got out and joined the babbling stream of schoolchildren winding into Oslo Spektrum.

As he got closer to the entrance, he could hear music being played over the loudspeakers inside. He recognised the song even though it was almost drowned out by all the noise the children were making.

When the bell rang, up we sprang, and moved off in a gang, happy and gay and jolly and fine, all standing in one line. We stood like beads on a string, not one of us said a thing . . . !

Wow, Finn thought. That song really must have been written ages ago, and it definitely didn't fit with how things were now, both at school and here today. They were channelled into the building, and it was only when the crowd entered the arena itself that the stream dispersed. Children ran all over the place looking for somewhere to sit in the stands, which were already packed with wild school pupils jumping and singing. To Finn the entire building seemed to be rocking. They had been given a single-sheet programme at the door. Finn had put his in his pocket, but a lot of the children had scrunched theirs up into balls and were now throwing them around in the stands, making the place look like an indoor snowball fight. You would be forgiven for thinking the audience had been chosen based on who could make the most noise.

The extensive floor space had been divided into lots of different sections. All over Oslo Spektrum there were quizzes taking place: children were asking questions and thinking and giving answers. They were now only minutes away from Viktory taking to the stage.

'There you are, Finn! Hi!'

Junita lit up when she spotted him and ran a hand through her wavy fair hair. Viktor didn't seem as happy to see him.

'Cutting it a bit fine, aren't you? Just try not to ruin everything,' he said.

Finn returned his glower, but said nothing. Junita leaned towards him.

'We're going to be a good team. You're a great addition,' she whispered.

Finn wondered whether Viktor was aware that it had been Sunniva, Camomile and him who had reported his father's dirty deed. Or whether Ernst was so embarrassed that he hadn't mentioned it.

*   *   *

230

Junita was right. They were a good team. If possible they even complemented each other better than Sun Factor 50 had. Not least because Junita was a real nature geek and Viktor was good at history. As usual, Finn knew a little about everything, although he had flashes of brilliance with more esoteric knowledge. Such as when he remembered that the blackbird was Sweden's national bird. Or that arigato was Japanese for thank you.

An elderly man was the quizmaster for the first round, and he asked them thirty questions in total. How wonderful it was to focus on the competition, how liberating it was to think about something other than desperate prime ministers and missing children. It was almost impossible to avoid being swept up in the atmosphere. Finn looked around. It was a bit like being at a concert, except that all the noise was coming from the stands and not the stage.

After approximately ten questions they were in the lead, and the Urra spectators had started to sing 'We Are The Champions'. And fortunately they weren't far off the mark. Viktory won the first round three points ahead of a team from Jessheim School.

'Yay!' Junita cheered.

'Piece of cake. But it's only gonna get harder,' Viktor said.

But the quarter-final was even easier. The eight sections had now become four larger sections, and pupils from Uranienborg School were stealing the show both on stage and in the stands.

'Go team!' Junita said, giving Finn a high five when they had the quarter-final in the bag.

Even Viktor seems pleased, Finn thought.

Participants weren't allowed in the stand between rounds, so when Viktor went to buy a hotdog, Finn and Junita were left alone at their table. The competition and chatting to Junita had distracted Finn from all his woes, but when Junita went to the loo and he was left alone, reality hit him like a brick to the face. He was so worried about Sunniva. Where are you now? he wondered.

Suddenly he regretted having come to Spektrum. Surely they had no time to lose? His mind was made up on one thing: when his dad came home this afternoon, Finn was going to tell him everything, and he wouldn't stop until Theodor Bjørnstjerne Popps understood that this was actually happening and that Finn was telling the absolute truth. He would also ask his dad to get someone to shadow Chief Constable Malthe. Or maybe to arrest him immediately and force the truth out of him. And then make sure the rest of the police force devoted all their energies to finding the children.

Yes, that was what he was going to do. It was about time he reaped the benefits of being the prime minister's son.

CHAPTER 54

EVEN THOUGH MOST TEAMS had now been knocked out, their supporters had been asked to ensure the atmosphere didn't take a nose-dive. They didn't seem to mind. Finn could see that the audience were being given fizzy drinks and popcorn. Viktory had even managed to drum up a fan base outside the hard core from Urra. This had a lot to do with Junita, as most of the Urra fans were male. Some of the boys were wolf-whistling at her, and a lot of them had learned her name as well. Rhythmic chants of 'Ohhhhh . . . Junita!' could be heard from the stands. Finn noticed her ears had turned pink.

'OK, focus now and we'll make the final,' Viktor said as the semi-final started, his jaw set.

'Yes, of course,' Junita said quickly, to show that she was alert and not bothered by the whistles and chants.

They were still playing old songs over the loudspeakers in the background. Maybe the old quizmaster was responsible for the music as well? Finn had to close his eyes to concentrate on what was being sung.

No, no, my son, this isn't done. Don't cross the mat until you've taken off your hat. Next time think twice, that would be nice.

233

After a few minutes the song faded out and a fanfare sounded to indicate the semi-final was underway.

Viktory got off to a bad start. None of them knew that the Eiffel Tower was 300 metres tall, and Viktor glared at Finn when he couldn't remember who had won the Football World Cup in 1984. Sport was supposed to be his area.

Even their supporters fell silent. But then Junita answered 'gold' when the old quiz master asked what the chemical element *Au* was. And Finn whispered '*GoldenEye*' when they were asked the name of Pierce Brosnan's first James Bond film.

'Another point to Viktory,' said the grey-haired, po-faced quizmaster.

'We can do this,' Finn said as they moved up to third place.

Their rah-rah gang cheered and jumped up and down. It was a wonder the quizmaster could hear himself think. They were tied in second place with one question to go, only one point behind the leaders. Only the two best teams would progress to the final.

'We *have* to get this or we're out,' Viktor said, leaning forward.

The quizmaster took an unnecessarily long dramatic pause before starting to read.

'Who was the first person to sail through the Northwest Passage?'

Oh dear. Finn could tell from the faces of the other teams that it was difficult for them as well. Viktor and Junita just shook their heads. The Northwest Passage was the quickest sea route between Europe and Asia. It twisted around the islands north of Canada and joined the Atlantic and Pacific oceans. That much

Finn knew. But who had sailed though it first? Finn had a feeling he had heard it, read it or seen it on TV at some point. He also had a gut feeling it might have been a Norwegian. If that was the case, there weren't many to choose from. When it came to daring polar expeditions, it was generally Fridtjof Nansen or Roald Amundsen.

The other two looked at him, their eyes imploring. He went with his gut.

'Roald Amundsen,' he said.

'What?' Viktor asked, sceptical.

'Have you got any better ideas?' Junita asked.

Viktor thought about it for a couple seconds before shaking his head.

Two of the other teams answered 'Columbus', and the remaining team plumped for 'Vasco da Gama'. Well, we know they're wrong, Finn thought. He had been the first person to sail around the tip of South Africa.

The quizmaster lifted the card that would seal their fate for the rest of the National General Knowledge Competition, and announced:

'The correct answer is . . . Roald Amundsen.'

Junita leapt out of her chair, threw her arms into the air and screamed with delight at the same time as large sections of the stands exploded with cheers. Then she leaned over Finn and gave him a big hug.

'You're so clever!' she told him. Now it was Finn's turn to blush. Viktor stayed where he was.

'Yeah, nicely done. But we'd have managed with Iver as well,' was all Viktor said before wandering off.

Finn watched him go. What was his problem? he thought, irritated.

'Ignore him. He's just in a bad mood because of what happened to his dad,' Junita said.

She was right. Finn felt a pang of guilt. It couldn't be easy having your father in prison. He decided there and then that he would try to forgive Viktor. Even though he was behaving like a prat.

They were getting everything ready for the grand final. A raised podium was hastily being set up in the middle, with bright spotlights illuminating the four tables. Finn and Junita went to get a drink. Even though it was a break, Spektrum was anything but quiet. Buckets of popcorn soared across the rows of seats, children played tag in the aisles and scattered scuffles had broken out between opposing fans. Quiet returned to some extent when they announced over the loudspeakers that the final would start in three minutes. Finn used both his eyes and ears to search out the gang from Urra, who were now roaring a homemade chant for Viktory. He turned and was about to climb back up on stage when something caught his eye. He had seen something in the stands. He turned to look at the group from Urra again, then he rubbed his eyes and tried to focus.

He couldn't believe what he was seeing.

But there was no mistaking it.

Big Jimmy was standing with the Uranienborg School supporters.

CHAPTER 55

FINN DROPPED HIS PLASTIC bottle on the table and ran back off the stage. What the hell is going on? he thought as he ran. Big Jimmy was back? Where on earth had he been? Had he escaped from the kidnappers? And where were the others?

A barrier had been set up around the stage and the quiz participants had been warned to stay inside it as long as they were in the competition. Finn couldn't have cared less, he jumped over it without a second thought. The Urra fans were a little way up in the stands, and it was easy to see Big Jimmy among them. He wasn't called 'Big' Jimmy for nothing. But while the others sang and jumped around, he stood completely still and just watched. Finn ran up the aisle steps. It was no mean feat. Many of the children had camped down, and there were empty popcorn tubs and pop bottles everywhere.

'Jim-Erik!' he shouted as he got closer, but he couldn't make himself heard over the din.

A fanfare sounded from the loudspeakers. Oh no, Finn thought, the final's starting in one minute. When he reached the right row, he tried again.

'Jim-Erik!'

Big Jimmy looked around as he realised someone was shouting at him and spotted Finn waving at him from the aisle. Big Jimmy pointed at himself and raised his eyebrows. Finn nodded frantically and waved even more frenziedly as he gasped for breath. Big Jimmy squeezed along the row and smiled when he reached Finn.

'Finn, how nice to see you! Well done on reaching the final,' he said in a friendly voice.

Now it was Finn's turn to raise his eyebrows. How could he just turn up and act as if nothing had happened? Finn was perplexed.

'What . . . where've you been?' he asked.

'Er, I . . . what do you mean?' Big Jimmy asked.

'What do I mean? You disappeared. Your family were heartbroken. And now you're here!'

Big Jimmy grew serious.

'Oh, you heard about that, huh? Yes, I ran away from home. But I felt bad about it, so I came back.'

As simple as that. He ran away, felt bad about it and now he was back here? It *couldn't* be that simple.

'But weren't you kidnapped? By the flies . . . I mean, the men in gas masks?'

Big Jimmy's eyes flickered.

'Gas masks? I have no idea what you're talking about.'

Then he smiled again.

'I ran away and now I'm back. That's all there is to it.'

Then the tannoys crackled.

'Could . . . could Finn Popps please make his way to the stage

238

now? I repeat, Finn Popps to the stage, please. The final is starting now,' said the speaker, sounding harassed.

How is that possible, Finn thought.

'Where are all the other children? The others that were kidnapped? Or . . . ran away?'

The noise rose to previous levels around them. Finn had to shout to make himself heard.

Big Jimmy frowned.

'I really don't know what you're talking about, Finn. But hurry or you'll miss the final!'

Big Jimmy pointed to the stage as if Finn were confused about where he was supposed to be. Finn fought a wave of frustration. Something didn't add up. A lot didn't add up. Big Jimmy the bruiser was now the very essence of friendliness. He pointed at Big Jimmy and shouted as authoritatively as he could.

'Don't you go anywhere! You hear me? I need to talk to you after the final,' he said, before turning and rushing down the steps.

'Good luck, Finn!' he heard Big Jimmy call behind him.

The quizmaster for the final was a plump, dowdy woman wearing a blue jacket and thick, blue-rimmed glasses. She was visibly irritated when Finn came running on stage, his face shiny with sweat. For a moment Finn thought she looked familiar, but he guessed it was probably because she looked a bit like Baba's friend Margot from the bingo.

'What the hell are you playing at, Finn! We could've been disqualified!' Viktor hissed.

'Yeah, where were you?' Junita asked, worried.

Finn couldn't even begin to explain.

'Sorry,' he said, raising his palms.

The woman with the blue-rimmed glasses stood between the four tables and prepared to ask the first question. Finn glanced up into the stands. Big Jimmy was still there. Stay there, he begged.

'OK. Now's the moment,' Viktor said through gritted teeth.

Finn nodded and tried to concentrate. This was the final after all. They had a fair chance of winning the entire thing – the National General Knowledge Competition. This was big. Especially for someone who loved quizzes as much as he did. It went through Finn's mind that Sunniva would have been proud of him. I'll find you soon, he thought.

The woman in blue cleared her throat.

'Let us begin,' she said.

CHAPTER 56

IN SOME SPORTS, SUCH as football, or dodgeball for that matter, you can occasionally see from a player's or a team's actions whether they have prepared a strategy in advance. It might be the way they warm up, the way they run or the way they throw or kick the ball. It is a lot more difficult with quiz teams. Finn tried to suss out the other three teams – from Bergen, Narvik and Bærum respectively – but they weren't giving anything away. They just sat ramrod straight on their chairs waiting for the first question. He noticed that two of the team members from Grav School in Bærum were wearing glasses and vaguely wondered whether that meant they had read a lot of books. Or that they had been born with astigmatism of course.

The woman in blue adjusted her own glasses and cleared her throat again before speaking.

'First question: How many legs does a spider have?' she asked in a gruff voice.

Easy peasy, Finn thought. And let's hope it stays that way. They had all been given paper and pens, but as Viktor was the team captain, he wrote down their final answer.

However, it soon got a lot worse than eight-legged creepy crawlies. Much worse. They exchanged despondent looks when

241

asked for the names of the members of the eighties Norwegian band A-ha, and their hearts sank even further when the team from Bergen named all three. Viktor pulled at his usually neat hair when it transpired that none of them knew what the population of England was. He even protested aloud when she asked: 'What was Bergen called in the old days?' The team from Bergen, on the other hand, grinned from ear to ear before answering 'Bjørgvin' with an extra roll of the 'r'.

Every time Biddy Blue read out the correct answer, the supporters in the stands responded with either tumultuous cheers or dejected boos.

Finn didn't know where they got the energy from. The final round was also twice as long as the preceding rounds, with two sets of thirty questions. Viktory started doing a bit better towards the end of the first set, and by the time the break came round they were in third place. There was still hope. They were only three points behind Dunnonuffin from Bergen and one behind Wizkids from Bærum.

Finn was so absorbed by the competition and the atmosphere that he almost forgot to check if Big Jimmy was still in the stands. But he was still there, in the same place. Finn struggled to believe that Big Jimmy had been telling the truth. He had to know more than he was letting on. And why on earth was he so cheerful?

A fanfare sounded. The second round of the final was only a minute away.

'Sorry about the squirrels,' Junita said, referring to her failure to answer one of the nature questions.

242

'Don't worry. None of us has been on top form. Right, Finn?' Viktor said acidly.

'No, not one of us,' Finn said snippily. He certainly hadn't been any worse than Viktor.

'But we'll turn it around, won't we?' Junita said, looking hopeful.

'Yes, we will,' Finn said with conviction.

I'll do it for Sunniva, he thought.

They got off to a good start, and soon caught up with the team from Bergen. Finn had been able to make use of two of the more unusual capital cities he had swotted up.

'In which religion is Vishnu a god?'

Viktor and Junita exchanged uncertain glances.

'Buddhism?' Junita suggested.

'Hinduism,' Finn said. He had seen a documentary about India on National Geographic and remembered the god of love's four arms.

Viktor could see that Finn was absolutely sure.

'Good,' he said, writing down the answer.

But unfortunately, Dunnonuffin did know something. About Hindu gods and other things, so even though Viktory were answering the questions correctly now, it was no good, the team from Bergen were always a point ahead of them. By the time they reached the twenty-second question, Viktor was starting to despair.

'We'll never beat them!' he whined.

The other two teams were now mere spectators to the battle

for supremacy between Norway's two biggest towns, neither with any potholes in their roads.

'Who wrote *The Brothers Lionheart*?'

Too easy, Finn thought in disappointment. Dunnonuffin were sure to get that one as well. But their team captain, a girl with a lot of freckles, glanced nervously at her teammates before reading from her piece of paper.

'Astrid Lindquist,' she said hesitantly.

'Yessss!' Viktor cried.

For a moment there he reminded me of Sunniva, Finn thought. The Urra supporters cheered. Many of them already knew that the team from Bergen had given the wrong answer.

'Astrid Lindgren,' Viktor said when it was their turn.

Finn silently thanked the Swedish author from Vimmerby in Småland. The teams were tied. Oslo Spektrum was heating up, and not just with tension and excitement: it was quite literally getting warmer. A lot warmer. Sweat was running down their faces, and Finn wished he could take off his T-shirt, it was so hot.

Even after Biddy Blue had cleared her throat four times, there was no sign the audience were going to quieten down. It was only when an irritated voice came over the tannoy system telling them to 'shut up' for the next and final question that things settled again.

Biddy Blue read in a loud, clear voice.

'What is . . . an android?'

She had to be joking. Finn mentally hugged Camomile. He looked at the clock. Quarter to three. They were supposed to be meeting outside in fifteen minutes. He would probably be a bit late getting out, but the first thing he would tell his brother was that they had won, and all thanks to him. Then he realised that he *couldn't* actually say that, because Camomile didn't actually know what he was. Finn would have to make do with a real hug.

Providing Dunnonuffin didn't also know the answer.

'I don't know,' Junita whispered.

'Me neither,' Viktor bemoaned.

'But I do,' Finn said, smiling.

Then, in a loud, clear voice he said:

'An android is a humanoid robot.'

'A rosebush', 'a tool' and 'a kind of carnivorous duck' were the suggestions from the other teams.

Biddy Blue cleared her throat again, and for the first time that day, there was silence in Oslo Spektrum.

'This is the deciding question,' she announced.

It was all a bit much for Junita, who held her face in her hands. Finn closed his eyes and thought about palm trees, white sandy beaches and clear blue waves lapping against his toes. But then Sunniva appeared. As if to remind him he couldn't relax until he had found her.

'The correct answer is . . .'

All eyes were fixed on the plump little woman. Finn could see she was enjoying keeping them in suspense from the way the corners of her mouth were twitching. Enjoying being the only person who knew the answer. Apart from Finn.

'. . . a humanoid robot!'

For a tiny instant, Biddy Blue looked at Finn and smiled.

CHAPTER 57

OSLO SPEKTRUM EXPLODED AROUND him. They had done it. They had won the whole thing. It was almost surreal. Junita was hanging around his neck, and when she finally let go, Viktor held out a hand. Finn shook it.

'Well done, Finn. And thank you, we'd never have done it without you,' Viktor said.

'No problem. We'd never have done it without you either,' Finn said.

Viktor smiled. They waved to the Urra supporters in the stands to thank them for their support, which raised the noise level even higher.

Biddy Blue beckoned them over.

'Well done, children! We're going to award you your prize straight away, so don't run off,' she said.

Finn noticed that the other teams had already been escorted out of the arena. It seemed there weren't any silver or bronze medals in this competition. Only gold. Wow, Bora Bora, Finn thought. And to think he had only been abroad once, to Karlstad in Sweden with Baba to go shopping in the sales for a suit.

The lights in Oslo Spektrum were dimmed apart from some

spots that made the victory podium look as if it were glowing. The tannoy system crackled again, and a man's voice echoed around the arena. He wasn't so irritated now.

'We're ready to announce the winners of the National General Knowledge Competition. And we are proud to congratulate . . . Viktory, comprising Junita, Viktor and Finn from Uranienborg School, Oslo!'

More wild cheering from the stands. Finn, Junita and Viktor climbed up onto the podium and waved to the audience as Biddy Blue came towards them to hand out the prizes. She presented the certificate to Viktor, which stated that they had won a trip to Bora Bora. Then she gave Finn a bouquet of flowers. She looked at him and winked.

'We have another little surprise,' she said, before turning and walking over to a big bag to get something.

It was now so hot in the stands that a lot of the boys were bare-chested. However, Big Jimmy had kept his his cool, and his clothes on, and was now talking to the girl next to him. Finn realised who it was and was shocked again.

Hedda!

Big Jimmy was talking to Hedda! She was back! Suddenly he felt dizzy. What was going on?

Finn squinted at the Urra supporters to see if any more of the missing children were there. He was mainly looking for Sunniva, but he couldn't see her or any of the others. However he did notice something he hadn't considered before. There were no grown-ups in sight. No teachers with the students. No one supervising them. That went a long way to explaining the unruliness of the spectators, but even so, it was strange. The only grown-ups were the quizmasters, who were mostly elderly people. And where were they now? Finn looked around. There. They were standing together in a group of maybe twenty next to the podium. They were all holding something, but Finn couldn't see what it was. But he thought a couple of them looked familiar. And when he looked at Biddy Blue again, he realised where he had seen her before. She had taken off her blue glasses.

Now she looked like she did the last time he had seen her.

When he had run as fast as he could to get away from her and everyone else in the cabin in Maridalen.

Something was wrong. His head was spinning. His vision blurred, and for a moment it felt as if Spektrum were shaking even though the children were sitting relatively still now.

Someone poked him. It was Junita.

'Finn, what's happening to your flowers?'

Finn looked down at the flowers.

They were already wilting.

CHAPTER 58

FINN REALISED WHAT WAS happening in an instant. Within ten he had confirmation that he was right. Everything was happening in slow motion. Biddy Blue pulled something out of the bag. Finn already knew what it was. The group of elderly quiz masters were putting on their masks.

'Gas! Gas attack,' Finn shouted at Junita and Viktor, throwing his flowers away and jumping down from the podium.

They gaped at him in amazement, but Finn could see the life draining out of them. People started groaning in the stands, and some had already fainted.

'We need to get out! They're gassing the whole of Spektrum!' Then Viktor fell.

He stepped into thin air and tried to catch himself, but he was unconscious by the time he hit the ground. He lay motionless.

'What's going on?' Junita sobbed and took a few shaky steps. Finn grabbed her hand. They had to get out.

'Don't breathe! Try to hold your breath,' Finn said, pulling his T-shirt over his mouth. He wasn't sure it would help. After all, they had already breathed in the gas, and it wouldn't do much good holding it in their lungs, would it? But it had to be better than breathing in more. That said, he was getting dizzier and dizzier, and the ground was swaying. He was only just managing to stay upright. Panic rippled through the stands. Children were falling like dominos, screams were interspersed with whimpers, and no one knew what was happening. It was a terrible sight.

Junita gasped for breath.

'Finn, what's going on?' she shouted.

Don't breathe, Finn thought, pointing at the main entrance to explain that they had to get out.

They climbed down from the podium. Finn saw the grown-ups with their gas masks on and dragged Junita in the opposite direction. They staggered off, making slow progress, and then Junita fell onto one knee. Finn pulled her up. It was a lot darker now they were out of the spotlights. Finn couldn't hold his breath much longer. The gas was even denser now. His eyes were streaming, and he could taste the gas when he gasped for breath. The room started to spin and it hurt to keep his eyes open. Now he understood why it was so hot – they had switched off the ventilation system to ensure the gas would be effective. He looked up at the stands. What only minutes earlier had been an area full of boisterous, lively children was now a scene from a horror movie, with children strewn around everywhere.

Except for two.

Big Jimmy and Hedda were still standing, seeming unperturbed by what was going on around them.

* * *

A terrible silence was spreading, with scattered faint whimpers from the stands. Then a song was heard. It didn't come from the loudspeakers but from the main entrance, where the doors were opening. It sounded like a distant choir, but Finn couldn't hear what they were singing. Help is on its way, he thought.

Then Junita fainted. He only just caught her. He didn't have the strength to carry her, so he laid her down carefully. He carried on, keeping close to the ground where the air was cleaner.

He could see something moving by the main entrance. Someone was coming in. No, not someone, lots of people. A whole army of people marching in rows. It *is* the army! Finn thought, overjoyed. Dad's worked out what's happening and he's sent soldiers to save us.

But they weren't soldiers.

They were children.

Thousands of children came marching in, and they were the ones singing. No, Finn thought, don't come in here! You'll be knocked out. Go back.

But there was something strange about them. Something about the way they walked, as if they were sleepwalking. Something about the way they sang.

In the dim light inside the arena their eyes seemed to have a faint glow. They spread out, like an enormous swarm, heading for different sections of the stands before starting to climb. Their singing grew louder and clearer. It was only then that Finn heard what they were singing.

Hearts of lions, minds of flint, arms and legs of steel, backs strong and erect, eyes undaunted, what a sight they are! Ready to brave hardship, brave sleet and frost and heat, these are the boys that our Norway wants!

Again Finn's vision blurred, and he knew he couldn't crawl any further.

When his eyesight returned, he saw that two of the children were walking straight towards him. A girl and a boy. The girl was about twenty metres ahead of the boy, and as she came closer, Finn almost fainted in shock.

The girl was Junita.

I'm dreaming, he thought as Junita walked right past him. He turned. The other Junita was lying a few metres behind him where he had left her, unconscious on the floor. The new Junita stopped next to her and stood perfectly still.

He heard footsteps behind him. He knew who it was before he turned.

Finn looked round, straight into his own eyes.

CHAPTER 59

IT FELT AS IF he were drifting in and out of reality. Finn didn't know what was real and what was a dream. The huge flies lifted him onto their backs and carried him to a cold, dark room. It shook and smelled of petrol, his eyes stung, and he could sense there were other people around him. Then everything went soft and quiet, and he rose with thousands of other children. Like migratory birds they flew over the city, and all the flies were gone. He could feel the wind in his hair, but it wasn't cold, the sun warmed their faces as they glided through the air together, Big Jimmy, Hedda, Iver, Einar and all the others. And of course Sunniva. He held her hand as they flew towards the clouds and the city grew smaller and smaller beneath them.

Suddenly it was dark again, and he was freezing. He had to be awake now, he thought. Eventually a pair of strong arms lifted him up and slung him over a shoulder. He could smell tobacco, and it felt as though they were going upstairs. Then he drifted back into unconsciousness.

He woke up again when someone threw water in his face. Not once but twice. Finn tried to open his eyes, but they were stinging and he couldn't. He tried to blink away the pain, and when that didn't help, he tried to lift his hands to rub his eyes. But they wouldn't move. They were tied behind his back. And he seemed to be sitting on a chair.

'Finn?'

His vision was still blurry, and it hurt to keep his eyes open, but the voice was unmistakable.

'Sunniva?'

He heard footsteps and sensed a huge, dark shadow in front of him. Then someone threw water over him again.

'Time to wake up now, lad,' said a deep, rumbling voice.

Finn knew that Chief Constable Malthe was standing in front of him. The water soothed the pain in his eyes, and slowly his vision returned. The outline of the broad-shouldered man became clearer, almost as if someone were adjusting a camera lens to focus the image. Chief Constable Malthe was holding a glass, and there was a bucket of water on the floor next to him.

It was a large, empty room. Unfurnished except for the chair to which Finn was tied. There weren't even any windows. All the light came from a lamp on the wall. Finn could feel the rope cutting into his wrists.

He spotted Sunniva; she was wearing shackles and was chained to an iron ring in the wall. Then Finn did a double take. Bojan was next to her. He too was chained to the wall, but his body was hanging limply from his arms. He must have been unconscious. Finn sent Sunniva a quizzical look.

'Are you OK?' he asked.

'Well, I've had better days,' she said calmly.

Finn was confused. Where on earth were they?

Then he remembered what had happened at Spektrum. The wilting flowers, Viktor falling, Junita, the elderly quizmasters and the army of children marching into the arena. What had happened? What had happened to all the children?

He could feel the anger welling up inside him.

'Are all of you completely insane? What are you doing?' he shouted.

The tall policeman just shook his head.

'Now, now, calm down. If you hadn't been so damn nosy, neither you nor your prickly little friend would be here.'

'What about Bojan? Why's he here? Isn't he . . . the Colonel?'

Malthe laughed.

'That oaf? The Colonel? You have to be kidding. He's the only person who's been even nosier and more bothersome than you.'

Finn was stunned. His eyes were still stinging. He wished his hands were free.

'But . . . he was with you at the cabin!'

Malthe looked at Finn in surprise.

'The cabin? You were there?'

Malthe slammed a fist into the wall.

'I knew it! I knew Bojan wasn't the only one there. We heard a shout, but he swore he was alone.'

'So he wasn't with you?'

'Aren't you paying attention, boy?' Malthe snapped. 'Bojan was spying on us and we caught him red-handed. And even though we've bent his ear a bit . . .'

Malthe nodded in the direction of the gym teacher lying unconscious on the floor.

'. . . he hasn't said a word. So it was you he was protecting, was it? Didn't help much though, did it?'

Malthe laughed again.

Finn felt his cheeks burning. They had been completely wrong about Bojan. And what was worse, it was probably their fault that the gym teacher had been seen at the cabin. It was Camomile's shout that had alerted them. And now he knew why Bojan had shouted 'Ruuun!' He had been shouting at them, not at Malthe & Co. On top of that, he had sacrificed himself; allowed himself to be captured to protect them. Finn looked at Bojan, guilt gnawing at him.

But if Bojan wasn't the Colonel, who was?

Finn looked at Sunniva.

'Who's in charge? And what's GAG?'

She shook her head weakly.

'I don't know. I've hardly seen anyone since I was kidnapped. I've been down in the cargo hold with the other children.'

Sunniva's eyes narrowed as she turned to look at Malthe.

'Until the world's most cowardly chief constable came to get me . . .'

Chief Constable Malthe took two quick steps towards her and lifted a hand.

'Watch it, you insolent little . . .'

Finn was sure that Malthe was going to hit her, but the policeman caught himself in time. He smiled instead.

'I may as well get the Colonel now, so that you can talk to him yourself,' he said, walking towards the big iron door that was the only way out of the room. He opened it, but turned in the doorway and looked at Finn.

'He's been particularly looking forward to having you here,' Malthe said, before closing the door behind him with a loud clang.

CHAPTER 60

THE STINGING IN FINN'S eyes had given way to itchiness, which he tried to blink away. It didn't help much. He turned to Sunniva.

'What's going on? Where are we? Where have you been?'

Sunniva tried to smile, but all she managed was a strange grimace.

'Look at the door, Finn.'

He glanced at the iron door via which Malthe had just left. There was a name printed in the middle of the door: *Angelica*.

Angelica. It took a few seconds, but Finn caught on eventually.

'Are we . . . are we on a boat? Angelica . . . Angelica's not a woman. It's the name of a tanker.'

Sunniva nodded. Finn groaned. They should have figured that out. Angelica down at the harbour. Of course it was a boat.

'But that's about all I know,' Sunniva said. 'They kidnapped me at night and I was in a huge cargo hold when I woke up. There were only a few of us at first, maybe twenty including Big Jimmy, Hedda and Iver. But a few hours ago they wheeled in a crazy number of unconscious kids.'

'They gassed the whole of Spektrum,' Finn told her.

'They're plumb cuckoo.'

'But why? What are they going to do to us?' Finn asked.

'I don't know. They haven't said.'

There was silence for a few seconds. Finn had a lot more questions, but he was aware that Sunniva didn't know a lot more than him.

'What about you?' she asked. 'What've you been up to since I last saw you?'

Finn told her what had happened in the days since they had last seen each other. About the ride on the back of the dustbin lorry, the cabin and the meeting in Maridalen, Bojan showing up and how they ran for their lives through the forest.

'You're almost as crazy as they are,' she said.

Finn mustered a weak smile.

'We did what we had to.'

Then he told her what had happened at Oslo Spektrum during the National General Knowledge Competition.

'You won?' Sunniva repeated, impressed.

'Yes, but the celebrations were pretty short-lived. They gave me some flowers while I was standing on the podium, and when I saw they were starting to wilt . . . well, you know.'

Sunniva nodded.

'From then on it was a bit . . . chaotic, to put it mildly. And, the craziest thing about it, and I'm still not sure whether I dreamt this or it really happened, was that thousands of kids suddenly came *into* the arena. And they were singing . . .'

'Don't tell me . . . old Norwegian children's songs?' Sunniva interrupted.

259

'Yes, how did you know?'

'We've heard them on the boat as well, just not seen them.'

'And you won't believe me, but one of the kids . . .'

Finn didn't get any further. A loud noise warned them the door was about to open. Chief Constable Malthe stepped into the room. Finn felt his hackles rising at the sight of the huge policeman.

'Well, kids. Time to meet our Great Leader, as it were.'

They could hear footsteps outside the door, and then Finn realised there was also an extra thunk for every second step. As if the person were walking with . . . a stick.

A small, well-dressed, elderly man appeared in the doorway. Bushy eyebrows hung like hairy balconies over his craggy face.

'Headmaster Bentson,' Finn and Sunniva gasped in unison.

CHAPTER 61

THE OLD HEADMASTER ENTERED the room without looking at them, hobbling along in a grey suit and beige shirt with a white handkerchief sticking out of his jacket pocket. A stooped man with a big beak and huge hands followed him.

'Headmaster Bentson? Colonel Bentson, if you don't mind. I was in the army longer than I've worked at that school,' he said, banging his stick on the ground again. 'And in a way, I'm back in the army now.'

Bojan groaned in the corner and shifted a little. He seemed to be coming to. Bentson's face assumed a stern expression.

'Just look . . . all the parasites together in one room. You managed to crawl here eventually then, did you?' he said, looking at Finn and smiling.

'Parasites!' Sunniva snarled, yanking hard on the shackles that prevented her from attacking Bentson. 'Stop insulting us and tell us what the hell you're playing at, you . . . you geriatric psychopath!'

Bentson regarded the incensed girl shouting at him for a few seconds before turning to the stooped man.

'Just listen to her, Vulture! What kind of way is that to speak to your elders and betters?'

He turned to Sunniva again and took a step closer.

'What I'm playing at? What *we're* playing at?'

Bentson slammed his stick hard down on the floor.

'We're tidying up your mess!' he yelled. 'We're tidying up before it's too late! Before all of Norway is consumed by a generation of wild, unkempt animals like you who make life intolerable for the rest of us!'

For a moment Finn was scared that Bentson would completely lose his head and turn into one of the wild animals he was so afraid of. The man called Vulture stood by the wall nodding emphatically at everything Bentson said. The headmaster, or rather the Colonel, continued.

'Didn't you see them at Oslo Spektrum? Don't you see them sitting around you at school every day? How they babble, scream, make a racket, push, bellow and . . .'

Bentson searched for more words. He found them eventually.

'Today's Norwegian children have no manners whatsoever. Basic etiquette is a thing of the past. All they think about is "me, me, me" or "more, more, more"!'

Bentson looked at Finn.

'It didn't help that someone's father started a political party promising them exactly that,' he said acidly. 'That's why we . . .'

'Who's "we"?' Finn interrupted.

Bentson stood twirling his stick in one hand.

'Who indeed? *We* are a group of people who have certain common values. First of all, we don't much care for young people today. *We* are people who contributed to making this country great and now have to watch it fall apart. Except for a certain chief constable, most of us are headmasters and headmistresses, although we've had some of the school janitors doing the dirty work for us as well. Dirty work they failed to complete satisfactorily in your case. Isn't that correct, Vulture?'

Bentson threw an irritated look at the man with the big nose and stoop. Vulture. Couldn't have come up with a better name myself, Finn thought. And speaking of names . . .

'And you call yourselves . . . GAG?'

Bentson looked across at him in surprise.

'So you know that too, do you? As I mentioned, we're a group of older people who don't like children. Very few of us even have our own children. And none of us have grandchildren. So . . . GAG.'

Bentson smiled. Finn looked blank.

'Grunters Against Grandchildren,' Bentson said slowly, and then laughed. It wasn't a nice laugh.

GAG. Grunters Against Grandchildren. It was almost . . . childish. Finn felt his anger rearing its ugly head again.

'So you're going to ruin it for everyone who has grandchildren?'

Malthe took a step forward.

'We don't kidnap all of them. We just take the ones that won't behave. And believe me, bad behaviour isn't just in the classroom! Criminals are getting younger and more senseless,' Malthe said.

'But what you're doing is a hundred thousand times worse!' Finn shouted. 'You can't take thousands of children away from their families!'

263

'That's not what we're doing,' Bentson said calmly.

He looked at Malthe, who cleared his throat.

'We're not taking them as such. We're just exchanging them,' said the huge policeman, and then they both started laughing.

'Well put, Willy. That's exactly what we're doing. We're exchanging them,' Bentson said.

'You're not just insane, you're a monster. And what do you mean by "exchanging them"?' Sunniva asked as calmly as she could. Finn had never seen her eyes so narrow before.

Bentson's top lip quivered, and his right hand gripped the stick so tightly that his knuckles turned white.

'Watch your tone, young lady, or you'll soon see what I'm made of,' he said, without taking his eyes off her.

'We're exchanging the children for better models. Children brought here on this ship from a faraway country.'

Finn was confused. What was he talking about? They were exchanging children for other children? Was this a dream after all? Had an army of children really come marching into Oslo Spektrum? And how could he have seen himself among them?'

Sunniva spoke up.

'Can someone cut the crap and tell us what's really going on?' she asked.

Bentson smiled.

'It's really very simple. We're exchanging the children . . . for robots,' he said.

CHAPTER 62

THREE OR FOUR LOUD bangs followed Bentson's revelation. The whole room shook. At first Finn thought someone was bombing the tanker. Then the din settled into an even roar, and he realised it had just been the ship's engines starting up.

'Oh, there we are. Almost time to set sail,' Malthe growled. 'Hope you're ready for a cruise.'

'Where are we going?' Sunniva asked.

Bentson banged his stick on the ground once again. It seemed that was how he announced he had something to say.

'We, missie, are taking a little trip to North Boresia.'

North Boresia. Robots. Finn knew there had to be some sort of connection, but he couldn't quite work it out. He thought about all the unconscious children in the cargo hold. What was Bentson going to do with them? And in North Boresia? He had a bad feeling. What was it Malthe had said? They were going to 'exchange' them. For what?

'Are you going to exchange the children on the boat for robots from North Boresia?' he finally asked.

Bentson leant his stick against his leg and clapped slowly.

'Well now. Finally someone has an ounce of understanding,' he said.

'You're insane. Don't you see how many families you're destroying?' Sunniva exploded, furious.

Bentson smiled, his eyes positively gleaming.

'That's what's so clever about it! The families won't even notice. In fact, they're going to be delighted that their little brats are finally behaving like well-raised specimens of the species "Norwegian youth"!'

He was warming to the topic now. It was as if the insanity was breaking through the well-dressed façade.

'The robots are identical copies of their children! We even had to make a Sunniva when we realised we'd have to take you! Hahaha, I bet your mum will be so pleased when she gets home from Spektrum, just like all the other children, hahahaha!'

Bentson was laughing loudly now without restraint. Even Malthe and Vulture looked a tad unnerved.

'Rubbish! She'll notice straight away!' Sunniva yelled.

Finn thought about Camomile and how real he was. He really wasn't sure Vera would notice that Sunniva the robot wasn't the real Sunniva. After all, they weren't talking about robots, but . . .

'Androids,' he said without thinking.

Bentson stopped laughing abruptly and turned to look at him.

'They're not robots. They're androids,' Finn repeated.

'You're absolutely correct. *Humanoid robots.* I hope you appreciated that last question at the Spektrum. It was our little inside joke, hahaha!'

266

He's not all there, Finn thought. Then he remembered that the old man had filled a boat with kidnapped children. Of course he wasn't all there.

'And no one's better at making them than the North Boresians. I have to admit, for someone with such an utterly hopeless father, you're astonishingly well informed. Not to mention nosy. Willy could have done with people like you in the police force,' Bentson said, laughing again. He was in his element now.

'But what the police force *doesn't* need is traitors like Malthe,' Sunniva pointed out.

Malthe glowered at Sunniva as Bentson continued.

'All we had to do was get all the delinquents, all the hooligans in one place. Hence the National General Knowledge Competition. With a hand-picked audience,' he smiled.

It had all been a ploy, Finn thought. A lot of the other old people were head teachers at other schools. They had picked out the wildest, most disruptive pupils. And it couldn't have been a coincidence that there was suddenly a place for him in Viktory. Bentson had wanted to make sure that he would be at Oslo Spektrum.

But that still didn't explain all the events of the past week.

'Why bother kidnapping children in the week before the final at Oslo Spektrum?' Finn finally asked.

'Guinea pigs!' The headmaster pointed his stick straight at Finn. 'We, young man, know the importance of homework. We needed to make sure the androids worked as perfect copies. And they did.' He rubbed his hands together gleefully. 'Oh yes, Jim-Erik's copy was so perfect even I couldn't tell them apart.' And then he frowned. 'Until of course it because clear which of them was polite and well-behaved.'

'But . . . what will North Boresia do with all the children?' Finn asked.

Bentson tapped his stick against the ground in a cheerful manner.

'Kim Il-Ding and I studied together in England many years ago. And even though our lives have taken different courses since then, suddenly we found we had mutual interests. We wanted to get rid of thousands of wild, ill-mannered children and he . . . er, he wanted them.'

'You still haven't answered the question. What is he going to do with them?' Sunniva asked.

The headmaster, or the Colonel, walked over to her.

'Those hooligans we have in the cargo hold will become North Boresia's best soldiers.'

Finn and Sunniva exchanged incredulous looks.

'The wildest, most brutal and most fearsome soldiers in the world. Kim Il-Ding wants Norwegian children with Viking blood flowing through their veins. All they need is a few years of hard North Boresian discipline.'

Bentson laughed.

'You didn't think the dictator of North Boresia came all the way to Norway just to drink coffee with Taxi Teddy, did you?'

Finn closed his eyes. So that was why he had come. To meet Bentson. And to leave Camomile behind as a spy while he was at it. What is it with grown-ups? he thought. Talk about being badly behaved.

Another thunk with the stick. Finn really wanted to tear it out of the old man's hands and break it in two.

'Now then, my good people. Time to make a move. We've got a long trip ahead of us,' he said, moving towards the heavy door. Vulture hurried to open it for him. Bentson was about to leave, but then paused for a moment before turning.

'Now I think about it, it might be quite a short trip for some people,' he said coldly, eyeing them for a few seconds. Then he left with Malthe and Vulture. The heavy, metal door was locked from the outside.

Finn imagined Bentson standing outside smiling. A cold, evil, villainous smile. Just like in films. But this wasn't a film. This was real. And they were locked, tied and chained up, and convinced something even more awful was about to happen.

CHAPTER 63

THE SUN WAS SHINING on Oslo like never before. It was as if it were making up for all the days it had been away, as though it were trying to say: 'Sorry, I haven't forgotten you' and 'Help yourself, take as much as you want' at the same time. And people thought primarily it had been the clouds' fault and forgave the sun straight away. They smiled at it through closed eyes, letting it warm their pale faces as they waited for the bus. They also smiled at each other when they got on the bus, and some of them even said hello to someone they had never met before.

But now the sun had retired for the evening and sunk behind Nordmarka, pleased with the day's efforts. The sky was studded with stars, and a deep yellow moon illuminated the white ground. We know there are a lot of strange things between heaven and earth, but neither the sun, moon, stars nor people of Oslo knew that one of the strangest of all was now inside Oslo Spektrum, where thousands of robots were getting ready to go home to their new families. Or that thousands of real children were currently being held prisoner on the cargo ship *Angelica*, which was getting ready to take them to North Boresia and an uncertain but probably rather cruel future in the North Boresian army.

Two of these children were locked in a room without windows along with a mute gym teacher, and one of the children was thinking about something his father had said: it is amazing what you can do when you put your mind to it.

'You're out of your tiny mind,' Sunniva said, shaking her head.

'But we have to stop them! We can't give up now!' Finn said.

But even though he didn't like it, Finn had to admit she had a point. Bojan and Sunniva were wearing shackles, which in turn were threaded through metal rings in the wall. He was sitting with his torso and legs tied to a chair and his hands bound behind his back. The only other object in the room was a plastic bucket full of water that Malthe had used to wake him up. They sat in silence for a few minutes. They could hear the drone of the engines, but the ship hadn't actually started moving yet.

'When Malthe threw water at you . . . didn't he use a glass?' Sunniva said.

Finn tried to remember. He had been so groggy that he couldn't remember what had happened.

'Can you get closer to the bucket and check?' she asked.

With a considerable amount of difficulty, Finn managed to heave his way over to the bucket. He looked inside. Sunniva was right.

'Yes, there's a glass here.'

'Good,' she said.

He was about to ask her why it was good when he caught up with her train of thought. Glass. Broken glass. Rope.

'You want me to try and smash it?'

271

'Yes, Einstein.'

That was easier said than done. All he managed to do on his first attempt was to knock over the bucket, sending the water cascading across the floor and the glass with it. He bounced the chair towards the glass and kicked it as hard as he could against the wall. It shattered.

'What now?'

He was sitting with his back to Sunniva.

'Try to tip the chair over.'

'You mean try to tip myself over?'

Finn didn't wait for an answer. He started rocking the chair from side to side. Eventually he tipped over to the right and slammed into the concrete floor, hitting his head in the process. He could feel a pounding in his temples, and was vaguely aware of something hot running down his cheek. However, he was still able to move his hands despite his wrists being tied, and wasted no time using them to look for a piece of broken glass. He finally found a piece large enough to use as a kind of saw on the ropes tying him to the chair. After ten minutes he had cramp in his fingers and was fighting an overwhelming urge to give up.

'Don't stop, you're almost there!' Sunniva shouted.

A minute later the rope gave. He extracted himself from the chair and struggled to his feet.

'Well done! Just your hands left to go,' Sunniva said.

They were still tied behind his back. He got to work with the piece of broken glass again, and five minutes later he had cut through the rope and, unfortunately, into his wrists – but luckily not deeply enough for there to be any cause for concern.

It was great to be able to move freely again. He dashed over to the other two. Even though he stirred every now and then, Bojan was still unconscious.

'Hate to break it to you, but you're not going to get us out of these,' Sunniva said, tugging at the shackles. The sound of metal against metal was depressing. He would need a sledgehammer to smash them open.

The door was locked from the outside, as expected. Finn's sense of newfound freedom evaporated as quickly as it had come.

'The hatches in the wall,' Sunniva said, nodding towards the wall.

There were two round hatches in the outer wall, one down by the floor and one halfway between the floor and the ceiling. Both had levers that Finn assumed could be used to open them. He tugged at the lever on the lower hatch, but it had rusted into position. He grabbed the chair and stood on it so that his head was level with the second hatch. The lever finally yielded when he used all his bodyweight, and he pushed the glass open. He was rewarded with a blast of ice-cold air. He could see the quayside far below. They hadn't started moving yet, but it was only a matter of time.

'Shout for help!' Sunniva urged.

Finn tried to shout, but it was no use. There was no one to hear him, and even if there had been, the noise of the engines would have drowned him out.

'Could you jump down?' Sunniva asked.

'No, we're too high up,' Finn told her, sticking his head out for a better look.

Then he saw someone standing on the quayside far below. And it wasn't just anyone.

'Camomiiiiiiiiiiiiiiiiile!'

He could see the top of his brother's yellow hat. Camomile was walking to and fro as if looking for something. Me, Finn thought. He's looking for me.

'Up heeeere! Camomiiiiiiile!'

It was hopeless. The engines were really roaring now, even louder than before, almost as if they were getting ready to . . . no, please don't move! Finn prayed desperately.

There was a slight jerk as the boat edged sideways from the quayside.

Finn had an idea. He searched his pockets. They were still there. The programme and pen from the quiz final. He flopped down onto the floor and wrote the first thing that came to mind as quickly as he could: 'Angelica is a boat. We're on board. Help! Finn.'

Then, quick as a flash, he folded it into a paper aeroplane and climbed back onto the chair. The boat had now moved thirty or forty metres from the quayside, and Camomile was already getting smaller and smaller. He's too far away, Finn panicked, took aim . . . and hurled the aeroplane as hard as he could.

Just then, the ship started to turn. The last he saw was the paper aeroplane maintaining a steady course, straight for the freezing-cold water.

CHAPTER 64

TIME FLIES WHEN YOU'RE having fun. And goes very slowly when you're being held prisoner on a ship on its way to North Boresia. Now and then he peered out of the hatch they had managed to open, but all he could see was the lights further inland along Oslo fjord. In addition to the two hatches there were some air holes up by the ceiling on the opposite wall. But the holes weren't much bigger than a child's football.

'What's this room for, anyway?' Sunniva asked.

Finn tried to think. He had once seen a programme on the Discovery Channel about big ships where they had said something about what these sealed rooms were for. But he couldn't quite remember what it was.

'I don't know,' he said after a few seconds.

For the time being they couldn't do anything but wait. But what were they waiting for? Finn had a terrible feeling about Bentson's parting words: that the trip would be shorter for some than others.

He tried to wake Bojan, but it was no use. Instead he tried to ease the gym teacher into a more comfortable sitting position against the wall.

'How do you think Bojan got caught up in all this?' Finn asked, sitting next to the tall man to prop him up.

'Malthe said something about it before you woke up. They were sure they wouldn't have any trouble getting him to join them as he seemed frustrated by disobedient children.'

'Do you think they told him their plans?'

'I don't expect they told him everything. But clearly they said enough for him to suspect something was wrong,' Sunniva said.

Finn glanced sideways at the broad-shouldered man next to him. The huge metal whistle was still hanging around his neck. Finn reached out and turned it for a closer look. Then Bojan twitched, causing Finn to jump so violently that the gym teacher tipped over onto his side again. But this time he woke up. He blinked a couple times before focusing on Finn and Sunniva.

'Hi,' Finn said, getting up.

He responded with a small nod, but said nothing.

'Do you know where you are?' Finn asked.

Bojan nodded again and levered himself up onto his feet. He was clearly stiff and sore. He stretched as much as the shackles would allow. When he was finally fully upright, the iron ring was level with his hips.

Finn knew he had to say something.

'I'm sorry we were so loud at the cabin. We just got so scared when we saw you,' he said. 'We thought you were . . . their leader.'

A weak smile formed on Bojan's lips and he nodded slowly to indicate that he understood and that it was OK. But still he didn't say anything. Finn started to wonder whether he had really heard Bojan shout by the cabin.

Then he noticed that Bojan kept glancing up at the air holes in the wall. Was he afraid that they would seal them up? Surely it didn't matter now that Finn was free and had opened the hatch? They wouldn't lack air.

They stood in silence, a silence so saturated with unpleasant thoughts. Finn racked his brains desperately for something to say.

Then a faint whistling sound became audible over the roar of the engines. Bojan eyed the air holes warily. The whistling grew louder, and then it took on a gurgling quality, still getting louder, as if the source of the sound were coming closer. Bojan was transfixed by the five air holes now.

'What are you looking at? What's happening?' Finn asked nervously.

The answer came three seconds later. Not from Bojan, but in the form of five powerful jets of water shooting from the air holes. Which weren't air holes at all.

After a few seconds Finn realised what was happening. But it was Sunniva who put it into words.

'They want to drown us!' she cried.

CHAPTER 65

AT SOME TIME OR other we have all been told that we use only around ten per cent of our brain capacity, and that the remaining ninety per cent just sits there waiting to be used and make us super humans who can do, understand and remember everything. However, Finn knew it was a myth and that most of us use almost our entire brain.

But sometimes it is still a big mystery just *how* our brains work. Why, for example, do they suddenly decide to remember something you saw on the Discovery Channel at least two years ago as you're about to drown?

'I think we're in a kind of ballast tank!' Finn shouted as the water poured in. 'It fills up with water when the ship has no cargo! To balance the ship at sea,' he said.

Or it's used to drowned unwanted passengers, he thought. But he didn't say that.

He remembered now. The hatches on the wall were used to get rid of the water again. But they were only any good when there wasn't water streaming in at the same time.

Knowing what sort of room they were in didn't really help. They were still locked in and about to drown. End of.

'Try the lower hatch again!' Sunniva yelled.

Finn ran over to the outer wall, grabbed the rusty lever with both hands and heaved until his entire body shook. It wouldn't budge.

'I can't, it's stuck!' Finn cried in despair.

'The water's coming in so fast I don't know if it would've helped anyway,' Sunniva said, pulling at her shackles again.

The cold water was still blasting through the holes on the wall and had already reached Finn's ankles. For the first time since he had met Sunniva, he could see that she was genuinely scared. And even though he wasn't chained up, his situation wasn't a lot better. Jumping into the black, freezing water below was as certain a death as staying here.

Their only option was to fly. Or climb.

Finn carried the chair back to the hatch, put it down in the water and climbed onto it. He stuck his head out of the hatch and immediately had to close his eyes against the freezing cold December air. It was three, maybe four metres up to the deck. Finn could just see a railing when he craned his neck.

'Can you see anything? Could you climb up?' Sunniva shouted as Finn pulled his head inside again. He rubbed his face, which had stiffened in the cold.

'It's too far up,' Finn said.

'Could you use the rope?' Sunniva said.

The rope that had been used to tie Finn to the chair was now floating in the water. He picked it up. It was certainly long enough. He made a lasso and coiled the rest, then climbed back onto the chair and stuck his head out again. It was a long way up to the railing. And how would he tie the rope to anything? There wasn't anything for the lasso to catch onto; the railing just continued horizontally. But he had to try. Maybe it would catch onto something he couldn't see. He held one end of the rope in his left hand and used his right hand to throw the lasso and coils of rope as hard as he could up into the darkness. He had to pull his head back inside again quickly to avoid being hit in the face when it came rushing back down again.

'It's no good,' he said, flopping down onto the chair. 'I can't get the rope around anything.'

Sunniva responded by pulling desperately at her shackles.

Finn looked at her, his eyes vacant. Was this how it would end?

'The whistle,' Bojan said.

They both turned to look at him. Sunniva looked most surprised. It was the first time she had heard him speak.

'Use whistle,' he said in broken Norwegian as he leaned forward to show them what he meant. The huge whistle swung to and fro from the metal chain around his neck.

'It is heavy and chain is strong.'

Finn hurried over to him and lifted the chain over his head. It really was heavy. He could see what Bojan meant. If he attached it to the end of the rope, it might be heavy enough to wrap around the railing up there.

'Come on, Finn! You can do it!' Sunniva cried, more out of despair than hope.

The chair was floating in the water now. He replaced it under-

280

neath the hatch before climbing onto it again with the heavy, wet rope in his hands, this time with the whistle tied to the end of it. He looked at it for a moment. There was something engraved on it: 'Na Luka Od Bojan.'

Finn stuck his head outside again, into the roar of the wind, the waves and the engine noise. He braced himself and counted to three. One, two, three! The whistle and rope soared into the air, and for a moment Finn dared to hope. He heard a crash as the whistle hit the side of the ship further up, and then it plummeted back down again.

'Come on, try again!' Sunniva shouted from inside.

He coiled the rope again and got ready. One, two, three and . . . throw! The rope and whistle disappeared into the darkness. Finn made to duck back inside again so that the whistle wouldn't hit him in the face. But it didn't come back. A faint clang announced it had hit something hard, but all that came back down again was the end of the rope. Finn gave it a tug. The whistle and metal chain had wrapped themselves around the railing.

'It's caught!' he cried excitedly.

'Climb!' Sunniva yelled.

Finn made to wriggle through the hatch.

'Finn!'

It was Sunniva. He turned to look at her. The water was up to her thigh now and her teeth were chattering.

'I just wanted . . .' she started. 'Just be careful.'

Finn nodded and tried to smile. He wasn't sure whether 'be

careful' quite covered it when you were about to climb up a wet rope on the outside of a tanker going full speed on a dark December evening. Especially not when you also had to be on the lookout for a gang of old people who wanted to kill you.

He climbed through the hatch, keeping the rope taut. It was only then that he realised quite how cold it was. The fact that his legs were already sopping wet didn't help. When he was all the way out he put his feet against the side of the ship and started climbing up, one step at a time. He slipped twice, and both times he thought it was the end. But he just hung there from the rope for a few seconds until he found a new foothold. He finally reached the railing, where the whistle had wrapped itself around the lowest bar. Finn climbed over and fell onto the deck in exhaustion. He knew he had no time to lose. The water flowing into the ballast tank wouldn't wait for him. How high would it be now? He quickly retrieved the whistle, knowing it meant something to Bojan, and was about to start running when a powerful beam of light was shone in his face. Followed by an all-too familiar and particularly unwelcome voice.

'Hey, you there! Stay where you are!'

CHAPTER 66

OF ALL THE OPTIONS Finn was entertaining, 'stay where you are' wasn't even on the list. He shot off in the opposite direction to the torch and voice of Chief Constable Willy Malthe. The deck was wet and slippery. Finn had to take extra care not to fall. He could hear heavy footsteps behind him, and the light from the torch flashed around him as if he were at some sort of disco.

'Stop!' the chief constable shouted.

Not likely, you headcase, Finn thought, hurtling towards the first door he spotted. He was glad it was Malthe chasing him. The policeman was so big and fat that it was impossible for him to run that fast. Finn tore the door open, trying not to think about what might be waiting for him on the other side.

But at last he was in luck. There was a set of stairs behind the door. He hurried down them, almost tripping over a coiled rope at the bottom. It was attached to a small, red plastic ball, perhaps originally a fender from one of the lifeboats. He guessed that Sunniva and Bojan were a couple levels down. He visualised Sunniva trying to keep her head above water, the chains holding her down and . . . no, he couldn't think about that just now. Above him he heard Malthe starting down the stairs. Please be open, he pleaded when he found the right door. It was heavy, but it opened, and then he found himself in a long corridor with several doors leading off it. He ran over to the first one. Locked. But it didn't look like the heavy door that Bentson had locked behind him. Finn carried on along the corridor, skipping the next door, which was like the first, and then he spotted a big, thick door with a metal wheel attached to it. Bingo, he thought.

'Stop right there!'

Malthe had reached the corridor. No, no, no! Finn thought. So close and yet so far! He began to turn the metal wheel. It was heavy, but little by little it turned to the right. The footsteps were coming closer. Finn looked over his shoulder and saw Malthe only fifteen metres away. The policeman was walking now. And smiling.

'Well, well,' the policeman panted. 'I don't know how you got out, but it's all over now.'

Speak for yourself, Finn thought, turning the wheel to the right with all his might.

An immense force burst open the door, and the wall of water that flooded out of the room hit Malthe's huge body like a sledge-hammer. Finn tried to cling onto the metal wheel, but was thrown to the ground. However, luckily for him, the door didn't swing back against the wall. Instead it acted as a kind of screen, channelling the water away from him and to the left, where it formed a torrential river and carried Malthe away. Finn got to his feet, struggling not to be swept away to the right even though far less water was going that way. On the wall quite close to him he spotted a small cabinet with a red symbol representing a fire. He waded over and opened it. He had never been so happy to see a fire axe. Finn grabbed it from its bracket, then waded through the open door.

The water had stopped rushing out. He could see Malthe lying motionless at the end of the corridor. The water came up to the middle of his calf when he finally entered the room he had left only five minutes before.

Once more he recited a prayer of gratitude to whoever might be listening.

Please don't let it be too late, he thought.

CHAPTER 67

THE FIRST THING FINN saw was Sunniva's long, wet, black hair.

'About flipping time too!' she said.

She glared at him. Then she smiled. She must have had to hold her breath nearer the end, Finn thought. Her hair was only dry from the ears up.

Bojan's face brightened when he saw the fire axe. He lifted his hands so that the chain connecting the shackles was taut through the metal ring in the wall. Finn aimed and struck without a second thought about how this could all go wrong. Luckily his aim was true and the chain severed immediately. Then he did the same with Sunniva's chain before returning the whistle to Bojan.

'Thanks,' Bojan said, hanging it around his neck again.

'We need to hurry. Malthe was chasing me, but I think he's unconscious now,' Finn said.

They waded out of the room.

'OK. We have to find the other children. They're in the cargo hold,' Sunniva said.

'The stairs are this way,' Finn said, leading them towards where Malthe had been lying. After a couple of metres he stopped.

There was no chief constable in the water.

'What are you waiting for? Come on,' Sunniva said, passing Finn.

They ran along the corridor. Finn was worried about what had happened to Malthe, but Sunniva was right, they couldn't stand around waiting for him. Bojan sprinted into the stairwell.

'Stop, NOW! And don't move a muscle!'

Chief Constable Malthe was standing halfway up the stairs. He was soaking wet and breathing like a whale with a huge cartoon-style lump over his left eye. But that wasn't what made them stop stock still on the tiny landing. Finn stared, frozen in fear, at what Malthe was holding in his right hand.

The chief constable had swapped the torch for a gun.

Then they heard voices and footsteps further up the stairs. Oh no, here comes the whole old folks' home, Finn thought.

'Gerhard, I've got them!' Malthe shouted, without taking his eyes off the three escapees.

He aimed the gun at Bojan, who was standing closest to him.

'And don't worry, I've got the situation under control!'

Water was still flowing into the stairwell from the corridor, dripping down between the steps beneath them. Then Finn noticed something red floating next to Sunniva's leg. It was the plastic fender he had almost tripped over while running. Sunniva bent down and picked it up. It was still attached to the rope.

'I said don't move!' Malthe snapped.

They heard Bentson's stick long before he hove into view. Several other head teachers followed him, as well as Vulture and another small, scruffy man wearing a red cap, who Finn guessed must be the man he saw with Vulture at Einar's apartment and in his own house. Finn also recognised some of the others from the quiz, including Biddy Blue. Grunters against Grandchildren. Old people who hated children. Finn summoned the most venomous glare he had in his armoury.

Bentson stood looking at them and shaking his head. For a long time. Then he smiled. And said two words.

'Shoot them.'

At first, Finn couldn't believe his ears. Then he remembered that Bentson had already tried to drown them. Some of the old people turned away, but Finn noticed that Vulture just grinned. Bojan glanced at Sunniva and she nodded back. Finn was mystified.

Malthe lifted the gun and aimed at Bojan's heart. Then everything happened at once. Sunniva threw the red, plastic fender as hard as she could at Malthe's hand, as only the very best dodgeball player in Uranienborg School could. As it hit Malthe's hand, the gun went off and a loud bang echoed around the walls. At the same time, Bojan charged towards Malthe uttering the same cry he had shouted back at the cabin.

'Ruuuun!'

Finn and Sunniva didn't hesitate. They practically dived down the steep steps.

'I know where they are!' Sunniva yelled.

They raced on and jumped the last five stairs to the next landing. Then another shot was fired over their heads. But they couldn't stop, not now, they had to keep going, they could already hear the patter of running feet as the bingo mob from hell took up the chase. They hared down the stairs, jumping some and hitting landing after landing, most without doors.

'Here!' Sunniva said when they reached a blue door. She opened it and led them into a new corridor at least as long as the one they had just come from.

They belted down the corridor, Finn staying behind Sunniva, who knew where they were going. She didn't stop until they reached the far end, where there was another large door with a metal wheel in the middle. Sunniva started to heave the wheel to the right as hard as she could.

'Help me, it's heavy!'

Then they heard a voice behind them.

'No! No, don't open it!'

Bentson appeared at the other end of the corridor and limped towards them at an alarming pace. Behind him followed a whole flock of old folks. Finn couldn't see Bojan. Or Malthe.

'Don't open that door! It's dangerous!'

At first Finn wondered whether Bentson was trying to warn them of some real danger behind the door.

Then he realised that was exactly what he was doing.

Except that what was behind the door was only dangerous to the headmaster. He stood beside Sunniva and heaved at the wheel with her.

'One, two, three!' he cried. The wheel loosened and spun to the right.

'And now, on four!' cried Sunniva as they opened the door

289

together, releasing all the children who could have become, but never did, the wildest, strongest and most dangerous soldiers that North Boresia had ever had.

CHAPTER 68

IT WAS A SAD sight.

Finn and Sunniva were standing in the wheel house looking down onto the deck. It was unbelievable to think that the old people tied up below had *almost* managed to execute their plan.

They had kidnapped thousands of children, some of them snatched from their own homes in the middle of the night, most from Oslo Spektrum. And they had *almost* managed to do it without anyone noticing either, by replacing the children with identical copies.

Almost.

And the children had *almost* thrown every member of GAG into the sea as well. When they found out what had happened and who had kidnapped them, some of the biggest children had grabbed Bentson and hoisted him aloft. He had screamed like a man possessed and begged for mercy, but they weren't listening. They carried him to the railing, some holding his arms and others his legs. Then they had swung him to and fro while he shrieked in fright. Sunniva yelled at them to make them stop, but they weren't listening to anyone, they counted to three and threw him . . . straight at the wall of the wheel house.

291

The old man was almost unrecognisable. He was now sitting, bound hand and foot with Malthe, *inside* the wheel house so that they could keep an eye on the two ringleaders. The well-dressed, strict and, as it had transpired, completely insane headmaster was now a mere shadow of the megalomaniacal, cold-hearted GAG leader Finn had witnessed earlier that evening. Now, his suit was filthy, his shirt rumpled and his eyebrows, normally so authoritative and bushy, were dripping wet and droopy.

Much like the rest of him, and Malthe.

Sunniva looked over at them every so often, and each time she said the same thing.

'You should be ashamed of yourselves.'

After the children had overpowered Bentson and the other old folks in the corridor, Finn and Sunniva had run upstairs again to look for Bojan. They had feared the worst, and even though there were a lot of steps, they had ignored their exhaustion. Once again, Bojan had sacrificed himself for them, and this time his action had been decisive. Finn had heard gunfire, and he remembered that Chief Constable Malthe hadn't come down with Bentson. Maybe he had shot Bojan and tried to run, Finn thought. Maybe Bojan was lying somewhere bleeding. Or even worse, maybe he was . . .

They found him more or less where they had left him.

Sitting on top of Chief Constable Malthe.

'We heard a gunshot. What happened?' Sunniva asked breathlessly.

Bojan lifted the whistle hanging around his neck.

'Small gun, big whistle,' he said, smiling.

Finn took a step closer and realised what he was seeing. The whistle hadn't just got a new dent. It had stopped a bullet, which was embedded in the metal.

Bojan was now standing with them in the wheel house, helping them to make sure that the three North Boresians steering the ship kept the right course. Not to North Boresia this time, but straight back to Oslo.

The ship glided across the calm surface of the water, which was so still that they could have counted the stars reflected in it if they had wanted to.

'Who's Luka?' Finn asked.

Bojan blinked at him in surprise. Then he looked down at the whistle and turned it around to caress the engraving.

'Luka. I'm . . .' Bojan started, before pausing and turning to look out into the night. 'I *was* his grandfather.'

After they had been sailing for an hour, the entire ship was suddenly illuminated by a powerful floodlight. It was as though the sun had risen. There was mild panic among the children on deck.

'What's happening?' Sunniva asked. She peered out of the wheel house window with Finn.

Then a familiar voice rang out.

'This is an order! I command you to give yourselves up immediately!'

There were at least four military helicopters hovering above them as well as five or six helicopters from various TV and radio stations. Light was being shone on them from all angles, and in one of the helicopters they could see a small man with a comb-over and a large megaphone.

'Okey dokey, I repeat. Give yourselves up immediately! This is Prime Minister Teddy Popps, and you haven't got a hope in hell!'

THE VERY LAST CHAPTER

'IMAGINE BEING ABLE TO make robotth that are that much like humanth! I can't believe itth pothible,' Camomile said, thaking his head.

Finn and Sunniva exchanged quick glances.

'Yes, imagine that. It's quite something,' Finn said.

They were sitting on the roof of 18 Inkognitogate, on the polar bear skin that had saved Finn from the flies that night, talking about everything that had happened. Or rather, now they weren't saying much at all, because they had already discussed what had happened many, many times, both that day and every other day that had passed since the fateful evening on Oslo fjord.

It had been a wonderful few days. Not least thanks to the sun, which was fully in charge up there now and started every day by chasing away the few small clouds that were stupid enough to put in an appearance. It spent the rest of the day hanging idly in the clear blue sky like a drowsy yellow beach ball floating out to sea before finally disappearing over the horizon with a little yawn.

The pretty young weather girl on TV2 said that Norway hadn't had such nice winter weather 'since the Winter Olympics in

Lillehammer in 1894', which had prompted a stream of not-so-pretty and not-so-young women to call TV2's switchboard and demand that the weather girl be sacked as 'everyone should know that Lillehammer hosted the Winter Olympics in *1994*, even if they are young and beautiful'.

But that's how it is. Some people remember things and others forget. However, the three children now sitting on the roof of the prime minister's residence with the sun's pale cousin hanging over them like a half-eaten wheel of cheese would never forget what happened in the first couple weeks of that December. (One of them hadn't forgotten either that Lillehammer had hosted the Winter Olympics in 1994 and that Norway had won ten gold medals, eleven silver and five bronze.)

They all remembered how the newspapers in both Norway and the rest of the world had written 'Prime Minister Popps saves thousands of kidnapped children from being shipped to North Boresia', and printed pictures of the missing children under headings such as 'Home safe to mum – thanks to Popps'. They also remembered Prime Minister Popps saying on TV2 that he had 'long suspected that something terrible was happening', and that there was 'always mischief in the air when such young children ran away from home', and that he had sensed at once that 'the fat chief constable and the uppity headmaster weren't to be trusted'.

They also remembered that he had said, as a little aside in a little interview in a very little local paper, that he wanted to thank his sons Finn and Camomile as well as their good friend Sigrid for their help.

What *wasn't* reported anywhere was that Camomile saw a dustbin lorry leaving Oslo Spektrum when he'd arrived to meet Finn after the quiz, and had ran after it. Or that Camomile had run all the way home from the harbour with a cut on his forehead, clutching a paper aeroplane and shouting that Teddy had to 'thtop Angelica thtraight away!' Teddy Popps hadn't understood what Camomile was talking about at first, and when he had finally worked out what he was saying, he had just assumed his new son had finally lost the plot. It was only when Miss Syversen had come home from Maridalen after finding both the cabin and GAG's written plans for replacing all the children with imported androids from North Boresia that he had pulled his finger out and got his arse in gear. Especially after Miss Syversen had yelled that it was about time he 'pulled his finger out and got his arse in gear'. That had helped.

Yes. Some people remember things and some forget. Finn had pretty much forgiven his dad for forgetting what *really* happened. To be precise, that the children had saved themselves long before the prime minister came swooping down in his helicopter.

But that's just how it was. Being prime minister was a demanding job, and he knew that his dad found it a bit less stressful when he did popular things that people appreciated. And this had been immeasurably popular. In the days that followed, every single Norwegian had wanted to both vote for and marry Teddy Popps. The provinces of Jämtland and Härjedalen, which Norway had lost to Sweden in 1645, even submitted a written application to become part of Norway again.

297

There was good news and bad news for Headmaster Bentson, Chief Constable Malthe and all the other old folks. The good news was that it would be a very long time before any of them had to countenance a child again. The bad news was that that very long time would be spent behind lock and key.

'If Mr Bentson thinks Norwegian society is lacking in discipline, well, he'll be getting a right good taste of it now,' Teddy Popps had said to thunderous applause.

The kidnapped children were back home safe and had been exchanged for the androids, one by one. A few of the parents asked if they could keep the new, better-behaved version of their son or daughter instead, but for the most part there weren't any problems. After a few days the newspapers began to speculate on what Teddy Popps might do with all the androids, but they soon let the matter rest when all the holes in all the roads in all the towns in Norway were suddenly filled. Then they wrote 'A New Triumph for Super Ted', as they now called him. The leader of another political party grunted something about child labour, claiming that children had been sighted filling in all the holes in the middle of the night, but Teddy Popps dismissed the accusations as 'absolute bunkum'. 'Utter tosh,' he added.

Finn rather thought that his dad was starting to get the hang of being prime minister. And three days ago something had turned up in Sunniva and Vera's letterbox which suggested that Teddy had not forgotten who had *really* saved both the day and all the children a few days earlier.

It was a sealed dinner invitation, identical to the one that turned up on the reception desk at Hotel Bristol, the one that came through Bojan's door and the one that was handed to Miss Syversen.

And only an hour ago, after they had all eaten a delicious three-course meal, courtesy of Baba, culminating in banana fritters and ice cream á la Gran Canaria, Teddy Popps tapped his glass with his dessert spoon, cleared his throat loudly and ran a practised hand across his comb-over four times.

'My dear compatriots,' he started, as if practising for his New Year speech. 'Not forgetting Max and Bojan,' he added.

'I know that this has been quite a December for some of you.'

He sent a shy smile to those concerned.

'And that I . . . er, maybe didn't always listen to what some of you were trying to tell me.'

This time he looked at Finn, Camomile and Sunniva, who rolled their eyes.

'Anyway. I know there are still a few days to Christmas, but I wanted to surprise you with an early gift.'

That's what he said. And then he said some more.

Now Finn, Sunniva and Camomile were sitting on the roof gazing into the starry Oslo night as they thought about the last thing the prime minister had said.

'He said "everyone", right?' Sunniva said.

'Yup,' Finn said.

'Mum too?'

'Yeth. And Mith Thyverthen and Makthwell,' Camomile added.

'And Baba, Bendik, and Dad himself, of course,' Finn said.

'Don't forget Bojan!' Camomile added.

'And Bojan, of course,' Finn said.

'But when?' Sunniva asked.

'On Christmas Day.'

She turned towards him.

'And the government's paying for the lot?'

'Yup. For "Heroic efforts to protect Norwegian citizens".'

Sunniva smiled.

'I liked that bit. Heroic efforts.'

Her smile grew even wider.

'Hats off to your dad, guys. He's one smart cookie.'

Finn smiled as well. Because even though Baba had been a tad disgruntled and said she would much rather be sipping brightly coloured cocktails in Gran Canaria, Finn was fairly sure they would have those in Bora Bora as well. And that was just where they were going. All of them.

They sat on the roof for another hour. They didn't say much, but it was nice to sit looking at the stars and out across the rooftops. After around forty minutes, Finn saw a shooting star streak across the sky, just above Holmenkollen. He closed his eyes.

And didn't have a wish in the world.